His to Steal
The Unforgettable Series
Book 1

Autumn Archer

1

Lana

"Come on, babe, it'll be fun. We've talked about it for ages. Let's just go for it."

Lana took a deep breath after Rory's pep talk, her fingers twisting the strap of her purse.

His enthusiasm buzzed like a physical force, sounding so sure—so eager.

She wished she could mirror his confidence, but her pulse thrummed in her ears as he rapped his knuckles against the steel door.

A door latch clicked, and a high-pitched squeak cut through the silence before the heavy scent of expensive cologne and liquor hit her.

Bluesy beats pulsed through the opening, thick and sultry, mingling with the low hum of conversation.

A man appeared in the doorway—a short, balding figure in a perfectly tailored obsidian suit.

His tiny head, perched atop a stiff pinstriped collar, reminded Lana of one of those dashboard bobbleheads.

His gaze, however, was anything but comical. It was sharp, assessing.

"Names," he barked.

"Rory O'Hare and my plus one, Lana Craig."

A beat of silence stretched before the man gave a curt nod. "Right this way, Mr. O'Hare."

Lana exhaled, shifting closer to Rory as they followed their escort inside. The hardwood floor gleamed beneath the low, ambient lighting.

She barely had time to take in the gleaming chandeliers as the doorman led them through a set of hefty fire doors and into a swanky lounge.

A wave of heat and sensation crashed over her.

Decanters glowed amber on backlit glass shelves, casting warm reflections over the sleek, central bar. Scents of aged whiskey and something musky and masculine saturated the air.

Intimate clusters of velvet couches held figures draped in silk, leather, and confidence. Watchful eyes flicked toward the newcomers like they were appraising every detail.

The intensity of those gazes prickled over Lana's skin, setting her nerve endings alight.

Her breathing turned shallow, and she forced herself to inhale through her nose, exhale through her mouth.

"Rory, I don't know... if I want to do this anymore."

She reached for his hand, desperate for grounding comfort. But he didn't reach back. His hand remained buried in the pocket of his tailored trousers.

"Try to relax, Lan. You're so uptight." His voice

carried a mix of amusement and mild exasperation. "It's supposed to be fun, right?"

Lana swallowed.

"Yeah," she replied, but the word tasted uncertain on her tongue.

Truth was, part of her *was* intrigued. The exclusivity of it all, the quiet hum of indulgence in the air was a different world. One she didn't fully understand but had, admittedly, been curious about.

In the safety of their home, the fantasy had sounded thrilling. But now, being watched by wealthy strangers, her heart was thumping, and her senses were on high alert.

And yet, there was a tiny, insistent whisper inside her. *What if...?*

Rory, however, had no hesitation. He had wanted this for ages. The cost, the planning—it had all led to *this*. And he wasn't about to let her back out now.

A shift in movement drew her attention.

"I'll leave you both with Donna Marie. She'll take care of you." Bobblehead's voice was a smooth dismissal before he melted back into the crowd.

"Well, who have we got here then?"

A tall, willowy woman strode toward them, her tawny hair slicked back into a severely high ponytail. Thick, fluttering lashes framed tiny eyes that assessed Lana from head to toe.

A fire engine red nail traced over the list of names on a diamante-encrusted iPad as Rory did the introductions, referring to Lana as his plus one again.

3

Damn him.

They had lived together for over a year, and in her eyes, that made her more than just a *plus one.*

But Donna Marie didn't seem to care about that. The woman's gaze lingered on Rory's fitted white shirt and navy trousers, her inflated lips curving into a flirty smile.

"Love, you'll have the best craic tonight. We've got plenty of couples who are looking forward to meeting you both."

Lana's skin prickled, a jealous heat surging up her neck. She smoothed her palms over her hips, hyperaware of the snug fit of her dress.

Around them, men and women lounged in dim corners, sipping liquor, their laughter lilting over the hum of background music.

Outsiders might mistake this for a VIP cocktail bar. But the truth was far less innocent.

These people were here for one thing—consensual partner swapping, threesomes, or whatever the mood dictated.

Donna Marie's nails clicked against the screen as she tapped through something official-looking. Then, without looking up, she asked, "Do you need me to run through the terms of your contract again?"

Her brows attempted to arch, but the work she'd had done made that impossible.

Lana hesitated for half a second. Something in her gut told her she should pay attention, that she should have read every line of whatever contract they'd signed to be here.

However, stopping to listen to a list of rules would only make her anxiety worse. Maybe even have her heading for the exit.

Anyway, Rory would keep her right like he'd promised.

So, instead, she forced a breezy smile and shook her head. "No, it's okay."

Donna Marie shrugged as if it made no difference to her. "Suit yourself, love. Let me know if you change your mind."

Meanwhile, Rory trailed behind Donna Marie like a dog in heat, barely glancing back as she led him deeper into the club.

"Hey! Wait up!" Lana called after him, but he didn't slow.

The air was heavier now, thick with conversations, and something else—something sultry, electric.

She inhaled, forcing herself to move forward.

It's meant to be fun. I agreed to this. Rory and I are solid. Nothing will come between us. Not if we both play by the rules.

But even as she repeated the words, her gaze snagged on Rory's broad shoulders at the bar.

He was leaning in, shaking hands with a porcelain-skinned beauty whose poker-straight raven hair gleamed under the soft lights.

Lana couldn't see her full face, only a side profile— plump lips, high cheekbones, a body that some talented artist could have sculpted. She couldn't have been older than twenty-three.

Lana's stomach lurched.

Jealousy coiled hot and fast in her belly, making her feel both foolish and furious at the same time.

With a heavy sigh, she dug into her bag, fumbling for money to buy herself a drink.

If Rory could throw himself into this so easily, maybe she needed to loosen up, too.

"You look like a rabbit in the headlights."

Lana jerked at an unexpected touch, her breath catching in her throat. She spun around, finding herself face to face with a woman likely in her mid-forties with choppy peroxide dyed hair framing high cheekbones, and shrewd, honey-brown eyes.

She was elegant but not intimidating, her thigh-length lavender dress clinging in all the right places, a subtle confidence radiating from her expression.

Lana shifted her purse from one hand to the other. "That obvious?"

"A little," the woman admitted, a smile tugging at her glossy lips. "First time?"

Lana nodded, her gaze darting toward Rory. He was still at the bar, his focus consumed by the raven-haired beauty he'd just met.

He hadn't even glanced back to find Lana.

Disappointment knotted in her stomach.

The woman beside her followed her gaze, then exhaled through her nose in something between amusement and sympathy. "Ah. That's the hardest part, isn't it?"

Lana blinked up at her. "What is?"

"Watching them go off-leash for the first time," the woman replied.

Lana's lips parted, but no words came out.

Because *yes.* That was why her mind was spinning, and her stomach was queasy.

She was watching the guy she shared a life with flirt with another woman. And even though they'd agreed to this—had fantasised about it in the dark, whispered about it over wine—the reality hit differently.

Lana swallowed hard, her throat dry. "I guess I just thought... we'd stick together, at least at first."

The woman hummed, thoughtful. "Some couples do everything together. Others like to work the room."

She studied Lana for a moment, then added, "I'm Janice, by the way. If you need an anchor, you're welcome to sit with me for a while. No pressure."

There was a calmness about Janice. She had a way about her that made Lana feel *seen* instead of just... observed.

Her fingers grazed over the cool metal clasp of her purse as she glanced back at Rory. He still hadn't looked for her. Hadn't even checked in once.

A mix of jealousy, uncertainty, and hurt twisted in her chest.

Taking a deep breath, she met Janice's eyes. "I'm Lana. And that guy over there is my boyfriend, Rory."

Lana studied Janice beneath the soft lights. "You don't have a single wrinkle."

The woman smirked. "That's because I have access to the best Botox in the country, sweetheart. Perks of the trade when you own multiple salons. You should try it."

Lana let out a small, surprised laugh. Janice had a way of saying things so bluntly that it was impossible to be offended.

A bartender in a crisp white shirt and black vest approached, his salt-and-pepper beard trimmed close to his jaw. "What'll it be, ladies?"

"First round's on me. What are we having?" Janice asked.

Lana hesitated, still half-distracted. Across the room, Rory kept his hand on the raven-haired woman's lower back, his posture relaxed and his grin easy.

The nervous energy in her gut churned, but she forced herself to refocus.

"I'll have a gin and tonic, thanks."

"Boring. She'll have a pornstar martini." Then, turning to Lana, Janice added, "You need something fun, not a sad little G&T."

Lana rolled her eyes but couldn't help smiling. "Fine. A pornstar martini."

"That's my girl." Janice sat at the bar when the bartender moved to make their drinks.

Letting her shoulders relax for the first time since stepping foot inside the club, she exhaled. Despite the opulent setting, the designer dresses, and all the second glances, Janice was a friendly face.

"So," Janice continued, drumming her nails on the polished countertop. "Tell me about you. What do you do when you're not standing around in high-end sex clubs looking like a deer in the headlights?"

Lana snorted. "I work in an office."

Janice gasped in mock horror. "No! An *office*? How dull! No wonder you're trying to spice things up."

"It's not as bad as it sounds." Lana giggled.

"Let me guess... Customer service?"

"Admin assistant."

Janice winced as though Lana had confessed to a prison sentence. "Sweetheart, you need an upgrade."

"Not all of us have the capital to start up our own beauty empires."

Janice's face softened. "Maybe not, but that doesn't mean you can't be your own boss one day. You're young, you've got time."

Lana shrugged, swirling her cocktail after the bartender placed it in front of her. She wasn't sure she had the ambition for something bigger.

Life with Rory had always seemed comfortable. Enough. But as she sat there, surrounded by wealthy, powerful people who were pushing the boundaries, she couldn't help but wonder—*was comfortable enough?*

She took a sip of her drink, the sweet tang of passion-fruit hitting her tongue.

Janice leaned in. "So, tell me, what gave you two the push to come along tonight?"

"Honestly? Curiosity." Lana ran a fingertip around the rim of her glass. "It was more Rory's idea, but I... I guess I wanted to try something different for once, you know?"

Janice nodded. "And now that you're here?"

Lana's gaze moved to the crowd again. To the huddled couples, the hands grazing over bare skin in dim corners.

Despite her unease, a strange sense of excitement crept beneath the nerves.

She met Janice's eyes and admitted, "I don't know yet."

A few cocktails later, perched on a tall stool, Lana had almost forgotten why she'd joined the club Verto Veneri in the first place—the reckless, nerve-tingling plan to hook up with a sexy stranger.

Alcohol hummed in her blood, blurring the edges of her nerves.

Janice popped an olive between her teeth, chewing as she considered her. "You might be lucky enough to catch a glimpse of the owner, Marcus McGrath. He's something else."

She let out a dreamy sigh and fanned herself with a napkin. "The things I'd let that man do to me."

Lana arched a brow over the rim of her glass. "The owner actually mingles with the couples?"

"Well, not anymore," Janice said with a wistful shake of her head. "When the club first opened, he used to be visible. But now he's got a waiting list of new members longer than Royal Avenue. The guy doesn't need to show up anymore. It's a shame, really, because he's quite the eligible bachelor."

With her gaze far off, Janice idly rotated the diamond-studded wedding ring on her finger.

"Did he ever take part?" Lana asked before sipping her drink.

"Not that I know of, though the man has a reputation. Marcus McGrath doesn't need a club like this to get his kicks."

"Meaning?"

Janice smirked. "Meaning he never has the same woman on his arm. I bet if he walked in right now, you'd want him, too."

She popped another olive in her mouth, voice thick with amusement. "I'd happily kneel at his Italian hand-stitched shoes."

Lana let out a snort, but Janice didn't flinch.

"As if being gorgeous wasn't enough, he's also filthy rich, too," Janice added. "I wouldn't be surprised if he were a billionaire."

"He sounds like an arrogant arse to me." Lana rolled her eyes and finished her third martini.

"An unattainable, *powerful, arrogant* arse." Janice confirmed, leaning in and lowering her voice. "And let's be honest, sweetheart...aren't they the most dangerous, delicious kind?"

2

Lana

"Where did he go?" Lana whispered.

Slightly swaying, she placed her empty glass on the bar. Alcohol and adrenaline made her dizzy.

Her eyebrows snapped together, and her gaze searched the room, trying to pinpoint Rory.

A wave of anxiety swept over her, and her heart sank.

Rory wasn't there.

A second ago, he'd been leaning against a velvet-backed booth, talking to the raven-haired girl with toned legs.

Now—they'd both gone.

Her pulse pounded, fingers gripping the edge of the bar.

Don't overreact.

But the nagging pain in her chest refused to ease. She swallowed hard, pushing back the sting of something close to humiliation.

Despite that, she had joined with her eyes open.

They both agreed to this. As long as they had full transparency between them, it wouldn't violate their rules as a couple. So there was no reason to be upset.

Still, the thought of Rory disappearing into some shadowy lit corner with another woman made her chest tighten. He didn't even let her know or ask if she was okay to be left alone.

He'd been eager the moment they walked through the door, his excitement outweighing her nerves.

She let out a slow, measured breath and raised her chin, pretending his disappearance didn't bother her.

Janice nudged her arm. "You alright, sweetheart?"

Lana summoned a smile, even though her cheeks felt stiff. "Yeah, of course. Just noticed he's gone off somewhere."

She waved a dismissive hand, ignoring the ache behind her ribs. "Anyway, tell me more about this Marcus McGrath guy. I'll probably Google him later."

If she focused on something else—someone else— maybe the sting of Rory's absence wouldn't cut so deep.

"He has a good-looking younger brother, too," Janice announced when the bartender set down fresh drinks. "They have money and excellent genes. It would take a supermodel to trap one of those two."

"Looks and money aren't everything," Lana murmured. Then, with a wry smirk, she added, "Besides, I'm not looking to 'trap' anyone. Some men don't need to be trapped. They want the freedom to roam but still expect someone waiting at home. Isn't that the essence of this place?"

Janice let out a knowing laugh. "You're not wrong. But let's be real—it's not just men who want their freedom. Women like to keep their options open too."

She shot Lana a pointed look, one brow arching. "Maybe the real trick isn't trapping someone...it's making sure you never feel trapped yourself."

The room tilted as Lana sucked her chilled cocktail through a black straw.

"I need the loo," she said, grabbing her purse.

"Okay," Janice said. "I'm going to network now, anyway. As much as I've loved meeting you, I didn't come here for a girly night. My husband likes to watch me with other men, so I need to find myself a younger guy with lots of stamina."

She cackled, the sound rich and unapologetic. Then her expression softened. "I'd like to see you again. Call into the Lisburn Road salon for a chat. I'm there most afternoons."

Lana smiled, about to thank her, but Janice leaned in, wrapping her arms around her shoulders in a firm hug.

"And remember," she murmured, "you're young and beautiful. Most guys would be possessive of a girl like you. If it doesn't feel right, don't do it."

"Of course." Lana nodded, though unease trickled through her.

Possessive. That wasn't Rory. He didn't have a possessive bone in his body.

Lana pulled away, slipped off the bar stool, and adjusted her dress. "Thanks for keeping me company. I would've been lost without you. Have a good night."

"You too, sweetheart," Janice replied, winking. "And if you find a billionaire to whisk you away, be sure to introduce me to one of his friends."

Lana laughed, shaking her head as she turned toward the washrooms.

Her heels clipped against the walnut planks, each step feeling more purposeful, even as the buzz of alcohol made the edges of her vision blur.

She wouldn't fall apart just because Rory had vanished. If he wanted to act like she was invisible, fine. She wasn't a fragile wallflower.

The music faded when she stepped into the ladies, the heavy door clicking shut behind her.

A wave of quiet washed over her, dulling the pulse of conversation and bass thumping from the speakers outside.

She strode to the wall of mirrors, resting her hands on the marble countertop.

Overhead recessed lighting illuminated the row of empty cubicles behind her and cast a glow over her flushed cheeks, mascara-coated lashes, and slightly unfocused blue eyes.

She sighed, fingers tracing the cool surface.

Dutch courage had spilled into a drinking binge. But on the plus side, she wasn't as nervous.

Lana rifled through her bag, unscrewed her lip gloss, and focused on the precise movement of the wand as pink liquid stained her full lips.

Sober up, Lana, for God's sake, or you'll pass out before getting your clothes off.

She ran the tap, waiting until the water turned icy before shoving her wrists under the stream. The shock prickled her skin, sharpening her senses and slowing the tipsy fog in her brain.

Straightening, she met her reflection in the mirror again. Determination flickered within her blue eyes.

"Right, ready or not." She took a deep breath, dried her hands and adjusted her cleavage in the plunging neckline. "Woman the fuck up and talk to more people."

Someone perfect for a hot, commitment-free night was out there somewhere.

As she pushed out of the washroom, still muttering about checking out the men, her shoulder clipped the doorframe.

A firm grip caught her waist, steadying her. The touch alone sent an involuntary chill down her spine.

"Easy there," a voice murmured close to her ear.

Lana spun around, expecting—hoping—for some tall, brooding stranger.

Instead, she found herself face-to-face with a pale, older man, and a set of watery grey eyes peering at her through wire-rimmed glasses.

He was short, stocky, and radiated an unearned confidence.

A hand shot out from the sleeve of a moss-green jacket, hovering expectantly near her stomach. "You called for a man?"

Lana believed in gut instincts, and hers was sounding the alarm. Something about this guy sent a bone-deep shiver through her, like walking into a draft of cold air.

"Yeah," she said lightly, resisting the urge to recoil. "I want to look for my man. My boyfriend."

She flashed a tight smile, forcing herself to play it cool.

His grip tightened, the gold pinky ring on his finger pressing into her skin.

He hummed under his breath, rubbing a hand over his receding salt-and-pepper hairline. "Benny Bingham."

The name meant nothing to her, but the way he said it—like it should—made her stomach clench.

Lana could handle a little arrogance, but this was something else. He was staring at her like she was a shiny new toy, something to be tested, handled, maybe even broken in.

She forced herself to meet his gaze, even as her instincts screamed don't engage.

"Lana. Lana Craig." She yanked her hand free, keeping her voice neutral.

Benny's beady eyes raked over her, slow and assessing, sliding from her heels up to the cascading waves of her blonde hair.

Then, as if it was the most natural thing in the world, he reached out, catching a loose curl between his fingers and letting it fall.

A faint tug against her scalp. Not painful, but deliberate.

"What a beauty," he murmured. "It's great to stumble upon new blood. Is tonight your first?"

Lana clenched her jaw, her pulse hammering in her throat.

This guy creeped her out. His age doubled hers, and though he was handsome for his years, his vibe and sense of entitlement made her tense.

By the cut of his suit, he was rolling in cash. But money meant nothing when the attraction was zero.

And Benny Bingham? He was a firm no.

The hairs on her neck rose. "Umm...yeah, first time," she replied, a tight smile barely moving her lips.

"Perfect! I enjoy getting to know the newbies before anyone else. You're so voluptuous and fresh." He licked his thin lips like a lizard. "Where's your partner?"

A rush of prickles raced over her scalp, screaming at her to move. Find Rory. Get away from Benny. Now.

"Over there somewhere." She nodded behind him.

"Okay, I'll chat with Donna Marie to see if we can use the bridal suite on the top floor," he continued smoothly. "Would you like a few drinks first? Champagne? Or maybe you're into cocaine? I can get whatever you need."

His bushy eyebrows lifted like he was doing her a favour.

Lana cleared her throat, keeping her tone level. "No, thanks. I'm good."

Benny grunted low in his throat and stepped in, crowding her space. "Come on, don't be shy. We can order room service. Let's go straight upstairs."

Her jaw dropped. The scent of his cologne, thick and cloying, invaded her senses as he inched closer.

Definitely not.

"No way." She stepped back, only to hit the wall.

Now trapped, she lifted her chin, forcing steel into her voice. "I'm not hooking up with you. You're old enough to be my dad. I didn't come to Verto Veneri out of desperation."

"This?" She flicked a hand between them. "This is not happening."

The air shifted.

Benny's smug expression faltered, his nostrils flaring as he cracked his neck from side to side.

He took a slow, steady breath, but the tension seemed to tighten his tensions as he straightened.

When he spoke again, his voice had lost its forced charm, sinking into something darker.

"You won't last two minutes in this place." His mouth curved, but there was nothing amused about it. "I'll see to that."

A thread of genuine disgust wound through Lana's gut, but she refused to let it show.

She stood tall, folding her arms across her middle, eyes sharp. "Then I guess you'll have to find someone else to bankroll your ego for the night."

For a flicker of a second, something ugly crossed his face—frustration, anger, maybe even amusement at the audacity of her rejection.

Then, just as quickly, it was gone.

Benny backed up two steps, his smile as cold as his eyes. "Enjoy your night, Lana."

He turned on his heel toward the crowd and disappeared.

Her pulse pounded, and she blew out a gust of air, the encounter leaving an unpleasant taste in her mouth.

She needed to find Rory.

Lana pushed off the wall, her legs unsteady as she wove through the throng of people.

The air was sultry, and the lingering waft of alcohol was everywhere. Ice clinked against glass, laughter spiked through raised conversations, and the deep thrum of bass vibrated through the floorboards.

Her pulse thumped in her throat as she moved, every quick step taking her deeper into the club.

Eyes followed her. She could sense them crawling over her skin like phantom fingers.

Panic simmered beneath the surface, each second stretching taut.

She scanned the room, searching for Rory's auburn hair, for anything familiar to anchor herself to. But he was gone.

A knot formed in her stomach, and she palmed her belly. He wouldn't have left. Would he?

"Miss Craig."

A deep, clipped voice sounded to her right. Before she could turn, a man in a black suit stepped into her path, blocking her next move.

His posture was rigid, controlled, and the small earpiece looped around his ear made her breath hitch.

Security.

She stiffened. "Yes?"

"The boss wants a word."

Her mouth went dry. "The boss?"

"Mr McGrath."

The name landed like a spark in dry tinder, setting off an alarm in her head.

Lana's stomach flipped, a jolt of confusion threading through her thoughts.

Why her? Of all the people in this room, why did he want to speak to her?

Her pulse quickened, her breath coming faster as she glanced around, realising that although the club was packed, she was utterly alone.

Lana scowled. "Why does he want to see me?"

The security guy didn't so much as blink. "His chief assistant specifically requested you. Said the boss would need you in his office."

That wasn't an answer. Not really.

Her fingers curled into fists at her sides, her heart thudding against her ribs. Every instinct screamed at her to turn around and leave—but curiosity pressed down harder.

She hesitated.

"I wouldn't keep him waiting if I were you."

3

Marcus

"The membership list has surged over the past few months, Mr McGrath," Gordon, the accountant, announced, tapping his iPad.

"I've updated the figures and included a breakdown in your report. We also have a waiting list a mile long. Demand is through the roof."

Marcus remained silent, his back to the room, hands in the pockets of his tailored trousers as he gazed out at the Belfast skyline.

The city lights stretched before him, a glittering web of power and excess.

He owned his share of both.

Verto Veneri was no ordinary club. It was a sanctuary for the wealthy and wicked.

A place where monogamy was a suggestion rather than a rule, where business deals were inked between silk sheets, and where the most influential men and women in society surrendered to their darkest desires under the veil of exclusivity.

By day, these people played the roles of devoted spouses, high-powered executives, and public figures. By night, they indulged in whatever their appetites craved, all under his watch.

Marcus controlled the list of members with an iron grip. That exclusivity, combined with absolute discretion, had turned Verto Veneri into a global sensation in the elite's world.

Desire had its price, and Marcus ensured he benefited from it.

The Fitz Hotel was a prized gem in the McGrath empire—a five-star sanctuary of indulgence with sister properties scattered across Ireland, Europe, and beyond.

Yet, hidden within, was the ultimate prize—Verto Veneri, a high-class club with a notoriously long waiting list, even for the rich.

A curated den of desire, it catered to those who craved more than luxury, who sought pleasure without limits, discretion without question, and indulgence without consequence.

He and his brother Jamie had clawed their way into this world, carving out success with nothing but grit and a refusal to fail.

Gordon cleared his throat. "Would like me to prioritise acquisition opportunities in Dublin? Or would you prefer to look stateside?"

Marcus finally turned, rolling the tension from his shoulders.

"Find me options," he said, voice low and certain. "If there's nothing worth buying, we'll build."

Gordon nodded, pushing his glasses up the bridge of his nose. "Understood, Mr McGrath. I'll compile a list."

Marcus reached for the cut-crystal tumbler on his desk, the amber whiskey catching the light as he swirled it.

He took a slow sip, letting the burn settle before speaking again.

"Anything else?"

Gordon hesitated. "I don't have details, but there was a minor incident with a new member tonight."

Marcus arched a brow but said nothing, waiting.

"Security flagged it," Gordon continued. "Something to do with Mr Bingham and a woman. I don't have specifics, but Mr Bingham made the report this evening. I thought you might want to handle it yourself, given he's an investor."

Marcus exhaled through his nose, setting the glass down with a measured clink.

"Bingham's an arrogant prick, but he's valuable. If a new member is causing problems, I want their file on my desk."

"Yes, sir."

Marcus dismissed Gordon with a nod, already turning back toward the night beyond his window. Pettiness was a distraction he didn't need. He had a business to run.

And yet, as he rolled the whiskey over his tongue, curiosity settled in his chest.

New couples always made things interesting.

The woman was probably another gold-digger, targeting rich men.

Isn't that what all women want? Find the man with the deep pockets and reel him in like a prized catch.

Marcus wasn't an idiot. He hadn't built his empire, and certainly not his club, to be a playground for desperate women hunting for a sugar daddy.

The terms and conditions were clear. Couples need a one-year relationship history to qualify. Proof of bank accounts and utility bills. Nothing was left to chance.

However, throughout the years, several women had resorted to extraordinary lengths for a chance to gain access.

Marcus's phone buzzed on his desk, the screen lighting up with his brother Jamie's name. He picked it up without hesitation and swiped the screen to answer.

"Marcus, you busy?" Jamie's voice came through, lighter than usual, but there was always that hint of mischief.

"Always," Marcus replied, his eyes still on the skyline. "What's up?"

"Not much," Jamie sighed, like he was kicking back and getting comfy on a couch. "I just saw some pictures of you on the yacht in Marbella with a new woman. I'm thinking you're collecting them like trophies, or maybe she's the one?"

Marcus's lips curled into a small smile. "The one? I don't have time for that shit. Who wants a woman clinging onto them after spending the night together? Or calling every hour, asking if I'm 'okay' or 'thinking about her.' Fuck that, I've got work to do."

Jamie laughed. "You say that now, but I don't know how long you can keep avoiding it. You know, I've always thought you'd settle down with someone, at least for a night."

Marcus scoffed, pouring himself another whiskey. "That's rich coming from you, Jamie."

"I'm younger than you," Jamie countered. "I have plenty of time before my dick stops working."

Marcus shrugged. "I don't need to settle. I'm not built for that. Business is my priority. The only thing I'm tied to is this club, my investments, and the next big move. There's no time for a girlfriend or playing house. I don't want a woman breathing down my neck, asking where I've been or why I'm not texting back. That shit's for bored guys who don't have the balls to make it big."

"Yeah, yeah," Jamie teased. "You're Mr 'Too Busy for Women,' but trust me, even you can't avoid it forever. Just don't end up as the lonely old billionaire."

"Lonely billionaire?" Marcus echoed with a laugh, leaning back in his chair. "I'm surrounded by people all the time. I don't need anyone trying to convince me I'm missing something. I don't have time for distractions. The day I do is the day I lose sight of everything I've worked for."

Jamie sighed. "Right, well, I don't get it. You could have your pick, but you're just too focused on what? More hotels, more clubs?"

"Exactly," Marcus said, a glint of amusement in his

eyes. "That's what matters, Jamie. Women come and go, but this? This is what keeps me up at night. Not some girl calling me for a date or wanting me to take her to dinner."

"Alright, alright," Jamie chuckled, no longer pushing it. "But you better be careful, bro. One day, you might find yourself wanting someone to fill the silence, instead of just more investments. Trust me, I've been there."

Marcus grinned. "I'm happy with the silence for now. The money's good, the clubs are growing, and that's enough for me."

Jamie clicked his tongue. "Sure, sure. Keep telling yourself that, big brother. Just don't come crying to me when you're sixty and too old."

"I'll make sure to remember that advice when I'm on my third yacht, surrounded by a new set of women, all perfectly happy with their roles. Now, if you're done playing matchmaker, I've got things to handle."

"Whatever, Marcus," Jamie said, but then the mood shifted slightly. "By the way, Dad's doing well. He's had a good few days. He's been a bit more active lately."

Marcus raised an eyebrow, shifting his posture. "Good to hear. I'll swing by to see him tomorrow."

"Yeah, you should," Jamie replied. "He's been asking about you. In fact, he's always asking about you."

Marcus didn't respond right away. He let the words hang in the air, then nodded to himself, taking a sip of his whiskey. "I'll make the time. Tell him I'll be there in the evening."

Jamie's voice softened for a moment. "No worries. Take care of yourself."

"I always do," Marcus replied, though his thoughts were already elsewhere.

He wasn't one to linger on the personal stuff for long. His empire demanded his attention, and that was where his focus remained.

"Okay, see you soon," Jamie said, before hanging up.

Marcus stared out the window again, but the moment with his brother lingered in his mind. He had his plans, his work, and his purpose. But family? That was a different matter altogether.

A knock on the door broke his thoughts, and a staff member poked his head inside. "I have a Ms Craig here for contractual dissolution."

Marcus didn't turn from the view. His voice was sharp, commanding. "Did you give her the file with the signed contract?"

"Yes, sir."

"Send her in."

4

Lana

Lana stood in the doorway, gripping the red folder tighter than necessary.

Inside were all the documents she'd provided for her membership—confidentiality agreements, bank account details, medical reports, and, of course, the signed contract.

The same one Rory had pushed her to sign weeks ago.

Clearly, Bingham hadn't appreciated her rejection. Deep down, she knew he was the reason why she was escorted upstairs. What an asshole.

He actually thought she'd be interested in him. The memory of his beady eyes crawling over the dress she bought for tonight made her stomach turn.

Now she stood in a modern office, its clean-cut, contemporary lines at odds with the unease curling inside her.

A high-backed chair faced the window, its occupant

uninterested in her arrival. Floor-to-ceiling glass framed the Belfast skyline, the city lights glimmering in the dark.

The Harland and Wolff cranes loomed in the distance, their canary-yellow steel bold against the night sky.

She stepped further into the room, the clip of her heels muted on the carpet. Without a second thought, she tipped forward and tossed the file onto the glass desk.

The damn thing skidded across the sleek surface, spilling over the edge, the papers fluttering to the carpet below.

"What the—"

The man in the chair shot up like a predator disturbed and did a one-eighty turn in her direction.

Her breath caught.

Holy. Shit.

"I—I didn't mean for that to happen," she said, her fingers flying to her mouth. "Sorry."

He was the kind of dark-haired man whose presence filled a room before he even spoke.

A navy waistcoat hugged his broad shoulders, tailored to perfection over a pressed dress shirt. The precise cut made the fabric stretch perfectly across his solid torso.

He wore his shirt open at the collar, revealing tanned skin glowing in the soft office light, and his sleeves were rolled up to his elbows.

Dark stubble shadowed his square jaw, while his hair —ruthlessly short at the sides—gave way to thick coal-black strands on top.

But his eyes made her freeze.

Intense. Emerald green. That locked onto her body, sweeping from head to toe like he was assessing her, dissecting her appearance.

After a beat, he crouched, never breaking eye contact, and gathered the scattered papers. His movements were fluid, controlled, the quiet command of a man who had no patience for disruptions.

"Ms Craig?" His voice was deep, edged with impatience, but undeniably smooth.

Lana swallowed. Hard.

"Uh-huh." She nodded, gripping the strap of her purse like a lifeline. "Is my boyfriend Rory joining us, too? He's the one who talked me into this."

The alcohol she'd consumed earlier hummed in her bloodstream, pushing warmth to her cheeks.

Marcus arched a sceptical brow, his gaze making a slow, deliberate sweep over her body.

"It seems he's occupied," he said. "Without you."

The fitted black dress she wore clung to her curves, the lace-trimmed hem brushing just above her knees. A plunging neckline only amplified the swell of her breasts with every shallow breath she took.

And he studied it all in silence.

That look he gave her. A lazy, analysing flick of his gaze. It sent heat rolling through her.

He straightened, legs braced apart, shoulders squared, unfazed by her presence. A man who'd experienced it all lacked nothing and tolerated no nonsense.

"And you read the contract, Ms Craig?" He tapped

the papers against his palm, watching her with an expression that suggested he already knew the answer.

Lana squared her shoulders, exhaling softly.

"Sort of." Her voice was steadier now, though still laced with nerves. "Rory got me to sign it, told me some of the rules, but I didn't think it was that serious."

Marcus exhaled, a slow, deep sound that made her stomach churn.

"Do you often break the rules, Ms Craig?" His gaze dropped to her mouth, lingering for half a second too long.

Lana's heart slammed against her ribs. Her breath came too fast, and she fought to steady it.

Her tongue shot out, sweeping over her lower lip, tasting the lingering sweetness of her strawberry gloss. His eyes flicked back up, and her pulse spiked.

The look he gave her made her skin flush.

She concentrated on a point behind him, suppressing fantasies about him being her choice for the evening.

"Look, I know why I'm here." Her voice was sharper now, edged with confidence. "That old guy downstairs? Benny Bingham? He made my skin crawl. That's not what I agreed to."

She flicked her hair over one shoulder, standing her ground. "I have standards, Mr McGrath."

His expression remained blank, but his eyes held hers.

"How do you know what you've committed to?" His tone was dry, almost amused. "A contract is binding, Ms Craig. You should always read the terms before signing."

He took a step closer, tilting his head a fraction. "You could have sold your soul to the devil."

Lana's throat tightened.

She swallowed hard, the sound loud in the charged silence between them.

Her lashes fluttered lower as she inhaled, trying to ignore the fact that the suited devil standing before her was the most attractive man she'd ever met.

After a few seconds, her gaze drifted back up to his face. His eyes, that arresting shade of green, caught the light just right, igniting golden flecks that shimmered like fire against emerald.

They were hypnotic. A contradiction—cool, calculating, yet burning with something she didn't want to think about.

She cursed herself for that ridiculous thought, blaming the alcohol for how her body was on high alert around him.

In reality, she reckoned he expected her to be yet another woman infatuated with him. But he owned the club; he wasn't a member. Fooling around with him wasn't an option.

He could smoulder all he wanted. Make her skin heat, her breath hitch, but she wouldn't fall for it.

"So, are you the Devil, Mr...?" She let the question hang between them, her voice softer than she intended.

A cocky, lazy smirk tugged at the corner of his mouth.

"Yeah. You can call me Marcus," he said, his voice so deep that it sent a ripple down her spine. "And you're in trouble."

Oh, fuck.

No wonder Janice was enthralled by him.

His voice alone made her tingle everywhere. Marcus was the kind of handsome guy that made women reckless.

She wet her lips, aware of his gaze tracking the motion.

"And I'm Lana," she pointed out. "What sort of trouble are we talking about here? Because I don't have a lot of money to pay a big fine, or whatever."

Though his face gave nothing away, the way his eyes settled on her was unnerving to the point she was breathless.

His lips quirked at the corners, seemingly amused by her predicament.

After a few agonising beats, Marcus broke the tense silence and started browsing her documents.

She sucked in a slow breath, trying to settle the erratic pulse hammering in her throat. But it didn't matter that his lashes lowered.

Her blood still surged and her body still reacted as if he were touching her rather than just reading her personal details.

"How long have you and Mr O'Hare been together?" His voice was calmer now, but his focus remained on the paperwork.

She frowned, counting the numbers in her head. "About two years and three months."

His eyes lifted, pinning her in place. "Do you intend to marry him?"

The bluntness of the question sent her off balance. Heat crept up her neck as she folded her arms across her chest.

"Marry him?" She forced a light laugh, deflecting. "What relevance does that have?"

Marcus tilted his head, his full lips pressing into a firm line.

"So, you're not in a serious relationship?" The shift in his tone was subtle, a distinct edge of irritation sharpening it.

Her spine stiffened.

"Of course, it's serious," she shot back, swaying a little. "I wouldn't have moved in with him if I didn't think it was going somewhere."

A shadow crossed his face before he rounded the desk, moving toward her with a smooth, unhurried confidence.

She had little time to react before his palm moved to her lower back, steadying her on the spot.

The moment his hand rested on the curve of her spine, a shiver catapulted through her body, her nipples hardening in response.

"Do you need a glass of water?" His voice was quieter now, but low and resonant vibration from his chest made her pulse thrum.

She inhaled his cologne—woodsy, musky, masculine.

Tingles burst over her scalp, her body reacting before her brain could catch up.

The Devil was dangerously close. And knew exactly what he was doing.

She lifted her chin, feigning a confidence she wasn't sure she had around a man like him.

"So, are you going to explain why I'm here, or do you just enjoy making women squirm in your office?" she asked.

Marcus's gaze dragged over her with lazy consideration.

"Oh, I enjoy making women squirm, Lana," he said, his voice like smoke and sin. "Especially when they've broken my rules."

5

Marcus

"Tell me what I did wrong, then. What rule did I break?" she demanded.

"For a start, you didn't read the contract."

"Rory read parts of it out aloud," she replied.

A dull, unfamiliar sensation sat heavy in his gut. She belonged to someone else. Was in a committed relationship with some asshole who didn't give a fuck about her safety.

Yet here she was, in his office, like temptation wrapped in lace and nerves. It shouldn't bother him—but it did.

Only a certain type of man would leave a woman alone in a place like this on their first night.

Despite that, Marcus had no claim on her. He didn't even know the woman. But he sure as fuck wanted to do bad things to her.

"When he fucks you, does he only do half a job, too?

Is that why you became a member?" Marcus asked, taking his hand away.

"That's none of your business," she said, frowning.

He took in the long, golden waves cascading over one shoulder, the cinched waist, soft glossy lips that had his cock twitching with ideas.

Those lips would look stretched around his dick. And moaning his name.

"It's my business when you belong to my club, Lana." Her name rolled off his tongue like a slow drag of whiskey, potent and fiery.

He didn't look away, watching the way her ocean-blue eyes reflected the light with a distinct restlessness.

"Is your relationship fake?" he asked. "Did you join Verto Veneri to find yourself a sugar daddy?"

Her eyes narrowed. "Are you serious? Not everyone is driven by money. Like I've already told you, Rory is my boyfriend. We live together and I've no plans to run off with a *sugar daddy*."

She rolled her eyes and inched closer to the desk like she needed the support—or maybe she was trying to put space between them.

As if that would help.

"Rory vanished shortly after we arrived," she admitted, a flush of frustration creeping into her cheeks. "He started chatting to a woman early on."

She tucked a stray strand of hair behind her ear.

"I'm not a prude, but I felt like someone threw me to the lions unarmed." She glanced up at him. "I have standards, you know."

Something about the way she said it sent a dark pulse through him. *Fuck, I bet you do.*

His jaw flexed as he let out a slow breath through his nose.

"Let me get this straight. You're a Verto virgin, and the man you consider a potential husband abandoned you the second he got here?"

The word *husband* left a sour taste in his mouth. He didn't like it. Didn't want to be one and didn't think she should be shackled to a guy who didn't put her first.

Heat burned beneath his skin, anger rising in his chest with a force that caught him off guard.

What the fuck was happening?

Usually, he wasn't interested in what people did in this club. He didn't give a damn who fucked who—so why did the thought of *her* being neglected, left alone to fend for herself, make him want to put his fist through a wall?

The pages in his hand crinkled under the pressure of his fingers.

"So he doesn't know you're with me?" His voice was low, lethal.

Lana raised her chin, but he saw the hesitation, the crack in her confidence.

"No..." she admitted, her voice softer now. "No one knows I'm here. Except for the guy who escorted me upstairs."

That was all Marcus needed to hear.

Rory O'Hare had no fucking clue what he'd left unprotected.

And that? That made her *his* to play with.

"The fact you couldn't find him probably means he's fucking someone else without a care in the world for you, beautiful."

There was no sugarcoating it. No softening the edges. Just the truth.

Her ebony lashes lowered first, then her head dipped, sending loose curls tumbling over her shoulder. A flicker of guilt twisted through him, fast and unexpected.

"This was all Rory's idea." Her voice was quiet, but not weak.

There was a thread of defiance in it, too. And a need to justify herself to me. She slid a hand over her hip and plucked at the fabric tight against her thigh.

The movement was slight, but fuck, it ignited a red-hot response in him.

"He promised me it would level up our relationship. You opened this place for that reason, right? So stop judging me, Mr McGrath."

Marcus dragged a hand over the unshaven stubble on his jaw, exhaling.

"I'm not judging *you*," he said. "I'm judging your boyfriend."

She might be petite, but she certainly wasn't fragile. With her soft curves and a hint of sass, the woman was designed to entice a man to control her.

And all he could think about was yanking those straps lower, sucking her nipples into his mouth, and bending her over his desk to hear what sounds she'd make the moment she finally let go.

"He loves me," she insisted, chin tilting upward, her blue eyes sparking like lightning in the dark.

Marcus resisted the urge to mock her statement.

"Rory said it will make our sex life better."

The word *sex* hung between them, thick as smoke, and his cock twitched in response.

"I know exactly why I joined your club, Mr McGrath. I had plans to have fun with a guy and maybe learn something new. Rory can fuck whoever he wants when we step inside Verto Veneri. But me? I draw the line at sleazy creeps like Bingo Balls."

Bingo Balls?

A rare, unexpected smirk ghosted across his lips. Laughter threatened to crack through his usual cold exterior, but he pushed it down.

His expression hardened again in an instant.

Lana's hand slid across her stomach, her mouth twisting in disgust at whatever memory she was reliving.

She was trying so damn hard to convince them both that she belonged there—that she wanted to be part of his world.

But her eyes? They told a different story.

The rigid set of her shoulders, the subtle way she kept touching herself, wasn't an invitation, more like a need for grounding.

It wasn't hesitation born from inexperience. She was vulnerable. And it caused an unfamiliar stir in his chest.

She wasn't his usual type. Not the polished, high-maintenance women who threw themselves at him, hoping for a taste of his wealth and power.

Lana was curvy and unsure—innocent, even. She wasn't trying to seduce him, wasn't angling for anything beyond an answer.

And yet, she had his full fucking attention.

Shifting her weight from foot to foot, her arms still hugged her belly. She tilted her head, her eyes narrowing a little as they moved over his shirt.

"What exactly are you trying to do here, Marcus?" she asked.

That voice of hers. Silky and Northern Irish, it wrapped around him—warm, smooth, with just enough rasp to make his dick full and hard.

It lacked the broad, brash accent of Belfast city girls. She spoke with a refined, deliberate accent, each syllable dripping with a sinful edge.

Men would pay a lot of money to hear a voice like that whispering filth across a phone line.

And him? He'd listen to her all night.

"Take a seat," he commanded. "We need to discuss the implications of your actions, Lana."

Without waiting for a response, he strode toward two white leather sofas, setting her documents beside a magazine on the glass coffee table.

She held back for a fraction of a second before moving, choosing the sofa opposite him and nudging an ochre cushion out of the way.

Distance. She was trying to put space between them.

Interesting.

He concealed a smirk and skirted the table's edge.

Pinching the knees of his tailored dress pants, he sank onto the sofa directly beside her.

His thigh nudged hers, making his veins fire up.

A hint of perfume hit him, the scent soft, fruity, and utterly fucking tempting.

He resisted the ridiculous urge to lean in, wondering if the scent deepened where her pulse beat at her throat.

Instead, he cleared his throat and sat back, watching the subtle rise and fall of her shoulders.

How she held herself tight, spine straight, knees pressed together, ankles crossed like she could somehow will away the charged energy simmering between them.

She was aware of it. Of *him*. Despite trying to hide it.

Her gaze drilled into the abstract painting on the wall, until finally, she angled around to face him, her ocean-blue eyes locking onto his.

"Well? What happens now?" she asked, frowning.

"When a client breaks my rules, we end their contract with immediate effect," he said smoothly. "That means they'll never step foot in one of my establishments again. No exceptions."

Her shoulders slumped. "Can I get a refund?"

Marcus let out a dark chuckle. "No refunds, beautiful."

Her jaw dropped somewhat before she recovered, her brows drawing together.

"Are you serious? How is that fair? That man wasn't my type, and you know it. Just because he wanted something to happen doesn't mean I have to agree."

"Absolutely. However, it's how you dealt with the

matter that's the issue," he said. "You would have known about the respect requirement if you'd read the terms."

She sighed. "Rory spent a *fortune* on the membership fee. He saved for months, worked long hours—"

"I don't run a charity," Marcus cut in, rubbing his jaw, amused by her attempt to plead her case. "And for the record, Mr O'Hare won't be allowed back, either. The contract is per couple. There's no flying solo in my club."

Her spine went rigid.

"Both of us?" She blinked, disbelief flashing in those pretty blue eyes of hers. "He'll be furious."

Marcus smiled, slow and knowing. "Not my problem."

"What would it take for you to reconsider?" she asked.

6

Marcus

"Perhaps we could come to an agreement?" Marcus leaned forward, his elbows braced on his knees.

Truth was, he couldn't give a fuck if her pathetic excuse for a boyfriend had to save up for the membership.

That wasn't his problem.

But this woman had his blood running hotter, faster—even though she wasn't his.

"That depends on what you want," she replied, biting the edge of her bottom lip, a subtle gesture that only made him want her more.

His gaze trailed lower, catching the delicate lace creeping up her bare thigh, a burn of desire growing within him.

"You're not in a position to negotiate, Lana," he said. "I have the power to throw both of you out tonight. Doesn't matter what your boyfriend's dick is doing at this precise moment, or how much he paid for the opportunity."

Instead of escorting her to the door, a fleeting thought raced through his mind. He'd happily spread her legs and fuck the woman over his desk to silence the dark lust swirling through his veins.

A shiver hit him, his body reacting to the image in his head. His muscles tightened as his pulse went wild.

She flinched as he dipped closer, his fingertips grazing her cheek before he pinched a few stray strands of her hair and lightly ran them between his thumb and forefinger.

When she whimpered, an electric current shot through him. And from her quick intake of breath, Lana reacted like the rush had hit her, too.

"I'll forget your abuse of the rules, Lana," he said, holding her gaze. "And give you a second chance."

She exhaled, as if lost, searching for something to steady her. Her ringless fingers fiddled with the bag in her lap, and the slight movement of her leg made it rub against his thigh.

"There's a catch?" she whispered, voice tinged with uncertainty. "Isn't there?"

"Not a catch, as such," he smirked, enjoying every second of her hesitation.

Lana's stormy blue eyes held his golden-green ones, and she lifted her chin in defiance to appear bolder.

"I don't have any money, if that's what you're after. So, what else do you want?"

Adrenaline surged through his veins, her question sparking something primal inside him. It shot into his chest like a live wire.

A growl rumbled low from the back of his throat, and her reaction was immediate—she stood, her heels wobbling as her eyes popped wide.

"I should go," she said breathlessly, her voice shaking.

Marcus rose, his towering height looming over her. "We haven't finished."

Lana tilted her head back to meet his gaze, a hint of a dare to cross a line in her eyes, mixed with a sheen of uncertainty.

"Really? I think you'll find you can't stop me from walking out that door," she said, the challenge in her voice strong, but there was a waver there, too.

The blue hue of her eyes darkened, and in that moment, Marcus knew she'd break his control.

Without thinking, he cupped her cheeks in his hands, his thumb brushing over the soft skin as he dropped his face close to hers.

"Let's test that theory, shall we?" he said, before his mouth crashed onto her glossy lips.

Fuck.

Her breath, warm and inviting, sent a surge of heat through him.

His hand jumped to her ass, and he yanked her closer, bumping his pelvis into her belly, claiming her mouth with a force that demanded submission.

At first, her muscles tensed in resistance, her palms lifting, as if she might push him away. But she didn't.

Instead, one hand curled into the fabric of his shirt, the other skated the landscape of his chest as her body melted into him.

She softened and kissed him back, responding with a hunger that turned his blood molten.

The taste of her—sweet like strawberries and laced with alcohol—was a mind fuck. He wanted more. Maybe everything she had to offer.

Kissing her hard, he explored her mouth with slow, deliberate licks, teasing her, pushing deeper, and stroking her tongue with growing urgency.

His left hand fisted the hair at her nape, tugging her head back, and his teeth grazed the spot beneath her ear, sending a visible shiver over her skin.

"You're not as innocent as you let on. Are you?"

She whimpered, a dirty sound that sent intense vibrations through his chest. Her body pressed into his, eager, needy, and it drove him wild.

Together, they deepened the kiss, the pressure raw and unrestrained, until he finally pulled away.

She traced the swollen, glossy outline of her lips, as if processing what had just happened.

He dipped his head to the curve of her neck, aware of the wild pulse beneath her skin.

"I bet you're wet for me, Lana." His words were husky, loaded with desire.

"No, I'm not," she said, though her voice trembled, betraying her. "It was just a kiss."

A low, cocky smile curved his lips as he watched her. "That was some kiss."

Marcus wasn't used to resistance. And this woman was playing hard to get—even though she could leave if she really wanted to.

Lana straightened, rolling back her shoulders, but her eyes were wide with a mixture of shock and want.

Her desire matched his.

"You can't stop me from leaving," she said, a little breathy, backing away.

When she half-heartedly tried to sidestep him, he grabbed her waist and dragged her chest into his.

"Here's the deal. If you're wet, then I won't destroy your contract," he said next to her ear. "It's as simple as that. A chance to figure out if this club is truly meant for a girl like you."

She frowned. "Why wouldn't it be?"

"Okay, then own up," he said. "Are you wet for me?"

"Burn the damn contract for all I care," she said, clearly bluffing, because she broke eye contact and stared behind him. "If I'm expected to deal with creepy assholes like that guy downstairs, then I'm out. I'm not that desperate."

His hand slid to her neck, and he thumbed the delicate curve of her throat. Goosebumps spread over her skin, and when the faintest groan escaped her lips, he nearly lost himself.

The pulse of desire in his veins was almost unbearable.

"You're not that desperate," he countered. "But you are desperate for something."

Her lashes fluttered, and she exhaled a shaky breath. "Are we done here, Mr McGrath?"

Without a second's hesitation, he grabbed the hem of her dress, yanking it upward until it bunched around her waist, exposing the soft, pale skin of her thighs. His blood raced.

He was breaking his own rules, but fuck it, he didn't care.

"You tell me. Are we done here, Lana?"

His hand slid between her thighs, fingers finding the damp heat of her panties. He didn't wait—sliding them aside and dragging his fingers through the warmth of her wet pussy.

And she didn't stop him.

Instead, she muttered under her breath and dug her nails into his biceps, clutching him like a lifeline. "Oh, God..."

"I knew it," he growled, his voice rough and dark with need. "Really fucking wet."

When she groaned, he realised she needed him to take the lead. To control the situation so she could justify her surrender.

Rubbing her clit, her body arched into his touch. She was so fucking responsive, so needy for more.

Her breath hitched, and he knew the ache burning between her legs was growing wilder, hotter.

His finger traced the curve of her inner thigh, light but electric, making his dick throb as he witnessed her greedy reaction.

"Tell me, Lana..." He pushed deeper, letting his finger linger, testing her—testing himself. "Do you always get this wet when you're fucking around on your boyfriend?"

His question hung in the air. He knew she shouldn't

be in his office—getting off on his hand—this wasn't how his club worked.

But rules are made to be broken once in a while.

She swallowed, and then her voice trembled as she spoke. "Maybe... maybe it's just you."

Her words hit him like a challenge, like she was trying to make sense of it all, even if she didn't have the answers.

A dangerous smile tugged at his lips. His palm swathed her throat, feeling her pulse beneath his fingertips, as if it was somehow syncing with his.

"I'm special, huh?" he asked, his voice low and teasing as he drove his finger inside with slow, sure precision. "You get wet for me, but not your boyfriend?"

She gasped.

Her body was responding to him in ways she couldn't deny. And the truth was there in her eyes, even if she refused to speak it aloud.

He watched as a slight shiver ran through her and her legs parted to give him better access.

"So what if I'm wet?" she whispered. "I joined this club for a reason. To try something different. To experience something new. This is...new for me."

"New, huh?" he asked.

Her nod fuelled him, made him want to push further, to see how far he could take her.

His expression darkened, a dark desire taking hold. Marcus hadn't experienced this sort of buzz in forever.

He withdrew his hand, loving how her bright blue

eyes turned navy, thinking it was over before it had even begun.

But when he brought his fingers to his mouth and sucked, savouring the taste, her pupils blew wide.

"I'm honoured," he said, smiling when her cheeks turned pink.

Lana lowered her gaze, a mask slipping into place, but he could sense the fire burning hot under her skin. He knew there was an ache between her thighs that begged for a release.

"No need to feel honoured, Mr McGrath," she said, cool, like she was trying to regain control of herself. "I'll have forgotten all about you by the morning."

"Really?" When his fingers skated up her thigh, she whimpered.

He leaned in, his breath ghosting over her ear. "Then maybe I should do something you'll remember."

7

Lana

"Oh, God…"

Lana's forehead dropped to his shoulder; her willpower utterly defeated when he pushed aside her panties again.

The pulse of his fingers made her veins burn hotter.

She rocked her hips into him, the sensation so deliciously electric it clouded her mind.

Every movement ignited a scalp-tingling rush that spread all over her. Even if she wanted to, she couldn't bring herself to pull away.

I'm supposed to be Rory's girl.

The thought hovered in the back of her mind, distant yet persistent. Despite that, she suspected Rory was doing more with the other woman.

That realisation alone made the guilt a little less heavy, a little easier to bury.

But still… This *was* wrong, wasn't it?

Technically, Marcus wasn't a member. But he was

the owner, and this was still in the realms of the club rules.

Her mind swirled in confusion as she writhed against him.

The faintest trace of musky cologne layered over the scent of whiskey and *him*, leaving an unforgettable mark on her senses.

His height made her seem small in comparison, but not in a way that intimidated her—no, it was oddly comforting. Almost protective.

This was the essence of forbidden lust, which made it far too tempting to refuse.

She gasped as his fingers pumped in deep. The whole situation was off the charts hot. Unlike anything she'd ever experienced.

God, I need this.

The pang of guilt was quickly consumed by the fire coursing through her veins, searing away the last of her doubts.

Lana's hips moved against his hand, chasing the friction, the heat, the *release*. She was so close to the edge, every inch of her burning with need.

"Please stop." Her voice was a breathless plea, but there was no conviction behind it.

Truth was, in the dark corners of her mind, she didn't want him to stop. She craved everything he offered for just one night.

"Really?" he asked, leaning back and holding her gaze.

The throbbing between her legs was almost unbearable now, building so high, so fast, she thought she might explode.

With his free hand, he cupped her jaw and squeezed. "Should I stop, Miss Craig?"

Her heart pounded in her chest, and when he angled his wrist just right, the pleasure spiked, sending her over the edge of her restraint.

"No..." She exhaled the word.

Her breath hitched, and an uncontrollable moan tore from her throat as his fingers slid in deeper, two of them now, stretching her in a way that made her legs tremble.

Electricity shot through her. The fierce heat differed from the warmth she had with Rory. She couldn't figure out if it was just the risk of being in a stranger's arms—or the stranger himself.

Rory took his time. Coaxed her, made sure she was ready. But Marcus—he turned her skin to fire with one look.

"Oh...my...god, please don't stop." The words slipped out before she could even register them, her body unravelling beneath his touch.

The bag strap fell off her shoulder and thudded to the carpet. Her hands found their way to his pressed shirt, smoothing over the fabric, aware of the muscular contours underneath.

"Hmmm... my dick would enjoy sliding in and out of this pussy." His voice was low, almost growling, sending a ripple of desire straight through her core.

The combination of his fingers and his words had her spiralling toward a place she couldn't control.

She was lost in his touch, his presence and the tingle of his breath against her neck. All of it struck a match and set the wrongs ablaze.

Lana ground her hips, hunting for a release. pulsing while his other hand fisted her hair, his grip firm as he pulled her closer, his mouth violently crashing over hers.

The kiss was raw, possessive, the kind that made her forget the world around her.

Their teeth clashed and their tongues played. It wasn't just a kiss—it was an awakening.

Her breasts pressed tightly to his chest as she hung onto him, each movement sending shivers through her. His thumb expertly rubbed the pulsating nub between her thighs, working her into a frenzy.

Getting off on his hand was wrong. She knew it was, but, fuck; the thrill was so unbelievably good. The fine line between guilt and pleasure had blurred beyond recognition, and she couldn't tell where one ended and the other began.

She rose higher, giving in to the rush of tingles. Her legs braced and her release tore through her in waves.

With her face buried in his shirt, she gripped him tighter, panting.

The deep, satisfied growl rumbling in his chest was loud against her ear, reverberating through her bones and making the sensation stronger.

But then, as quickly as the fire ignited, it was over.

His fingers withdrew, and he tugged her dress back down in a casual gesture that snapped the moment back into something cold and distant.

Her hands slid from his shoulders, down to his chest, finally falling away when she backed up.

Steadying herself, her mind swirled with guilt and a lingering desire she couldn't quite explain or get rid of.

Marcus nudged her chin with his knuckles, lifting her face to meet his gaze, his eyes dark green and intense.

He dragged his essence-coated fingers over her swollen lips, sending a jolt of heat through her, before he raised them to his mouth and sucked.

"Don't break the rules. This is your last chance," he rasped. "Are we clear?"

She cleared her throat and fixed her hair. "Yeah, crystal clear."

"Good night, Ms Craig." He stood back and raked a hand through his.

Her hands balled into fists, her body tensing with a mix of frustration and confusion. The cocky asshole had her climaxing in minutes and then dismissed her like it meant nothing.

Which it didn't. But the formality of his brush off stuck in her throat.

For a silent second, she stared at him, studying his confident, effortless stride as he sauntered toward the door, his gaze turning distant.

Marcus pulled open the door and tapped his fingers on the solid wood, a subtle gesture that spoke volumes of his control over the situation.

Still breathless, Lana bent to grab her purse from the carpet, trying to ignore the dampness between her thighs, the proof of her body's betrayal.

Straightening, she rolled her shoulders back and gathered what little composure she had left, sauntering past him without giving anything away.

Once she was in the corridor, she glanced over her shoulder, her chest tightening at the sight of him watching her leave.

Inwardly, she cursed herself for giving in to a gorgeous man who's so damn full of himself—and becoming one of his conquests.

She hated how quickly he'd reverted into that cold, detached businessman, dismissing her with a calculated calmness as if it was all part of his plan.

"I appreciate the second chance, Mr McGrath," she said, her voice steady despite the storm raging in her chest. "And don't worry, I'll never step foot in your office again."

But then, as if her body hadn't been through enough, his voice rumbled through the corridor.

"Lana..." His voice was like silk slipping over the gritty remains of her crushed self-control, pulling her back into the fire.

"Break the rules and you'll have me to deal with on a whole other level."

She kept walking, faster now, not sure if that was a dare or a warning.

Getting into the elevator, she let out the breath she'd been holding and sank against the wall. She pressed a hand to her chest, trying to calm her racing heart.

Lana couldn't decide if she was angry, still turned on,

or both. She was just...*confused* and unsure what to do next.

There was a fire burning low inside her. A flickering flame that needed stoked.

If Marcus could get her pulse racing, then maybe another man could, too.

8

Marcus

He'd taken a risk, and fuck, he dared her to break his rules—so he could break them, too.

That dress of hers clung to her body like sin, outlining curves that made his blood run hot. But that kiss. Her little moans. That was something else.

Now, with the door shut and the scent of her perfume hanging in the air, Marcus exhaled a deep, heavy breath. His dick throbbed against his zipper, and his pulse was uneven.

He ran a hand over his jaw, recalling her drenched pussy and inner walls gripping his fingers as if she had been waiting for him. The way she'd melted into him, hesitant but hungry, like she'd tasted the forbidden and needed him to fuck her before she changed her mind.

It had his body primed.

Her moans were stuck in his head, wicked and taunting. And that sweet taste of strawberry on her lips was a pleasant surprise.

He grinned at the way she'd fisted his shirt, responding to him like she was losing herself in something bigger than just a cheap thrill.

She seemed lost in the dark. And thought he was her lighthouse.

Marcus gritted his teeth, shaking the thought away. Getting her out of his office was the right move.

Sure, he was a bastard for finger fucking and then pushing her away, but it had to be done.

Reality hit. He had to forget she ever existed because he had no business fooling around with a Verto Veneri member. No business touching anyone outside the rules he'd put in place.

His fists flexed. The sensation of her wet heat had gone. In the moment, had she begged, he would have bent her over his desk, slapped her ass raw, and buried himself inside her until she'd forgotten every other man who came before him.

But that would never happen. Not with a woman who was in a relationship.

Marcus didn't get involved with the couples in his club. And that was that.

Dragging a hand through his hair, he told himself the encounter was a rare moment of weakness. A one-off incident, never to be repeated.

He stalked to his desk and snatched up the phone, jabbing the speed dial button with more force than necessary.

"Donna Marie, who did Rory O'Hare go off with

tonight?" His voice came out sharper than intended, irritation tightening his jaw.

"Uh, let me check. He's one of the new clients..." He heard her tapping at her keyboard. "Yeah, he took a suite with Jacqueline Simpson. They're in room 505."

Marcus's grip on the receiver tightened. Fucking typical. He had no idea why he even bothered to ask.

"Did Mr Simpson join them?"

"No, he's with someone else. Why? Is there something wrong, Marcus?" Donna Marie asked.

"It's nothing." He pinched the bridge of his nose. "Let me know when the new guy has left."

Hanging up, Marcus poured himself a whiskey, straight, no ice. He paced his office, his footsteps muffled against the carpet as his mind reeled.

Business. He needed to focus on business.

But every time he tried, his thoughts veered back to the blonde. The way she'd gasped against his lips, the way her thighs had trembled, the heat of her skin against his fingers.

He knocked back the whiskey, but the burn didn't take the edge off.

Fuck it.

Slamming the glass down, he strode out of his office and headed straight to the security room. The door buzzed open, and O'Brien and Donovan turned to greet him, their postures straightening as he entered.

"Mr McGrath," O'Brien acknowledged.

"Show me the Verto main lounge," Marcus ordered, his voice gruff.

Donovan didn't ask questions. He pointed to a set of monitors, their screens flickering between various camera angles. Marcus's gaze locked onto the one showing the club's bar area.

Lana.

She was sitting alone at the bar, stirring a drink with a slow rotation of her straw, her expression unreadable.

But he knew what she was doing. She was waiting for another man to approach her, to take her to a suite. She came to play, after all. And had every right to do just that.

A knot twisted in his stomach, the sensation unexpected and unwanted.

This was why he'd created Verto Veneri—to give couples a space to explore without secrets or lies. But watching Lana sit by herself while her boyfriend was screwing another woman upstairs angered him.

He told himself his concern was nothing more than a responsibility. A duty of care for his members. That was all.

Despite that, Lana looked like fucking prey, and the men circling the bar—men who were looking for an easy invitation—were predators waiting to pounce.

He had rules in place to keep things safe, to ensure consent, but he knew how some of these bastards operated. They'd recognise she was vulnerable and seize an opportunity.

Marcus's gaze stayed fixed on the monitor as Lana ordered a drink, his jaw tightening with every second that passed.

"We can watch the woman if there's a problem, sir," Donovan said.

"It's fine. I have a few minutes to spare. Last thing I need is a new member getting in over their head. We can't risk an innocent woman like her having a bad experience. She'd end up getting the club shut down."

But the longer he watched, the more he found himself hoping she would get bored and leave. Alone. Untouched. Unclaimed by any other man.

It made no sense.

He wasn't the type to fixate on a woman, especially not one who belonged to someone else. Yet a crazy notion of stealing her for himself whispered through his mind, irrational and daring.

But Marcus didn't need to steal women.

Nor did he do reckless things to have them.

And he sure as hell didn't want a relationship.

She was better off with her dumbass boyfriend, however undeserving he was. Because in the end, after a hot and heavy night, Marcus would walk away. That's who he was. A man who fucked, not a man who kept.

Except...

His pulse was hammering. His dick was still on high alert. And every muscle in his body braced, ready to move the second some other bastard made his approach.

He exhaled, dragging a hand over his course-haired jaw, forcing himself to look away from the screen.

"Who's that?" O'Brien asked.

Marcus's gaze shot back to the live footage where a man was getting comfy on the bar stool next to her.

His fingers curled into fists, and his voice dropped to a low murmur, surprising even himself.

"No one touches her tonight. Understood?"

9

Lana

Lana walked up to the bar. Her steps were smooth, but her mind scattered.

She pulled a ten-pound note from her purse and slid it onto the counter, trying to ignore the way her fingers trembled.

The bartender gave her a quick nod. "Same again?"

"Yeah, please."

As she waited, Lana's gaze drifted across the shelves behind the bar. The bottles, some labelled 'McGrath', caught her eye, and she couldn't help the wayward thoughts that followed.

She wanted to push him out of her mind, to bury him somewhere in the dark corners where fleeting encounters belonged.

But it wasn't that easy. In the aftermath, the memory of his lips consumed every second that passed. The press of his body against hers and the way she'd moaned for him.

Her thighs ached with the echo of their kiss. The heat he'd ignited still simmered, and no amount of alcohol would douse the fire.

His scent, his hands—damn, his hands—kept resurfacing, that naughty sensation of being touched by someone else.

She downed her drink, trying to ignore the mix of frustration and desire still dancing through her veins. Around her, couples moved in the shadows, disappearing in a flurry of lust and anticipation.

But where was Rory?

Marcus was right. Rory didn't care that she was sitting at the bar all alone. The fact she could have hooked up with someone else too didn't give him cause for hesitation.

She had been fooling herself, thinking that maybe tonight they'd share the experience together. But no. He'd wandered off, leaving her to cross paths with Marcus.

It hit her all at once. In the wake of her recent encounter, she was questioning everything. How could another man stir her emotions? Why did she have such an intense desire to overstep boundaries with Marcus?

As she sat there, Rory was cheating on her, yet all she could think about was Marcus. Would she have let him do more if he's pushed?

The thought made her pulse race. She closed her eyes for a second, trying to clear the fog, but it was no use.

Marcus was trouble.

And she was thankful their paths would never cross in the future. Billionaires don't pop up in her world.

Despite everything that had happened, maybe Rory was right all along. This might be fun with the right guy.

Lana hadn't given it much thought before, but now, with the image of Marcus's hands still fresh in her mind, she wondered if all her rigid rules were just holding her back from something better.

Which meant she needed to find a man who ticked off all the right boxes...but absolutely not Marcus McGrath.

She mentally reviewed her list.

1. **Tall but not lanky**–A build like Marcus's, but not Marcus.
2. **Dark hair**–Jet black hair that smelled fresh. Marcus's hair tempted her to lean in closer.
3. **Attractive**–There should be instant attraction. On the same scale as her pulse-pounding reaction to Marcus.
4. **Well-built**–A little muscle definition wouldn't hurt, right? And Marcus? Clearly defined muscles showed beneath his shirt. She'd smoothed her hand over the dips.
5. **Funny**–Was he funny? Or was his broodiness enough to keep her hooked without jokes?
6. **Clean**–His musky scent still lingered, intoxicating and hard to forget.

7. **Straight teeth**–He had perfect white teeth behind that sexy, cocky smirk.
8. **Below forty**–He didn't look a day over thirty-five, but then again, age is just a number... right?

She rolled her eyes and huffed at the constant comparisons. Honestly, it was embarrassing. Her obsession with him was a waste of time.

Marcus McGrath, the undisputed seducer of all women—including her—served as the benchmark for those who followed.

Truth was, it sickened her how easily he had affected her, how he knew he could tease her—and how she'd let him.

As she ran through her mental checklist of her fantasy man, the guilt settled in. Rory didn't tick every box. Not even close.

But he was a decent guy. Rory was good to her. She loved him, and maybe, just maybe, she *could* learn to love this strange, boundary-pushing idea of a relationship.

Still, as she weighed it out, despite his redeeming qualities—his humour, his height that could have been intimidating but somehow wasn't—he didn't exactly match up to the raw, undeniable attraction she'd felt a few hours ago.

Rory wasn't Marcus.

But Rory cared about her in his own way. They shared something real, something stable, something she could build a life on.

He'd convinced her this experiment, this wild night of 'playing around,' was a step toward growing closer, expanding their boundaries, bringing more fun into their sex life.

That was the reason she was perched on the barstool. For the future of their relationship.

Lana sipped from her glass, eyes scanning the crowd.

Perhaps she was being too picky. Age, after all, wasn't everything. Older men might have more experience, but they also came with baggage. Taking another gulp of her cocktail, she upped the age limit on her list to forty-five.

A sudden shift to her left caught her attention, and she noticed a man she hadn't seen before leaning against the bar. Light creases framed warm, chocolate eyes, and a pale blue shirt hugged his torso.

Streaks of silver in his dark hair slotted him into the early forties range, and his well-built body spoke of effort and discipline. He had the vibe of a man who knew exactly what he was doing.

"Hey, sweetheart," he greeted, offering a large hand. "Mind if I sit with you?"

His tone was polite, his eyes warm and unassuming. Lana glanced up at him, hesitated for only a moment, then nodded and accepted his handshake.

"Sure. I'm Lana." She smiled, noting the firmness of his grip.

"Carl," he said. "And the pleasure is all mine."

He didn't waste time ordering, but instead crooked two fingers at the bartender.

"Guinness, and whatever the lady is drinking." He gave Lana an easy grin.

Lana tapped her glass with her fingernail, shaking her head. "It's okay. I've already got one here. Thanks anyway."

Carl's lips curved at the corners, a polite smile that didn't feel forced.

"Let me buy you a drink, sweetheart. One more won't hurt." He winked, the charm effortless.

Lana hesitated, then gave a slight shrug, shifting to the edge of her bar stool. "Okay... Same again, please."

Carl settled in next to her, exuding a calm confidence that wasn't overbearing. He launched into conversation, his voice smooth as he spoke about his logistics business, which focused on the transportation of luxury goods.

His passion for his work was clear, and despite her growing restlessness, she listened.

"I own a fleet of vehicles, mostly based in the UK," Carl explained, then added with a grin, "The whole 'luxury transport' gig opened up some pretty interesting doors for me...both business-wise and...personally."

He winked again.

Lana nodded, her attention waning as he continued on about his business ventures. He mentioned his wife, Lorraine, a Scottish woman who apparently had a taste for the finer things in life.

Carl's words drifted into the background as Lana's mind wandered. Sure, he was easy to talk to—good-natured and kind—but there was zero spark. No electric charge kicking off between them.

In fact, he was verging on tedious. He was also...*safe*.

She considered Carl to be the type of man who she could remove her Verto learner plates. He was charming and grounded in a way that most men weren't.

The guy had a life and a marriage that worked for him.

That's what you need, she reminded herself.

Someone who didn't come with complications. A one and done adventure.

But her hot encounter kept gnawing at her. The memory of Marcus's touch still burned through her skin.

She forced her attention back to Carl, nodding as he rambled on about another logistics venture. Despite his looks, he was just too ordinary for her.

But the fact was, thinking about Marcus had lit a slow burning fire in her core and she wasn't sure how to get rid of it.

Carl's flirtatious smile and the way his hand lingered just a moment too long on her arm made her decision feel simpler. Maybe it was time to shift gears, away from the dangerous allure of Marcus and toward something safer, more predictable.

"What do you do for a living?" Carl asked, his attention fixated on her mouth as he raised his glass to his lips, the slight rasp of his deep voice sending a ripple of awareness through her.

Her pulse fluttered. More from nerves than anything else.

"I'm stuck behind a desk all day, shuffling papers,

unfortunately," she said, attempting to sound nonchalant while she flicked her hair behind her shoulder.

Carl's eyes darkened, his lips curling into a knowing smile. "You've never been to Verto before, right?"

Lana nodded, aware of his sweeping gaze drinking in her cleavage. "Yeah. Is it that obvious?"

The throb between her thighs had almost completely fizzled out. She wanted it back—she wanted that rush.

Carl leaned in, the low rumble of his voice sending warmth through her chest.

"You seem a little nervous," he said, his eyes sparkling with mischief. "But that's okay. Makes it more exciting. Too much of a good thing dulls the rush."

Lana sucked in a breath, the craving for something intense hitting her again. She exhaled, trying to mask the flutters in her chest and went for it.

"Would you like to be my first, Carl?" she asked, biting her lower lip with a playful look, hoping to mask the insecurity that crept beneath her skin.

The alcohol gave her a false sense of confidence, enough to throw herself into the moment.

Carl chuckled low, leaning back on his stool, amused by her boldness. He put his hands behind his head, his biceps flexing beneath the pale blue shirt.

"WOW, straight in there, Lana," he said with a dark, lustful gleam in his eyes. "I'm honoured. I knew you'd be up for it."

He swirled the black liquid in his pint glass, his gaze never leaving her. "I love meeting the new members.

Seeing the excitement through fresh eyes is a big turn on. Let's go get us a room. Deal?"

Lana's stomach swooped, but her mind kept racing—*Focus on the moment, Lana.* She played with the lengths of her hair, running them through her fingers to steady herself.

"Deal," she said, her voice just a little too breathless. "I'll go freshen up."

She slid off the barstool, tugging the hem of her dress down, aware of his eyes on her every step.

"I'll head upstairs and get myself ready. Donna Marie will give you the other key card." Carl leaned in, kissing her cheek.

"Okay," Lana replied, her voice tight as the reality of the night hit her.

"I'll see you in the room," she added almost inaudibly, trying to convince herself she was making the right choice.

But all she could think of was Marcus's height, his watchful green gaze, the heat in his touch, the way he'd kissed her—like he owned her.

Carl was a safe choice. But Marcus... Marcus was the fire she'd never have again.

10

Marcus

"The girl at the bar, Lana Craig—who's the man talking to her?" Marcus snarled into the phone, his voice low, cutting through the line like a whip.

"Carl Reed. Is there a problem?" Donna Marie's tone was cautious, aware that something was off.

This was the second time he'd called her tonight. Marcus only checked on members when necessary.

However, tonight wasn't normal.

He was obsessing over Lana. And watching her talk to another guy stirred intense, strange emotions within him.

His fingers curled around the receiver, his grip a silent reflection of the tension knotting in his stomach. She came here to screw a stranger and had paid for the privilege. He should let that roll off him. But it fucking tore at him.

"It's the girl from earlier," he muttered. "I'm monitoring her movements. Making sure she behaves. I don't want more pissed off members tonight. Did you smooth things over with Bingham?"

"Of course. I fixed Benny up with another new member. A lady closer to his age," Donna Marie half-laughed, her voice a little more relaxed. "He'll be happier now. Don't worry, I'll keep an eye on the girl."

"I'm already on it." His jaw clenched.

Marcus slammed the receiver back into place and turned toward the monitors. His eyes returned to the live feed.

Where the fuck did she go?

Donovan flicked through the different cameras. Marcus said nothing more, waiting for his security to do their job.

And then, there she was.

On the screen, Lana stepped out of the washrooms with that unmistakable confidence in her walk. Every step had a slow, seductive sway of her hips. Golden hair bounced with the rhythm of her stride, and he could almost taste that strawberry of her gloss.

His eyes tracked every move.

Her ass, that damn ass, deserved a spank for the way she had his full attention.

Marcus' fingers twitched as the thought of tugging her head back, making her beg for it, slid into his mind. He cleared his throat and pushed it down, watching Donna Marie hand her a key card.

A sharp pang of possessiveness slammed into his chest.

"What the hell is she doing?" Marcus muttered under his breath.

Lana was walking toward the lobby now, her movements slow and her veins full of alcohol. She was oblivious to the sick thrill shooting through Marcus while he watched every step she took, knowing he had the control.

Marcus ran a hand through his hair, needing a straight whiskey when she moved into elevator and the door slide shut

For a split second, Marcus allowed himself to breathe. She was gone—out of sight, out of his reach—and rising to the top floor.

The security men were quiet, knowing better than to speak. Marcus hated the pulse of tension rising in his chest, like a slow burn that wouldn't ease.

His fists clenched at his sides, watching as the elevator ascended. The higher she went, the angrier he became.

Her form in the camera was small but the floor she left behind was another drop in his blood pressure. His fingers twitched. His mind screamed for action, yet his body froze with something dark and powerful.

As the elevator doors opened, she hesitated. Just for a second, but Marcus saw it. That slight pause, that brief moment where she wasn't sure.

It struck him hard, like a punch to the gut. Was she nervous? Undecided? Had she even wanted to come here at all, or was joining Carl a drunken impulse?

His gut told him something wasn't right. She wasn't a

careless party girl looking for meaningless thrills. There was more to her. A deeper vulnerability. A quiet need to feel wanted. And that, more than anything, pissed him off.

The screen blinked as Lana reached the door of the penthouse, fumbling with the key card. She was tipsy, but she still tried, her fingers shaky, her eyes darting around as if waiting for someone to pull her out of this situation.

His blood ran hot, and his pulse quickened.

With alcohol clouding her judgment, she was heading straight into bed with a man who didn't deserve her. A man who didn't know the first thing about treating a woman the way she deserved. It made him sick.

Carl Reed was planning to fuck her in a suite he owned. Who the hell did he think he was?

"Donovan," he growled through clenched teeth, his gaze burning into the screen. "Deactivate that card immediately."

His words were clipped, a razor-edged command. He wanted to pull her out of that elevator by her fucking hair and take her back to his office.

Donovan hesitated for a moment, just enough to register the seriousness of Marcus' tone. "Sir?"

"Don't question me, just do it." The growl escaped before he could stop it.

He was halfway to the door before Donovan could respond, the fisted desk still echoing in the silence.

His heart pounded in his ears. It wasn't about her right to choose. It wasn't about whether or not she had a boyfriend. No one else was going to touch her in this fucking hotel.

He spun around, his eyes narrowing in icy fury. "Keep her out of that room, Donovan. I don't give a fuck how you do it. Just stop her."

The words had barely left his lips before he was striding toward the elevator, his long strides making the floor seem to tremble beneath him.

He stepped into the elevator, fingers already hitting the button for the top floor, knowing he had the power to do whatever he wanted.

As the elevator surged upward, his muscles tensed. His heartbeat pounded in his ears, each passing floor adding to the suffocating pressure building in his chest.

By the time the doors slid open, his entire body went taut when his eyes settled on the beautiful blue-eyed woman waiting for the lift.

Lana.

11

Lana

Lana pressed the button outside the elevator, her mind racing as she glanced back at the penthouse door.

The malfunctioning key card had to be a sign. Perhaps a random hookup with a stranger wasn't meant to be.

With Ken? Callum?

Whatever the hell his name was, she couldn't even remember and blamed it on the booze.

Waiting for the elevator to arrive, her thoughts spiralled. Was it the unknown that excited people like him?

The notion of sex with someone they weren't in love with–without expectations or sneaking around?

After tonight, she understood how people crossed those lines.

She'd been a victim to the fierce attraction that still burned through her. A strong desire to push the boundaries with another man. A playboy like *Marcus*.

She shivered and palmed her belly, cursing herself for thinking about him again.

With a soft sigh, she reached into her purse, fishing out her phone. But when she glanced at the screen, her heart sank. No missed calls from Rory. No messages. Nothing.

She swallowed the hurt and typed out a quick text asking him to call her. She waited, expecting a reply that didn't come. Of course, he didn't get back to her. He was somewhere in The Fitz, fulfilling his fantasies.

Eventually, the elevator doors slid open, and her pulse skittered to a stop.

Marcus.

He was right there, leaning against the mirrored wall, arm raised a fraction as though he'd been waiting for her.

His head was lowered just enough to make his jawline look even sharper, his broad shoulders making the shirt hug his muscles.

When she froze, his gaze snapped to hers, and all the air left her lungs in a quiet whoosh. She swallowed hard, trying to steady the frantic pulse picking up in her throat.

His hand traced the wall, a slow, controlled motion. She couldn't tear her eyes away. This man's presence radiated the same impressive dominance as before, an unshakable force that captured her attention without a single word.

And her body remembered. The way he'd taken control. How she saw stars when he'd pushed her to the edge.

Her skin prickled, and pulsating heat returned

between her thighs. Lana hated how Marcus was the man who set her alight. More so than Rory.

This insufferable, arrogant man was her dirty little secret.

Marcus's voice broke through her daze, a low rumble that sent tingles coursing all over her.

"We meet again, Lana Craig."

She stumbled back a step, her chin dipping to break the intense eye contact.

"Are you following me?" she asked. "There must be rules about men stalking female members."

"I own the place, remember?"

"Aren't you getting out now?" she asked.

"I'm waiting for you to join me."

The pull toward him was magnetic, absurdly strong. His green eyes were intense, framed by thick black lashes, the gaze of a man who was used to getting whatever he wanted.

But as she sighed and inched back some more, he prowled toward her, not giving her a moment to breathe.

"Get into the elevator, Lana."

His command was cold, stern—no warmth or invitation in it. More like an order. Her body reacted before her mind caught up.

The urge to obey warred with the fire that roared inside her. He wasn't asking. He was telling her.

"Excuse me?" she bit out the words. "You don't get to order me about. I don't care if you own this hotel. There's no way I'm getting inside that elevator with you."

His eyes never left hers, and a faint smile tugged at the corner of his mouth like he was enjoying this.

"Get in, Lana." His voice softened, but it was no less commanding.

Her jaw clenched.

"Why? Because I messed up again with the key card?" Her words were sharp, but the alcohol had loosened her tongue.

She pushed herself to stand taller, bolder.

"For your information, Mr McGrath, the key card wouldn't work. Which is more your hotel's fault than mine. That's the reason the guy I met at the bar is still waiting for me down the corridor." She jutted her thumb behind her. "Not because I was trying to break your rules. So...you can't kick me out."

She paused, taking a breath, her cheeks flushing with a mix of anger and embarrassment. "You...you brute!"

The low chuckle rumbling through his chest was like a spark to gasoline, deep and ever so sexy.

"Brute?" he repeated, a hint of amusement in his voice. "I've been called many things, but I don't think 'brute' is one of them. In fact, I don't think anyone uses that word these days. C'mon, get in."

A wild pulse fluttered in her throat, the heat rising up her neck. Her mind screamed at her to walk away, but the adrenaline pumping through her veins betrayed her. Truth was, she could lose control around him, and that scared her.

Rather than obey, she backed herself against the wall,

her spine pressing into the cool surface, trying hard to ignore the tension coiling in her body.

She swept her hair over her shoulder, letting it cascade over her breasts, a move she knew was seductive. She couldn't help it, though.

"I can't get in that elevator with you," she whispered, but the words lacked conviction.

He stepped closer, his presence overwhelming, and in one fluid movement, his large hand waited in the space between them.

"Let's go," he said, his voice a low rumble.

"Why should I?" she asked.

"Weren't you waiting for the lift to take you down?"

She blinked up at him, her breath shallow, and then she slotted her hand into his. The second their skin touched, a surge of electricity shot through her.

"Fine."

With his hand wrapped around hers, Marcus guided her inside the elevator and the doors closed, sealing them into the small space together.

She yanked her hand away and curled her fingers, savouring the warmth he'd left there. Moving to the opposite side, she did her best not to stare. To not notice how his presence left her nowhere else to look.

"I won't have sex with you, Marcus," she muttered under her breath. "If that's what you're thinking."

His gaze never shifted from the digital display, his eyes sharp and calculating as the elevator descended.

He said nothing, the silence heavy between them.

At minus one, the bell chimed, and the doors slid open. The sudden coolness of an underground car park made her shiver, a contrast to the simmering heat in her veins.

She blinked, confusion knitting her brows together. "Why are we here?"

Stepping forward, she wobbled. His hand was quick and firm on her elbow, holding her upright.

"Careful," he said, the tone not quite as caring as it could have been.

He led her out of the elevator with that same commanding grip. Every step she took felt rushed, as if she couldn't keep up with his brisk pace.

Her heels clicked against the concrete underfoot, echoing a rhythmic accompaniment to the sound of her thumping heartbeat.

Under a bright fluorescent light, her mind whirling as they passed a few parked cars. There was no one else around. Just Lana and a man on a mission—to do what?

"Why are we out here?" she asked.

When they reached a sleek black Mercedes Benz, her stomach fluttered.

"This is my private car," he announced. "My driver is inside, waiting."

Unhanding her, he strolled to the rear passenger door, opened it, and stepped aside. His eyes locked with hers.

"Get in."

"Where are we going?"

Marcus straightened, his expression giving nothing

away as he stared at her for a moment. When he finally spoke, his calmness twisted her stomach.

"*We* aren't going anywhere together. You're going home, Lana."

"Home?"

His words hit her like a cold bucket of water, and her heart sank, disappointment creeping in.

A wicked part of her had hoped for something else—a night that would burn hot and fast, wild and dirty. A one-night stand to give her the release she craved.

But no.

He wasn't looking at her with desire anymore. No, his features were tight and his eyes shuttered. A perfected look, his method for dismissing women he'd been with.

Marcus was dismissing her all over again.

Her throat tightened, rejection knotting her stomach.

"What about Rory?" she asked, her voice barely a whisper.

Marcus stuffed his hands in his pockets and scowled as if the mention of her boyfriend had struck a chord. He stared ahead, the harsh lines of his jaw tight.

For a long moment, he didn't answer, as if he was weighing his choice of words.

"Rory isn't part of this equation," he finally said, his tone matter of fact.

There was a moment of hesitation before he continued, his voice lower now, almost a growl. "You're here because of *you*, not because of him. I'm doing you a favour, Lana."

"A favour?" She half-laughed. "Sending me home

isn't a favour, Marcus. You're treating me like I'm a schoolgirl who made a mistake."

His gaze flicked to hers, intense and unreadable, and for the briefest moment, she saw a flash of something dangerous behind his eyes.

"I know you're not a little girl. But you're also not in control here. You never have been. The sooner you realise that, the better."

He was right. Since they'd met, he was the one in control, and she was just trying to keep up.

"Not everyone has everything worked out," she said, the sting of his words uncomfortable. "What happens now? Are we allowed back?"

Silence stretched as Marcus scratched his jaw, considering her. There was something in the way he looked at her now—something almost calculating.

"You'll go home tonight and read the contract," he said, his voice firm. "Next time you walk into my club, I suggest you put a limit on the amount of alcohol you drink. People make stupid mistakes when they're drunk."

She rolled her eyes. "I highly doubt your club has a one drink policy."

"No, it doesn't, but I'm writing it into your contract. And remember what happened the last time you didn't follow the rules?"

Her cheeks flushed. Maybe she'd break them again just to find out how far he'd push her.

"What will happen to Rory when he's finished?" she asked. "What happens to him, Marcus?"

12

Marcus

"I don't give a fuck about him," he snapped. "My only concern is ensuring you return home and think hard about what you're getting yourself into."

A flicker of hurt pride moved behind her eyes, and a weird pang fizzled through him again, unsettling in its intensity.

"Joining your club wasn't a half-baked idea, or even a whim," she chided. "Shouldn't the big boss be more welcoming to his paying members?"

She gazed up at him, all big blue eyes and boldness, like she needed him to drag her back into the elevator and watch him fuck her against the mirror.

But that wouldn't happen.

"I gave you a second chance, didn't I?" he replied.

Marcus wasn't trying to be an asshole to the woman who'd crawled under his flesh and licked his heart with her sweet, strawberry-flavoured tongue.

However, she was forbidden, and he had to send her away.

In blunt terms, he wasn't interested in fairy tales or relationship goals, and she was already with another man, considering marriage. She'd made a commitment to a guy, and that was her choice.

Fucking a client would be a major breach, and quite possibly ruin everything he'd worked so hard to achieve.

Those were the cold, hard facts. But when her lashes lowered and she bit the corner of her lip ever so slightly, his entire body clenched with a pained restraint.

"Why did you give me a second chance?" she asked, her voice laced with suspicion. "If you were going to send me home straight after."

Staring at her pretty face, he debated the question. One he didn't have a suitable answer.

When she shifted, unsteady in her heels, he stepped into her and caught her waist.

Too tight. For too long.

Lana sucked in a breath, and his gaze burned into the wild pulse in her neck.

One step—just one—and his mouth would be on hers. But he didn't move. Neither did she.

"Get in the car, Lana," he ordered, his voice rough as his hands fell away.

She hesitated, stubborn. "And if I don't?"

Lana folded her arms across her chest, her expression full of defiance and drunken bravery.

Marcus sighed through his nose. Of course, she'd prove to be difficult. He should've expected nothing less.

"You're drunk, Lana. It's time to call it a night."

She lifted her chin, all haughty stubbornness. "I'm tipsy. Not drunk."

He narrowed his eyes. "You've stumbled twice now."

"Try keeping up with your long strides in a pair of high heels."

"If I let you leave on your own, you'd likely break your damn ankle stepping off the pavement. Now please, get in the car. My driver will drop you home. Tell him your address when you get in."

She didn't move, holding her ground, staring at him like she was daring him to force her. His patience had already worn thin, and this was testing his self-control.

Then, before he could say anything else, his phone buzzed from inside his pocket.

He dug it out of his trouser pocket, glancing at the screen, cursing under his breath.

Isla. A woman he'd had a hot and heavy afternoon with in Marbella.

Fucking hell. He never gave women his number.

The name was visible, glaringly obvious, and he didn't miss the way Lana's gaze lingered on the name, then cut back up at him.

Her glossy lips pressed into a thin line.

"Nice," she said, her voice slow, taunting. "I guess I shouldn't be surprised. Being a billionaire playboy and all that. I feel sorry for her."

Marcus's grip on the phone tightened, but he ignored the call, shoving the device back into his pocket. "It's not what you think."

Lana let out a soft, mocking laugh. "Please. I don't think anything. I already know what sort of guy you are."

His brows lifted. "Yeah? Enlighten me, beautiful. What sort of man am I?"

She cocked her head, giving him a look so sweetly condescending it made his blood heat.

"Rich. Powerful. The kind of noncommittal man who uses his good looks to his advantage and fucks a different woman every night, all because he can."

Marcus smirked. "Are you jealous?"

She arched a brow at him, her voice dripping with mock innocence. "God, no. But poor Isla might be jealous if she found out Marcus McGrath was getting me off earlier."

He stepped toward her, crowding her body against the car, forcing her to tilt her head back to meet his glare.

"That woman—or any other woman, for that matter—doesn't get a say in what I do or who I do it with."

Lana's brows rose. "So you *are* admitting there's a lineup?"

A muscle ticked in his jaw.

"I don't answer to anyone," he said, voice low. "If I wanted to take you back inside, bend you over my desk, and make you scream my name until security has to clear the club, I'd do it. And no one—not even Isla, or Rory, or even you—could stop me."

Lana's breath hitched, but she recovered fast. "And the fact you haven't done all that means I'm just a minor inconvenience the big boss has to get rid of, right?"

His hands clenched at his sides. She was playing with fire, and the worst part? He wanted to burn with her.

Instead, he exhaled a heavy sigh. "Get in the car, Lana."

"I can get a taxi."

Marcus huffed out a humourless laugh. "Don't push me."

And for a second, he hoped she might keep arguing. That she might test him just a little bit further, so he'd have a reason to take.

But then she sighed dramatically and slid into the back seat, flashing him one last taunting smile before slamming the door shut.

Fucking hell.

A muscle in his jaw ticked, and he backed up a few steps, wishing he could see through the tinted glass, his own face reflecting at him instead.

Hands pocketed in his dress trousers, he forced himself to do a one-eighty and strolled back to the elevator, the thud of his designer shoes echoing around him.

Without giving in to temptation and glancing over his shoulder, he hit the call button and waited.

Behind him, the engine purred, and the car picked up speed. He knew better than to turn around—but, fuck it, he did anyway.

Marcus's head angled a fraction to watch the car crawl up the narrow ramp to the streets of Belfast city.

His head shook as he exhaled a long breath, finally able to breathe normally again.

Except...he couldn't.

The air had been warmer when she was next to him.

Inside the elevator, the doors slid shut, enclosing him in a space that held a trace of her perfume.

In the time it took him to ascend the floors to his office, he fantasised about her sweet groans, imagined her on all fours, taking all of him, and then cursed himself for the way his dick throbbed.

Maybe the rules were made to be broken.

His phone was in his hand before he even reached his desk. He hit the contact for Donna Marie, bringing the device to his ear.

"Didn't expect another call from you tonight," she said, voice edged with amusement. "Something wrong?"

"Where's Rory O'Hare?" Marcus asked, his voice flat, businesslike.

There was a pause.

"Still occupied. Why? I thought you didn't give a shit about that client."

Marcus exhaled through his nose. "I don't."

"So this sudden interest in his whereabouts has nothing to do with the cute blonde you just escorted downstairs in the lift?"

A muscle twitched in his jaw. Donna Marie was too damn good at her job.

"Is she still with you?" she asked, voice shifting into a more respectful tone. "Is there something you need help with?"

Marcus rolled his shoulders, pushing away the irritation prickling at his spine. "She's on her way home."

Silence stretched for a beat. Then a soft, shocked laugh came. "You sent her home?"

"Yes."

"Ohhh, I have to hear this." She sounded far too entertained. "The girl shows up at your club with her fella, catches your attention by rejecting Benny, and you decide to...what? Shred her contract and shove her in a car...but then her fella is still—"

"I don't have time for this," he snapped.

"What happened?" she asked.

His grip on the phone tightened. His patience was thinning fast.

"I sent her home," he said gruffly. "Because she'd had too much alcohol."

"Right." Donna Marie let the word stretch, clearly unconvinced. "The fact she's gorgeous and had plans with Carl isn't part of it?"

Marcus growled low in his throat. "Goodnight, Donna Marie."

Jaw clenched, he scrolled through his contacts and tapped on another name.

"Yes, sir?"

"I need a client file on Lana Craig," Marcus ordered, his tone clipped. "I want everything—her background, her family, her finances, every place she's lived, every person she's been involved with. I want to know who she is and who her employer is, too."

A slight hesitation. "Is there a problem, sir?"

Marcus grunted as he stared through the floor-to-ceiling windows of his office.

Yes. There's a fucking problem.

Even though he wanted to pretend Lana didn't exist, he couldn't.

13

Lana

The mattress sank. Cold skin brushed against her legs, startling her awake.

"Hey, babe," came a whisper in her ear.

Lana rolled over to find Rory snuggled up in their puffy duvet, his eyes slitted.

"You okay?" he muttered.

Seriously? Is that all he had to say?

After he'd fucked off and left her alone in the devil's lair, so he could play with a pretty brunette?

Her chest tightened, resentment tangling with the remnants of booze in her bloodstream. At least *her* escapade had been harmless—heavy petting, a little flirting, some toe-dipping into a world that, in hindsight, she wasn't sure was for her.

His? Not so much.

She swallowed against the lump in her throat. "I'm fine. Took you long enough to check in on me. Did you have sex?"

A slow breath left his lungs. "I sure did, babe. She was a right firecracker."

Her heart pinched, the bluntness of his confession cutting deeper than she expected.

"Oh, really?" she said, playing down the harsh jolt of jealousy. "In what way?"

She fluffed her pillow, landing a few extra punches into the plush fabric.

Rory gave a sleepy chuckle, stretching like a cat, too satisfied to care about the claws he was digging into her. "Shhh, babe, we can talk about this later. I need a few hours sleep."

Noticing a stream of light peeking out from under the curtains, she glanced at her phone propped up on the nightstand.

Rory had crawled into bed at six-thirty in the morning. He'd been out all night without sending her a brief "you good?" or replying to any of the messages she'd sent him.

Yet a stranger had pulled her from the chaos, made sure she was in a car, and watched until she was gone.

Marcus McGrath owed her nothing. He had no reason to care what happened to her.

Rory had plenty of reasons, though. The main one being that she was his girlfriend.

He should have held her hand until she'd settled. Kissed her nerves aways. Stayed by her side while they chatted to the other members.

Lana blinked, trying to push the thought aside as she climbed out of bed, her feet sore and her head pounding.

Pulling open the nightstand drawer, she grabbed a blister pack of painkillers and popped two out, washing them down with lukewarm water from a forgotten bottle.

Behind her, Rory had already sunk into a deep sleep, his breath evening out, unfazed.

She sat on the edge of the bed, staring at the wall.

Marcus's voice still echoed in her head.

"Get in the car, Lana."

Her pulse skipped, an uncomfortable warmth creeping up her spine.

She should be raging right now. Furious at Rory, at herself, at the whole stressful situation.

Instead, Marcus was haunting her thoughts now.

How he'd eyed her in the underground car park, as if tempted to fuck her in a shadowy corner even though his actions suggested the exact opposite.

And that? That pissed her off even more.

After dressing, she headed downstairs and made a cup of tea, though it went cold because her mind drifted.

As a distraction, she scrubbed the kitchen counters so hard her arms ached, mopped every crevice of the floor, and wiped down the windows, even though they weren't dirty.

But no matter how much she cleaned, Marcus McGrath lingered on her brain like a tattoo.

Those gold-flecked green eyes of his had been so cold when they first met—calculating, distant, indifferent.

But by the end of the evening, they'd burned.

The shower clicked on upstairs, and Lana glanced at

the wall clock, shocked to learn she'd been cleaning all morning.

Rory had finally woken up, and they'd both missed lunch.

Her belly growled as she rubbed her temples, the dread of their inevitable conversation pressing down on her chest.

They had talked about this very scenario—about what would happen if one of them crossed that line. Honesty had been the number one rule. No secrets. No games.

But now?

Now, she wasn't sure if she wanted to hear the details. Or if she should tell him about Marcus.

The floorboards creaked overhead and then Rory appeared in the kitchen, a towel slung low around his hips, his hair still dripping.

"Mornin', babe." His grin was easy, boyish, utterly unaffected like he hadn't just spent the night with someone else.

Like nothing had changed.

And maybe, for him, it hadn't.

But for her?

Something had cracked open.

"Hey," she said, her voice too even. "Do you want coffee?"

His grin widened. "Yeah, sure. I'll get it."

He poured himself a mug, the one she had bought him as a joke after an argument about paint colours.

She's Da Boss.

Her lips curled at the memory, but the warmth that used to accompany it was gone.

Rory moved into the sitting room and flopped onto the sofa, tipping his head back, exhaling. She followed and sat next to him, her muscles stiff.

His gaze lingered on her side profile, dark eyes searching.

And then, finally—

"You okay, Lana?"

Her stomach knotted.

He was asking. But did he *actually* care? Or was this just another box to check before moving on?

She angled her head to catch his eye. "Did you enjoy yourself last night?"

Her fingers tightened around her mug.

Rory grinned. "Yeah, did you?"

Her heart jumped. She wasn't sure she had an answer.

"I didn't have sex, Rory, if that's what you mean," she shot back.

But she did do something... with someone she couldn't forget.

Guilt swelled in her chest, warring with the tangle of emotions.

Rory's brows lifted, and he reached out, stroking her arm in a way that once would have soothed her. Now, it came across performative. Like an automatic response, not a genuine one.

"Babe?" His voice dipped into a practiced softness. "Are you pissed at me?"

Lana shifted, her body twisting to face him.

"You had sex with that doll girl, right?"

"Doll?" He snorted, shaking his head like she was ridiculous for asking. "Yes, Lana, I did. But that's why we went there. To experiment with different partners. *You* knew that. I really thought you would have embraced it more."

His expression shifted, like he needed to defend himself. "Don't make it into a thing. You'll get your turn."

Lana inhaled sharply, blinking fast against the sting in her eyes.

She didn't want to cry.

Because realistically, she didn't have the right to.

Even though they'd agreed to this, talking and *doing* were two different things. And now that she was sitting with him in the aftermath, with the man she had loved for years, all she could think about was how much this could tear them apart.

Her throat burned.

"D-did you enjoy it?" Her voice cracked before she could stop it.

Rory fidgeted with the towel, loosening the tight grip it had around his waist.

"Babe, I can tell you're upset. Maybe we shouldn't talk—" He exhaled, running a hand through his damp hair. "Maybe we shouldn't get into it."

Her temper snapped.

"Did you *fucking* enjoy it, Rory?" she gritted out, her pulse thundering. "You made a promise. We both did. No secrets. No lies."

Rory lowered his eyes, shaking his head as he sighed. "Look, Lana, it was a one-night stand. Of course, it was exciting. It's what Verto Veneri is all about. Right, babe?"

She stared at him; her nails digging into her palms.

Even though she'd signed the dotted line, she wasn't sure if she'd understood what that meant for them.

A single tear slid down her cheek.

Rory caught it with his thumb, his touch gentle, practiced. He had always been affectionate, always known how to soothe her. But now, she wasn't sure if she wanted to be soothed by him.

Sliding his hands into her hair, he leaned in, his lips pressing over the next fallen tear.

Soft. Warm.

"It was just physical. There was nothing behind it. I still love you, babe...always will. Okay?"

Truth was, Rory would get turned on even if she bent over to pick up trash. Sometimes a quick fumble and a fuck on the kitchen counter was fun. But mostly, she was emotion driven.

His breath feathered over her skin as he left a trail of kisses down her cheek, his eyelashes brushing her skin like a whisper.

"Did you kiss her, too?" she barely croaked.

Rory exhaled, his breath warming her damp skin.

"Yes, babe," he admitted, pressing another kiss to her jaw. "But not like this. Not with *meaning*."

Then his lips crashed into hers.

His mouth was hungry, demanding.

Like he *needed* her to believe this—to believe *him*.

But she didn't.

Not really.

Because everything inside of her was numb.

The red-hot heat she'd fallen victim to with Marcus was glaringly absent now.

And that terrified her.

Rory pulled back, his eyes dark and hooded.

"I want to hear how hard you got fucked last night, Lana," he murmured. "Tell me you did. Please."

His voice thickened, turning hoarse with sudden, desperate lust.

Her stomach twisted.

Was this his new kink?

"But I didn't, Rory," she whispered. "I swear I didn't."

Rory exhaled through his nose, his fingers gripping her waist.

"I know, babe. I believe you."

He kissed her as his hand jumped to her breast, squeezing hard.

"Pretend," he urged.

Her heart slammed against her ribs.

"Just tell me someone fucked you, Lana."

She sucked in a gust of air. Marcus's face flashed in her mind. The heat of his touch. The steel in his voice.

Her hands ran over Rory's bare chest, touching him while she kissed him back.

She wanted to please him.

To create a fantasy that would blow his mind.

In the end, they'd both returned home to each other. That was all that mattered.

That's what they had agreed.

Although everything inside her screamed that their relationship was broken.

"Yes, Rory." Her nails bit into his shoulders. "He fucked me hard. So hard."

Rory groaned, his grip tightening.

"Oh, Lana," he growled, his mouth trailing down her throat.

She squeezed her eyes shut.

And imagined someone else.

An intense heat burst over her skin, swelling between her legs, making her breath come faster.

She wasn't with Rory anymore.

In her mind, she was back in the office with Marcus— his hands on her hips, his mouth at her throat, his voice in her ear.

She let the fantasy escalate, let herself sink into it, teetering on the edge of something dark and delicious.

But reality slammed back into her as Rory shoved his damp towel to the floor, yanked off her sweatpants, and drove himself into her with a rough, impatient thrust.

Lana gasped, her fingers digging into his hips.

She forced herself to reconnect, to be present. To remember that this was her boyfriend.

Not Marcus.

Her nails scratched his skin as she pulled him closer, trying to reignite the fire that had died the second he touched her.

A feral gleam darkened his molten gaze.

His thrusts grew harder, faster, more relentless than

ever before. His fingers slid up, wrapping around her neck—tight, possessive, pressing against the frantic pulse beneath her skin.

Lana barely had time to process the shift before he pushed her backward, forcing her head off the edge of the sofa. The room flipped upside down in her vision.

Rory's grip on her throat tightened.

"You like that?" he growled, his fingers pressing against her windpipe.

Her eyes widened, alarm shooting through her veins.

She could sense how much he was getting off on it— the way his breathing turned shallow and his muscles flexed with power.

This wasn't the Rory she knew or how they made love.

He'd changed. His touch rougher, almost aggressive. And not in a way that turned her on.

A warning bell rang in her head.

As his fingers tightened around her neck, his expression darkened. Her panicked breaths weren't reaching her lungs.

She couldn't get enough air.

"Stop!" she gasped, grappling at his wrist and slapping his chest. "I...can't...breath..."

For a heartbeat, he didn't react.

Then, with an exasperated sigh, he let go, his dark eyes flickering with something unreadable before his lips curled into a playful smirk.

Lana lay there, stunned, her heart hammering.

Her body had gone cold.

The arousal that had burned inside her moments ago had shrivelled into nothing.

But Rory didn't seem to notice.

Or care.

He kept going, his hips slamming into hers, chasing his own release while she lay beneath him—silent, motionless, and utterly disconnected.

Seconds later, he groaned, spilling into her with a satisfied shudder.

She shoved him off.

Rory hit the floor with a thud, landing on the plush shaggy rug. He lay there sprawled out with a lazy grin, looking satisfied.

"What the *fuck* was that, Rory?" she hissed, scrambling for her sweatpants.

His eyes remained closed, his chest rising and falling in slow, deep breaths.

"Lighten up," he muttered, stretching like a cat. "Women like it, babe."

Lana's vision blurred with fury.

She snatched his towel and chucked it at his face.

"Well, I don't," she said. "Especially when you didn't fucking warn me first. You don't even know what you were doing. That shit is dangerous."

Rory dragged the towel off his face and propped himself up on one elbow, his expression shifting into something amused.

"I wasn't actually going to strangle you, babe." He chuckled, shaking his head. "You're such a prude."

Lana sucked in a sharp breath, that word hitting her like a slap.

She clenched her teeth, rage boiling in her veins.

The problem wasn't her because she craved new things, too. Ached for the kind of sex that left her breathless, dizzy, hungry for more.

But not like that.

Not with a guy who thought he could do whatever he wanted without even asking.

Lana stormed out of the living room, her bare feet pounding up the stairs as she climbed, putting distance between them.

"Fuck you!" she shouted over her shoulder. "If you *ever* try that again without warning me first, I'll knee you so hard in the balls that *you* won't be able to breathe. People have safe words for a reason, asshole."

Rory's laughter followed her up the stairs, making out like she was overreacting. Her blood boiled.

Reaching her bedroom, she slammed the door shut, flung herself on the bed and stared up at the ceiling—lost.

In the past, she'd had so few partners she could count them on one hand. And sure, none of them had been wild or particularly adventurous, but that didn't mean she didn't crave the thrill.

Fuck Rory for calling her a prude.

And fuck Marcus for not taking more when he'd had the chance.

Next time, she wouldn't hold back.

14

Lana

Lana sat at her cluttered desk, staring at the spreadsheet on the screen in front of her.

Around her, the open-plan office hummed with the usual Monday morning chaos—phones ringing, keyboards clacking, the occasional burst of laughter from the sales team in the corner.

The air smelled faintly of burnt coffee and someone's aggressively microwaved leftover curry.

She sighed and slapped a fresh sticky note on her monitor: *toothpaste*.

Rory had spent the morning rummaging through the bathroom cabinet like a man on a mission, his toothbrush stuffed in his mouth, grumbling about how she never replaced anything.

Rather than start a row, she'd let him huff and made a mental note to buy more.

At least he'd made her an omelette last night. And apologised for choking her. Sort of.

He'd claimed he was only trying something new, hoping to spice things up. And after a few minutes of grovelling, he'd sworn he wouldn't do it again. If that pacified her.

It didn't.

She never wanted to experience that kind of panic again. His fingers pressing too tightly, her lungs squeezing. The raw fear of not being able to catch a breath—there was nothing sexy about that.

But even now, a day later, a gnawing guilt still sat in her stomach, whispering that maybe she should have embraced the moment—trusted him.

It's not like she was against the whole throat cuffing thing. The problem was how he'd sprung it on her.

Lana sighed and focused on the endless numbers and columns. She studied them. Then reanalysed the same row, the important data all jumbling together into a meaningless blur.

Her brain refused to engage, hijacked by a very particular thought.

Verto Veneri.

That forbidden, secret world where she had almost—*almost*—let herself go.

She bit her lip, her gaze flickering to her coworkers. No one knew. No one could tell she was sitting at her desk thinking about a man who wasn't her boyfriend.

Not even Amanda, her friend who flitted from man to man like a mischievous, red-haired fae, collecting stories the way other people collected loyalty points, knew.

"Good weekend?" Amanda's voice chirped from over the adjoining desk divider.

Lana tucked her hair behind her ear and tilted to the side, peering around her monitor. "It was okay. You?"

Amanda stood, unbuttoning her denim jacket and sauntering toward Lana's desk. She shoved a mess of unread pages aside and perched herself on the edge, tugging up the knees of her skin-tight black trousers like she was settling in for a gossip session.

"Oh. My. God." Amanda leaned in, her voice dropping to a dramatic whisper. "Guess who I ran into on Saturday night?"

Lana smirked. "Don't tell me. James?"

Amanda's jaw dropped. "How the *hell* did you know that?"

Lana tapped her pen against her lips. "It's written all over your 'I had sex' face."

Amanda gasped, smacking Lana's arm.

"*Jeez*, is it that obvious?" She peeked over her shoulder as if everyone else saw it, too. "That must be why Richard grinned at me like a horny dog this morning."

Lana's gaze settled on Amanda's cleavage, which presented itself in her low-cut ivory top.

"I doubt it was the pretty face he was looking at." She arched a brow and smirked.

Amanda attempted to tug her neckline higher, then huffed when it refused to cooperate. Her eyes twinkled under the overhead lights.

"Well, whatever. James and I have amazing bed chemistry, you know. I'll tell you everything at lunch."

Lana glanced at the digital clock on her monitor—*five past ten.*

Two long, tedious hours stood between her and an escape from her squeaky office chair.

Amanda stood and stretched. "Deli at noon?"

"Yep. See you downstairs."

Amanda winked and sashayed back to her desk, leaving Lana alone with her thoughts and an unread report.

Then her desk phone rang.

"Lana, a delivery guy left a bunch of flowers for you," came Johnny's voice from reception. "What floor are you on?"

Lana blinked. "You sure they're for *me*?"

"Yup. Card says, *To Lana Craig, we will finish what we started.*"

Her heart stopped and her pulse pounded against her ribs.

Who the hell—?

Rory wasn't the flowers type. The best he'd ever managed was a half-dead bunch of carnations from a petrol station on her birthday.

And Marcus McGrath wouldn't send her flowers because they didn't have any unfinished business. He'd started and ended it all in the space of a few hours.

"Sixth floor, near the printer," she said, her voice steadier than she felt.

"Got it. Be right up."

Lana hung up and stared at her screen, the cursor blinking on the report she had to finish by the end of the day.

Her weekend had been a mess of mistakes and regrets.

But this?

This had just changed everything.

Moments later, Johnny, head of security, ambled through the office, his burly frame almost swallowed by a bouquet of yellow roses so large it obscured half his face.

"Someone's got a rich admirer." He set them on her desk with a grunt. "Bet these cost a few quid."

Lana's brow scrunched as she stared at the vibrant petals catching the light, their subtle, sweet scent filling the air like late spring.

They were beautiful.

And completely out of place in her life.

She reached for the tiny card tucked among the stems, her pulse quickening. No name. No initials.

Her stomach twisted.

If Rory didn't send them...then *who* did?

For the next hour, the bouquet became her accidental muse. She gazed at the pretty petals instead of the dull, black numbers on her spreadsheet, her thoughts drifting to all the people she'd been in contact with over the past week.

A coworker's voice shattered the haze.

"Pub time," he declared, slinging on his coat.

Lana jolted back to reality.

Shaking herself, she locked up her desk and checked

the time. She had a few minutes to spare before meeting Amanda for lunch.

On autopilot, she ducked into the ladies' washroom— her refuge, the only place in this sterile office where she could steal a moment of peace.

She dropped her bag onto the wall shelf and dug out her phone, thumbs hovering over the screen before finally typing:

Hey. What time will you be home? xx

Rory's reply was almost instant, a single, sharp vibration against her palm.

Zac wants to go for a few pints after work. Don't wait up x

Her lips pressed into a tight line.

And there it was. Their entire relationship summed up in text messages.

Rory and his mates. Then Lana.

She hesitated, debating whether to ask about the flowers. But she didn't. If they weren't from Rory, he'd probably start something.

Shaking off the thought, she reached for her bronzer, sweeping warmth over her cheekbones, blotting her pink lipstick, and finishing with a light mist of her favourite perfume.

By the time the clock struck noon, she was slipping into her leather biker jacket, scooping up her bag, and heading for the stairwell.

Amanda stood in the corner of the foyer, deep in conversation with Richard Gifford, the office enigma.

Broody as ever, Richard leaned casually against the pillar, his scalp-shaved black hair resembling a second skin.

He was all humour and effortless charm, his long lashes framing steel-grey eyes that rarely betrayed what he was thinking.

Until he looked at Amanda, then his eyes would darken, a subtle hint at how much he fancied her.

As the two stood talking, his lips curled into a slow, rakish grin, and Amanda's fingers twitched at her side, like she had to stop herself from touching him.

Lana sighed. Their tension was palpable.

Amanda liked to boast about being unattached, about never letting a guy get to her. But it was obvious to anyone with eyes that Richard had already carved out space in her heart.

She just refused to admit it.

Amanda flipped her red curls over one shoulder. "Lana! Let's get out of here before someone tries to make me do actual work."

Richard smirked but said nothing as he pushed off the pillar and strode toward the elevator.

Amanda's gaze trailed after him, her expression betraying her usual bravado.

Then she exhaled and snatched her bag from the floor.

"Right, let's make like a tree and *leaf*." She snickered. "I'm starving."

Lana ruffled her fingers through her long hair and hummed in agreement. "Me too."

The glass doors slid open, spilling them onto the pavement. A warm late-summer breeze caressed her skin.

And then—

Amanda's fingers latched onto her arm, hard.

"Holy crap, Lan."

Amanda's words faded while Lana's heart thundered, and her skin warmed all over.

Because there, parked across from their dull, grey office building, was a sleek steel-grey Lexus. And propped against it, one hand tucked into his trouser pocket, was Marcus McGrath.

He wore a navy-blue suit. Jacket open, cobalt lining catching the light. His confident gaze held her full attention.

Lana's stomach clenched.

Her pulse pounded against her ribs as he pushed off the car and strode toward her.

15

Lana

"Lana."

Something about the way he said her name sent a wicked shiver down her spine.

Amanda hovered close behind, squeezing Lana's arm. "Who the hell is that guy?"

Lana barely heard her.

Marcus stopped just in front of them, removing his sunglasses with one hand and sliding them into his jacket pocket.

Sunlight glinted off his gold watch.

She swallowed hard.

"Lunch?" he asked, but the raised brow and the slow drag of his green eyes over her body made the invitation seem less than innocent.

"With me?" she asked, shifting her weight from foot to foot. "Why?"

Marcus cleared his throat, rubbing the short hair at the nape of his neck. "To eat, Lana. That's all."

Liar.

His watchful gaze, that confident smirk, all of it implied more.

Amanda was openly gawking now, her jaw slack, her eyes darting between Lana and the man who had just turned an ordinary afternoon into something much more dangerous.

Lana tore her gaze away from Marcus, shooting her friend a silent plea.

"Can you give me a minute, please?" she asked.

Amanda frowned. "Ummm...sure, Lan. I'll head to the deli. See you in five?"

Marcus stepped in closer. The scent of his musky cologne wrapped around her senses. His hand brushed against her wrist, a barely there touch, but enough to send a jolt through her.

"Don't wait for her," he said, his voice flat.

Amanda's eyes widened to the size of saucers.

"Lan?" she mouthed. "Who is that guy?"

Lana gulped, her gaze jumping back to Marcus.

Nerves jumped in her throat as heat pricked her skin.

She'd love to go with him.

God, she wanted to go.

But she was Rory's girl.

Casual arrangements were acceptable when everyone agreed to them—when the rules were clear.

This, though? This had her veins pumping faster, hotter, and the lines blurring.

Marcus must have recognised the tug of war raging in

her eyes because he leaned in, his lips hovering near her ear.

"Just lunch, beautiful," he said, his voice a low rumble.

The warmth of his breath caressed her skin, sending tiny, delicious bumps all over her.

"I promise," he added.

Her head tipped forward the smallest fraction, drawn in by his pull, by the unbearable temptation of him.

"Okay, Marcus. Just lunch," she said, her voice softer than she intended. "But I don't have long."

She turned to Amanda. "See you back in the office."

Amanda shot her a 'you'd better explain this later' look before retreating, her head turning over her shoulder every few steps.

With his hand settled on the small of Lana's back, Marcus ushered her toward the Lexus LC, its sleek grey design an extension of the man himself.

The second she slid into the passenger seat, a shiver of anxiety ran through her.

His car smelled of fresh leather and something darker, richer—like it had never been driven before today, like it existed for this moment only.

Marcus sank into the driver's seat and glanced at her, not quite smiling as he covered his eyes with a pair of sunglasses. Still, the connection made her pulse quicken.

The engine purred as he pulled onto the busy streets of Belfast, stopping at a red light.

Without looking away from the road, he shifted gears. "You look stunning."

Lana laughed. "Hardly."

She knew exactly how she looked—exhausted, hungover from the emotional weight of her weekend, and dark crescents sat beneath her eyes.

"I take it your boyfriend enjoyed himself on Friday? I heard he pulled an all-nighter."

"That's because the owner didn't hunt him down and send him home," she countered.

Marcus smirked. "Yeah, only people I like get the VIP treatment."

Ignoring the heat creeping up her neck, she changed the subject. "How do you know where I work?"

Her finger tapped against the leather seat beside her thigh, a nervous habit, anything to distract herself.

A smirk touched one corner of his mouth. "I can find anyone, anywhere, Lana."

Her brows knitted together. "Why did you find me?"

"I thought we could have lunch together, having already been acquainted."

"Acquainted?" She half-laughed, trying hard not to give away how her pulse had spiked. "Is that what you call it?"

God, the memory of his hands, his mouth, the way he made her orgasm with his fingers—it all crashed into her at once.

Marcus gripped the steering wheel, his knuckles flexing. "We were merely introduced. I only got to know a little about you."

Lana's fingers curled into her lap as she stared out at the city streets, her cheeks turning pink.

"Your fingers got to know more than they should have, Mr McGrath."

His chuckle was deep and dangerous. It rolled through the car, sent sparks flying, and made her thighs clench.

"Are you flirting with me, beautiful?" he asked, voice dripping with amusement, but his green eyes stayed locked on the road.

Lana's pulse stuttered.

"No, I'm not," she shot back, too sharp, too defensive.

She folded her arms across her chest.

"Where are you taking me?" she asked. "The Fitz?"

Marcus reached over and tugged her seatbelt a little tighter against her body, checking she was secure.

"No, somewhere better," he replied. "More intimate. Unless you'd rather go back and have that dull deli lunch with your colleague."

Her head turned, and their gazes locked, the challenge gleaming in his eyes.

"When I think of lunch, I don't think of intimacy, Marcus."

He chuckled, the sound deep and dirty. "Don't worry. I have lunch waiting for us at my place."

Marcus shifted the gears as they cruised through the city. Lana let out a quick puff of air through her nose, crossing one leg over the other. "That's presumptuous, don't you think? What if I'd said no?"

His lips twitched. "Even if you didn't join me, I still had to eat. But for the record, I'm glad you did."

She narrowed her eyes. "So, what, you made lunch and assumed I'd end up in your car?"

Marcus let out a low chuckle, one hand drumming lightly on the leather steering wheel. "Exactly... which you are, right?"

Her stomach flipped. Jesus. He had no shame.

"And the flowers," she said, quickly changing the subject. "Were they from you, too?"

His brow creased. "Flowers?"

"Yeah. The yellow roses that came to my office earlier. Were they from you?"

He half-shrugged, as if the idea of sending flowers was beneath him.

"Sorry, Lana. I didn't send you any flowers. They must be from your not-so-better-half." A slow smirk curled up the corner of his mouth, like he was particularly proud of himself for the quip.

Lana sucked in her lower lip, chewing it in thought.

Rory.

The guy who tried to choke her during sex. Who'd been inside another woman hours before touching her? She almost laughed out loud. Rory thought a bunch of yellow roses could fix their problems. Then again, flowers weren't his style, even if he had the motive.

And yet, here she was, sitting in another man's car, hoping that he had sent them.

Shame struck her like a bolt of lightning.

"You'd know if I sent you flowers, Lana."

Her gaze snapped to him.

"They would fill your office," he continued. "You

deserve far better than cellophane-wrapped roses. I'd buy you a whole damn field of flowers."

Lana's breath caught, heart stuttering in her chest.

The way he said it so casually, so assured, like it was a fact. Like if he'd thought it through.

And yet—

"Anyway," he added, rolling his shoulders in an easy shrug, "you belong to someone else, so it wouldn't be appropriate for me to send you flowers."

Lana's head jerked back, a surprised laugh slipping from her lips.

"Oh really? No flowers, but taking me back to your apartment in the middle of the day for lunch is appropriate?"

Her lips twitched despite herself, the undeniable pull of him making it impossible not to smile.

"Look, beautiful," he murmured, finally glancing over, his eyes dragging over her like a slow caress. "I said lunch and that's exactly what I meant."

Lana swallowed hard.

Damn. Damn. Damn.

16

Lana

The car pulled into the Titanic Quarter, gliding alongside a sweeping curve of glass-fronted apartments that overlooked the water.

Marcus buzzed the intercom, his deep voice cutting through the static as he requested access to the basement car park. The gates groaned open, granting them entry. No hesitations. No verifications. Whoever controlled the doors already knew who he was.

The slow descent into the underground garage revealed polished concrete when motion-activated lights blinked on, making her acutely aware of how far she was from her little slice of life.

He pulled into a reserved space close to the elevator, killed the engine, and exited without a word. A moment later, her door swung open.

Marcus waited, one hand extended, his expression unreadable behind the sunglasses still perched on his nose. The way he held himself—calm, assured, commanding—made it impossible to refuse.

Lana placed her palm in his, and the moment their skin touched, he pulled her up, his grip strong but controlled. Their bodies brushed, her breath catching as her heels met the floor.

He didn't let go. Not right away.

His fingers flexed around hers, his head tilting—watching, waiting for something.

"Thanks," she said, smiling.

"You're welcome."

The air between them grew hotter, charged, alive with sparks. Then, just as quickly as he'd drawn her in, he stepped back and let go.

Pressing his hand to her back, he ushered towards the elevator doors. As they approached, gleaming doors parted as if summoned by his presence alone. The fruity scent of cleaning solution hung in the air, but as soon as the doors whispered shut behind them, her senses came alive with *him*.

That musky cologne of his caught in her a chokehold.

Lana forced herself to the far side of the elevator, gripping her purse with both hands as if that could somehow protect her from the sparks bouncing off the surrounding walls.

Marcus, however, stood relaxed, hands in his pockets, eyes concealed behind those damn sunglasses. The only giveaway was the subtle tension in his stubbled jaw. Otherwise, he was the picture of control.

Her thighs clenched, a shameful ache growing

between her legs at the sheer sight of him. It had been two days since Verto Veneri, and she hadn't been able to stop replaying the way he'd touched her, the way he'd looked at her—like he already owned every inch of her body, even before she gave in.

And now, he'd set his sights on bringing her to his place.

Lana inhaled a steadying breath. That didn't mean she'd surrender all over again.

The elevator glided to a stop, and before she could gather herself, Marcus was already stepping out, moving with effortless ease through the hall.

She followed; her heels muffled against the thick, charcoal-grey carpet.

As soon as he opened the door, he gestured for her to enter.

"After you, beautiful," he said in a deep, commanding tone.

Marcus's penthouse was nothing like she expected.

The space was vast, drenched in natural light from floor-to-ceiling windows that stretched along the length of the open-plan living room. The view of Belfast Lough was uninterrupted, the distant Isle of Scotland visible through the thin veil of clouds.

The decor was minimal, yet the furniture gave a high-end vibe. Muted tones of deep greys, blacks, and whites created a sleek, masculine aesthetic, punctuated by clean lines and luxury finishes.

Not a single piece of clutter. No framed photos. No signs of a single male living his best life.

She walked through the space, moving from the entrance hall to the open plan living and kitchen. On the cool white countertop sat a duo of bowls, two crystal glass flutes and a golden magnum of champagne, the black ace of spades, resting in an ice bucket.

Nerves fluttered through her.

This wasn't an impulsive lunch date. Marcus had planned it.

Was he thinking about her ever since that night? Or was this a typical player move? Then again, a rich guy like him could have lunch with any woman. Not the admin assistant with a boyfriend.

Marcus tossed his keys onto a small leather tray on the console table, strolling toward the kitchen like he did this all the time. Like he wasn't breaking every unspoken rule between them.

"This is your place?" she asked when he joined her by the marbled top island.

Marcus shrugged, casual as ever. "Well, yeah, it's one of them."

Her brows lifted. "So, it's not your actual home?"

He smirked but didn't answer, uncorking the champagne and pouring her a glass.

Lana turned her back to him, casting her eyes over the clean carpet and showroom new couch. There weren't any forgotten coffee cups, kicked off shoes, or half-read books. No warmth or homeliness.

"You don't actually spend any time here, do you?" she asked, glancing over her shoulder to find him.

Marcus leaned a hip against the counter, his eyes following her gaze. "It serves its purpose."

Lana turned back around and moved towards the filled champagne he was offering her. He appeared relaxed, but something simmered beneath the surface, hidden beneath that effortless confidence and those watchful green eyes.

"What purpose is that?" she challenged, tilting her head.

He smirked again, but it didn't quite reach his eyes. "Moments like this."

Moments like this.

Something about the way he said it made her chest flutter. Like she was just another fleeting moment in a place designed to forget them all.

Lana wet her lips, forcing out a whisper. "And this is just lunch, right?"

Marcus smirked, removing his sunglasses and placing them on the counter. "That's all, beautiful."

The whole setup—the champagne, the immaculate space, the way he carried himself like he had nothing to prove yet owned everything in sight—felt too deliberate.

She took the glass but didn't drink, merely watching him over the rim.

"Why did you really bring me here, Marcus?" Her voice was steady, but inside, her nerves twisted tight. "We don't know each other."

"Can't two adults enjoy lunch together and talk?" he asked. "I can answer any questions you have about Verto Veneri. About the terms set out in the contract."

Lana narrowed her eyes. "Is there a limit on the amount of champagne I'm allowed to consume while we talk?"

He grinned, catching her sarcasm. "Drink as much as you want. I'll always get you home safely."

Her blood ran red-hot.

She took a sip and bit back a smile. "I read through your contract, and I'm pretty sure an initiation lunch with the owner in a penthouse wasn't mentioned."

Marcus folded his arms, watching her in return. "You wound me, beautiful. Would you rather I took you to a sandwich shop?"

Lana's brow scrunched, thoughtful. "Maybe. At least that would've been...safer."

His smirk deepened, slow and knowing. "And tell me, Lana—why would you feel unsafe with me?"

Her fingers tightened around the stem of the glass. That wasn't the right word, not really. A better term might have been 'less impulsive'. The danger wasn't in being alone with him. It was in how much she *wanted* to be alone with him.

"I should have said no," she admitted, voice quieter than she intended.

Marcus closed the distance between them in one measured step and reached up, tucking a strand of her behind her ear.

His green eyes burned into hers, unapologetic.

"But you didn't," he murmured.

Her pulse thudded against her ribs.

"No," she whispered. "I didn't. And you promised

we'd only have lunch, not replay what you did to me in your office."

Marcus tilted his head, gaze dropping briefly to her lips before meeting her eyes again. "Are you waiting for me to apologise for that?"

Lana swallowed hard, forcing a smirk to her lips. "You don't seem like the apologising type."

His grin was slow and sinful. "I'm not."

She let out a breath, shaking her head. "Of course you're not."

Marcus backed up. "Drink your champagne, Lana. Your lunch will be ready soon."

Her fingers tingled as she raised the flute to her lips, knowing full well that taking a sip wasn't conceding to his order—though it wasn't resistance either.

Lana's gaze drifted toward the floor-to-ceiling windows once more, her breath catching at the breath-taking panorama. The shimmering water stretched beyond the docks, a vast expanse of endless blue, mirroring the sky above.

She had always felt a deep connection to the sea and its unrestrained beauty. A far cry from the cramped townhouse she called home, where a sliver of ocean peeked through rooftops like a tease, always just out of reach.

And yet, Marcus took the view for granted. The vast, open world, framed by glass and cold, impersonal luxury.

When Lana faced him again, she noticed he'd removed his suit jacket, leaving only a crisp white shirt, his sleeves rolled, exposing strong, sun kissed forearms.

She swallowed, heat curling low in her stomach as she caught the way his gold watch gleamed against his skin, the very picture of power and wealth.

A little too much power, perhaps.

"I need to be back in the office before two," she said, forcing her eyes away from the pull of him.

"One drink. One meal." His voice dipped lower, coaxing, teasing. "Then I'll take you straight back to your office."

He gestured toward the barstool, the subtle command laced in the tilt of his chin, the way his fingers curled around the edge of the counter.

She stepped forward, pulse quickening as she perched on the seat, the space between them shrinking by inches.

"I hope you're hungry," Marcus said, holding her gaze.

17

Lana

Lana swirled the champagne in her glass, watching the bubbles rise to the surface.

She set the flute on the countertop, dragging her lower lip between her teeth before exhaling.

She *was* hungry—but not for food.

Not for the linguine he was dishing out or the expensive champagne.

She was hungry for something far more satisfying, something that burned low in her belly every time Marcus glanced at her.

"Yeah, I'm starving," she replied, letting the last word roll off her tongue just a little too slowly.

His eyes flickered over her mouth, but he said nothing.

Lana took a slow, settling sip of champagne, letting the taste of desire fizz against her lips instead.

"Eat up, beautiful." He nudged a full bowl toward her.

A fork scraped against the marble as he slid it toward her, the metal catching the light. Lana reached for it, but the moment her fingertips grazed his, a fiery spark shot throughout her.

For a fraction of a second, neither of them moved—his touch was warm, searing, overwhelming.

Then, as if scorched, she clutched the fork like a weapon, withdrawing her hand.

Marcus's gaze danced over her face, his expression giving nothing away.

"This looks amazing. Thanks," she said, smiling politely.

She stabbed her fork into the mass of linguine and twirled, taking a slow, thoughtful bite.

"Mmm..." she hummed, savouring the rich, velvety sauce as it coated her tongue. "This is so good. Did you make it from scratch?"

A strand of linguine skimmed her chin, the sauce clinging in a pearl below her lips. His eyes widened as her tongue darted free from her lips, missing most of the mess.

In a flash, he reached forward and wiped it away, licking the sauce from his thumb afterward.

Her pulse jumped, and a rush of heat warmed her cheeks, spreading through her body.

They stared at each other for a silent beat until Marcus cleared his throat.

"I love to cook. Unfortunately, I don't always have the time. My chef handles most of it. He prepares meals in advance, freezes them depending on where I am in the world."

Her brows lifted in curiosity. "Does he travel with you?"

"Sometimes." A smirk ghosted his lips. "I make it worth his while financially when he does."

She dabbed her lips with a napkin. "If you travel a lot, where's the one place you always return home to? Your actual home."

Marcus leaned back, moving his gaze to the window as if he might find the answer written in the lough's shimmering reflection.

"I have places, properties...but home? That's a different thing. I never bring anyone there."

His voice dipped into something almost wistful, and for a split second, he wasn't the enigmatic, powerful man who oozed control—he was just a normal guy.

"What's the point of this penthouse if it's not your home and you don't rent it out for money?"

His lips twitched. "This place has its advantages."

Her eyebrows drifted up. "Like what?"

His gaze dropped to her mouth before meeting her eyes again. "Inviting an attractive woman to lunch, with no complications."

Lana swallowed, and her stomach knotted. *Complications*.

She exhaled and leaned her elbows on the cool marble counter. "You don't seem like a man who avoids complications. In fact, I'd say you seek them out."

"Maybe. Or maybe I just enjoy the company of a

captivating woman who looks far too good eating the pasta I made especially for her."

Lana laughed, but the sound caught in her throat when he smiled without breaking eye contact.

She wet her lips, nerves fluttering in her chest. "And here I thought you invited me here to promote your club."

"I did." He let the words hang between them. "But I'm a man who likes to multitask."

A shiver rolled down her spine.

Lana sat back and sipped her champagne, letting the moment stretch, then lifted her fork again and took another bite.

"Well," she mumbled between chews, "I hope you're good at it."

His smirk deepened, his voice a lazy drawl. "Oh, Lana...you have no idea."

"So...you enjoy cooking?" Lana searched for words, needing a distraction from the buzz rushing through her body. "Who taught you? Your chef?"

Marcus's gaze wandered over her. "I taught myself when I was younger. My dad worked long hours, so I fed my kid brother and had a hot meal ready for my dad when he came home."

Something about the way he said it—so matter of fact —made her chest tighten.

Before she could respond, he stood, crossing the kitchen in long, confident strides. The fridge door opened with a quiet hum, and he returned with a bottle of water, the muscles in his forearm flexing as he twisted off the cap.

"Want some?"

Her brow furrowed. "Aren't you having champagne? It's the nicest I've ever had, but I can't drink it by myself. Especially on a Monday."

One corner of his mouth lifted when she giggled.

"I won't have alcohol when I have to get behind the wheel with precious cargo in my passenger seat," he said, his voice huskier now. "You deserve the best champagne every day of the week, Lana."

Then, as if to break the tension, he winked—just the barest flick of an eyelid, a fleeting moment of charm.

Lana smiled helplessly. He was dangerous, but not in the way she'd expected. He wasn't just a figure of authority and wealth—he was a man who noted everything about her, catalogued and filed them away for later.

She reached for her glass and took another sip for something to do with her hands. "I thought you had a driver?"

"I buy cars to enjoy them," Marcus said. "Not to let someone else take the wheel for me. However, if I'm out for the night or doing business, I'll use my driver. If I have the choice, though, I'd rather be in control."

The way he said it sent an unexpected shiver down her spine.

Marcus angled his head, studying her.

She didn't know why she asked, only that she wanted to. "Where was your mother?"

The moment the words left her lips, his expression

darkened. His shoulders tensed and his grip on the water bottle tightened.

His lashes lowered as if he were shutting himself off from the question.

Then, his eyes found hers again—green flecked with gold.

"She died when I was nine," he said simply. "I took care of my kid brother, Jamie, while our dad threw himself into long shifts."

The casual way he explained his past made it hit even harder. No self-pity. Just hard facts.

Lana's fork clattered against the bowl as she let go of it. "You must be really close with your brother."

He nodded. "We have the same mindset. The same work ethic."

"I've been lucky," she admitted. "I've had both my parents my whole life. They moved to France last year, but they're only a phone call away."

She traced the rim of her glass, thoughtful. "Sounds like you had to grow up quickly. I can't imagine what that must have been like for you."

Marcus's gaze lingered on her for a moment longer before he rolled his shoulders back, shaking off whatever emotion had shuddered through him.

"Why did you join my club, Lana?" he asked, turning almost business-like. "Are you not satisfied with your current partner?"

Lana swallowed hard, surprised by his bluntness. "That's kind of personal, don't you think?"

Marcus didn't flinch. If anything, the glint in his eyes sharpened, like he enjoyed watching her squirm.

"Agreed," he replied.

He plucked a tiny piece of crayfish from his plate, popped it into his mouth, and chewed before swallowing.

"Would it be easier for you to answer if you knew me better?"

She hesitated, her pulse a slow, steady drumbeat in her ears. He was impossible to read, his expression a perfect mask of casual interest.

"It's not the sort of thing I want to talk about with you," she murmured.

Marcus leaned forward, clasping his hands together on the counter, his posture deceptively relaxed. Yet there was something about the way he watched her, as if expecting a negotiation rather than a conversation.

"Well," he said, his deep voice rolling over her skin like velvet. "You already know about my family. So, what else would you like to know before you answer my question?"

Marcus stared right at her, the casual stretch of his shirt pulling tight across his biceps, highlighting every flex of muscle beneath the white fabric.

"If you don't stay here that often, then why not stay in your hotel instead?"

"It becomes monotonous when my staff are constantly trying to impress me," he admitted. "It puts management under pressure, and that irritates me. My staff should focus on providing exceptional service to the guests, not running around trying to anticipate my every whim. I like to shut the door on business when I need to."

"A guy like you needs space?" she smirked. "Somehow, I find that hard to believe."

One corner of his mouth lifted. "Oh, yeah?"

She bit her lip. "You don't exactly strike me as a man who likes to be alone."

His smirk deepened. "You can't read me as well as you think."

"I can't read you at all." Lana tilted her head, swirling the champagne in her glass as she studied him. "No girlfriend? No marriage? That's a rather bleak outlook."

Marcus lifted his water bottle but didn't drink. "It's a realistic one."

She arched a brow. "And what made you so cynical?"

"Experience."

Lana pressed her fork into the last swirl of linguine, hesitating before asking, "So you don't think there's someone out there who could change your mind?"

Marcus let out a low chuckle, his stare unrelenting. "What is it you're really asking, beautiful? If I could fall? Or if I've already started?"

Her breath caught. The charged air and his closeness created a dangerous tension that caused her breath to catch. His fingers rested on the counter, mere inches from hers, the heat of him palpable even without contact.

"I'm just making conversation," she said, lifting her glass to her lips to mask the wild pulse point in her neck.

"Is that so?"

Lana swallowed a gulp of champagne, willing herself

to look away, but she couldn't. He had a gravitational pull, an intensity that made her forget how to breathe.

"I think," he said, voice dropping, "you're far more interested in my love life than you care to admit."

She set her glass down with a soft clink.

"And I think," she countered, mirroring his teasing tone, "that you're far more interested in my opinion of you than *you* care to admit."

Marcus held her gaze for a beat. Then, with deliberate slowness, he leaned in, just enough for his breath to ghost over her cheek.

"Touché." He smiled, and her stomach flipped. "I have my fun. Which doesn't involve love or marriage. I don't believe any of that."

The words hit her like an icy wave, stealing the air from her lungs. He didn't believe in love. Or commitment.

It shouldn't sting as much as it did, but it did—deeply. A faint ache bloomed in her chest, and she tried to brush it off, her eyes darting away from him, unwilling to meet his gaze.

She wasn't his. Never had been. So why did his statement hit like rejection?

Pushing the half-empty bowl aside, she set her fork down.

"That was better than eating at the deli," she said, her voice a little too light. "I should get back to the office now."

18

Marcus

Marcus noted the subtle flare of her pupils, a fleeting moment of an unguarded reaction before she reined herself back in.

What he said was true, though—he didn't believe in true love and all that bullshit.

He had never put himself in its path or allowed it to take root. His female interactions remained just that: interactions.

Nothing more. Nothing deeper.

After his mother's death, grief had been his lesson of love's cruelty, and it taught him an unshakable truth— feelings made you weak. They made you vulnerable. And that wasn't something he ever wanted to experience again.

So he poured his energy into making money, into expanding the McGrath empire, into mentoring Jamie so they'd never have to struggle in life.

Women were still a part of his life, but only on his terms—casual, transient, and devoid of emotional ties.

And yet...

He'd invited a blue-eyed beauty into his private space. A woman who, by all accounts, should have been just another passing temptation.

A brief indulgence before he moved on. But somehow, Lana was different. Something about her unsettled his mind and body.

She wasn't chasing him for attention, clinging to his wallet or demanding his time. Maybe that's why she was so goddamn irresistible.

Lana met his teasing with fire and wit instead of breathy laughter and eager compliance. She made him want to lean in, to unravel the mystery of her piece by piece. And that? That was dangerous.

In the unlikely event he considered settling down, she would be the type of woman he'd do it with.

Marcus stiffened. That thought was fucking ridiculous. He didn't do commitment. He didn't do forever.

Even if he did, Lana had a plan to marry the man she lives with. A man who didn't deserve her, sure—but involved with him.

And that meant she was off-limits.

Didn't it?

A fleeting thought of her climbing onto the counter and crawling toward him like a naughty little kitten flashed through his mind, so vivid it almost knocked the breath from his lungs.

His dick twitched, straining against his trousers, as he imagined her poised on all fours, waiting.

Fuck.

He needed to shut this down. But her eyes held a dirty secret.

"You keep looking at me like that, beautiful, and I'm going to think you're up to something."

Lana's brows lifted, her pretty lashes batting. "Looking at you like what?"

"Like you're imagining a better way to spend your afternoon than going back to that office."

A breathy laugh escaped her. "Now who's making assumptions?"

"I'm not assuming. I'm reading between the lines."

He let his gaze linger, sliding over her lips, her throat, the delicate curve of her collarbone. "And you're blushing, Lana."

She lifted her chin, playing it cool, but that shy little smile of hers was like gasoline to an open flame. "It's just the alcohol."

"Right," he replied, smirking.

Her tongue darted out to wet her lips. "Are you under the impression that every woman fantasises about you, Mr McGrath?"

Marcus chuckled. "Not every woman. Just the ones who can't stop staring."

She broke eye contact and stared at the bubble in her glass, a fact that sent satisfaction curling in his chest.

But he was playing with fire.

Marcus knew having lunch with her was dangerous

territory, but he was determined to put an end to this fleeting obsession. He assumed he'd lose interest—that she'd bore him or piss him off.

Instead, the spark between them burned just as intensely as ever. Clearing his throat, he stood and pulled his brain out of his full, hard dick.

"Thanks for having lunch with me, Lana. I'll take you back now." His voice was even, cool, betraying none of the chaos inside him.

Lana blinked, surprised by the sudden shift in his demeanour.

"Oh. Uh, sure." She hesitated for a fraction of a second, then offered him a shy, almost uncertain smile as she gathered her things.

That smile. Sweet, a little bashful. So fucking sexy.

Marcus clenched his jaw, lust crawling down his spine as his mind betrayed him again, conjuring a dozen images of what he could do to that pretty little mouth. How he could make her sigh, moan, beg.

How easily he could strip her and spread her legs open on this very counter.

The temptation to steal her out from under her boyfriend's nose was strong. But that wouldn't be fair to her. He'd ruin her future for one hot night in bed with him.

Releasing a slow breath, he turned away, adjusting himself discreetly as he grabbed his suit jacket, rolling his shoulders to shake off the tension.

Spending time alone with her, peeling back her

layers, watching the suppressed fire lurking in her eyes—and wanting to free it—was a mistake.

Because now, he wasn't just attracted to Lana.

He was hooked.

Lana slid off the stool, looking a little dazed like she wasn't entirely sure what had just happened. That same vulnerability she'd revealed in his office seeped into his bloodstream like a slow, addictive drug.

Her lips parted as if she was about to say something, then pressed together again, a shadow of hesitation flashing in her eyes.

He knew that look.

She was overthinking.

Trying to piece together why she'd spent the last hour locked in a push-and-pull game with him, why every fleeting glance and smile was a spark just waiting to go up in flames.

As she headed toward the door, her words came tumbling out in a breathless rush, like she had no control over them.

"I didn't want to join Verto Veneri at first," she said, oblivious to the way he hung on her every word. "Rory sold it to me as a thrill we'd both benefit from. But when we arrived, he didn't think twice. But it was that straight-forward for me. No one interested me until I met—"

She stopped speaking.

He already knew.

She didn't have to say it.

"Until you met who?" he asked, wanting to hear his name roll off her tongue.

Lana's body tensed. She glanced over her shoulder, wide eyes locked with his like she'd just backed herself into a corner.

He could see the war happening inside her.

To lie, or to tell the truth.

The way she was breathing, the way her pulse ticked rapidly at her throat.

The truth was all there.

"It doesn't matter anymore." She looked away and marched toward the front door, her shoulders set.

Marcus let her walk away from the question.

For now.

Because now he knew. Now, he was certain.

Lana wanted him.

She could fight it all she wanted and try to convince herself otherwise. But the truth was already out.

He prowled up behind her with leisurely strides, his blood humming.

She sensed his approach, and her spine instantly stiffened before she spun around to face him, her hair flying over one shoulder.

Christ.

She was stunning.

Her startled gaze found his, the pupils blown so dark a thin ring of blue crowned them. A rush of something fierce and primal surged through him.

Electricity snapped, alive and volatile, and fuck, he wanted to fuck her.

Instead, he kept his hands at his sides.

This wasn't an arranged club encounter where

everyone knew the rules—this was something else entirely.

But she didn't move away.

"I need to go, Marcus," she whispered, the words shaky. "Or I'll get in trouble with my manager."

His fingers grazed down the bare skin of her arm, a slow, intentional stroke.

A test.

A warning.

Or maybe a promise.

Her breath hitched, and damn it, his veins caught fire, heat flooding through him. So much for wiping out his fascination with her.

"Are you serious about marrying him?" he asked, his tone edged with an unusual possessiveness. "Is he your future?"

"I—I can't answer—" she stumbled over the words. "Th—that right now."

She exhaled, eyes searching as if she was drowning and didn't know whether to fight or let herself sink.

"I don't know."

Marcus stepped back, the devil on his shoulder whispering filthy promises, coaxing him to claim her, to sink his teeth into the hardened peaks of her nipples, to feast on the glistening heat between her thighs.

In the deepest, most depraved part of his mind, he was already fucking her—hard, relentless, driven by the intoxicating sound of her breathless moans and pleasured cries.

But then, guilt hit harder, and he remembered the reason he started Verto Veneri.

If he was going to have her, it had to be within the club's terms, shrouded in the contracts that made fucking outside her relationship acceptable. A neat little loophole to justify his urges.

Because he *would* have her.

And once he did, he'd move on.

One unforgettable, filthy night. Then done. Dusted. And out of his system.

"You deserve a man who'll put you first. If you marry him, I hope he's that guy," he said, leading her out.

Neither of them spoke. Not even during the five-minute car ride to her office.

When they pulled up outside the tall building, he jumped out, rounded the car, and opened the door for her.

His fingers wrapped around hers, steadying her as she stepped out. The contact was brief, but it sent a bolt of awareness through him.

Keeping his hand pressed to the small of her back, dangerously close to the curve of her perfect ass, he guided her toward the automatic sliding glass doors.

Towering over her, Marcus leaned in, his lips brushing the soft skin of her temple. "Have a good day, beautiful."

Lana gazed up at him, her ocean-blue eyes filled with temptation.

Fuck.

He gave her a curt nod, turned on his heel, and stalked back to his car, finally free of her pull.

"Seatbelt. Keys. Get the fuck out of here," he muttered.

But his hand stalled at the ignition, the hair on his nape pricking. He could sense her approach before he turned his head.

Lana stood at his window, brushing stray strands of hair behind her ear, her movements awkward, nervous.

Shit.

Marcus pressed the button to lower the window and smiled. "Forgot something?"

"I—uh." She cleared her throat, cheeks burning. "I just—God, I don't even know why I'm back here."

He smirked, cocking an eyebrow. "No?"

"Nope." She popped the 'p,' dramatically, shifting her weight from foot to foot. "I mean—maybe I just—"

A cute laugh bubbled past her lips, and she tucked a loose strand of hair behind her ear.

"So yeah, thanks for lunch." She shrugged. "It was a pleasant change to the daily grind. And, um... Enjoy the rest of your week."

"You too, beautiful."

And before she could say anything else, before she could stumble over another awkward goodbye, she backed up and waved before disappearing inside.

Marcus chuckled to himself, shaking his head at the grin spreading across his face.

Goddamn.

In that instant, Marcus knew, deep in his bones, he had to see her again.

And he knew exactly how to make it happen.

19

Lana

Wednesday arrived with a matte black envelope landing on the doormat.

Lana hesitated, her fingertips grazing the smooth surface as a knot tightened in her stomach.

She already knew what it meant.

Still, she peeled it open; her pulse spiking as she slid out the heavy cardstock, the gold cursive script shimmering in the morning light.

> *You are cordially invited to attend*
> *Verto Veneri*
> *Friday, 25 August, 8 p.m.*

She sucked in a breath.

Oh. My. God.

She hadn't expected an invitation so soon. Club nights were monthly—so this was a mistake, right?

Her fingertips brushed over the card as a wave of

unease washed over her. It had only been a week since her first night inside Verto Veneri, since she'd stepped into an unfamiliar world of whispered desires.

Since she'd met him.

And now, another invitation.

Moving through the sitting room and into the kitchen, she grabbed her phone from the countertop.

Rory had been absent more than usual, his presence at home more like an afterthought than a desire to be there.

Monday, he'd rolled in at two in the morning after drinking with his mate Zac.

He didn't return home last night.

The perks of owning his own workshop and employing a team of mechanics meant he could waltz in whenever he pleased, just as long as someone else picked up the slack.

And lately, that seemed to be all he did—waltz in and out.

When she first moved in with him, they were inseparable. They spent their nights curled up on the couch, tangled together beneath a throw, talking about their future.

But now? Now he was rekindling his old partying habits, slipping away into late nights and excuses.

Lana exhaled, pressing her lips together as she typed a message.

Hey—another invitation to Verto for this Friday!

151

Aren't they supposed to be
monthly????

She stared at the screen for a long moment before hitting send. Her phone stayed silent, the reply from Rory never coming.

His routine had become predictable. He probably lay unconscious on Zac's couch only to resurface by noon with a killer hangover that would leave him a hollower version of himself for the rest of the day.

With a frustrated sigh, Lana grabbed her purse and slung it over her shoulder on her way out the door. She didn't have the luxury of late nights and lie in's when she had a nine-to-five job to hold down.

She was tired of waiting for him. Tired of the silence and the emptiness.

The bus ride into the city was her escape, the steady hum of the engine offering a little comfort as she sank into the seat by the window.

She stared out at the blur of roads, trying to focus on anything other than the nagging invitation burning a hole in her mind.

Could she really return to The Fitz hotel and step into that world again, pretending she was okay with...everything?

Her pulse quickened. Marcus would be there.

She could already picture him, sitting in that office of his, wearing a tailored suit that made him look like he owned the world.

And he did. He owned *that* world.

A shiver raced down her spine, the memory of his green gaze sparkling with gold. Of course, he had golden specks in his eyes. The man was elite.

No. Thinking of him was dangerous.

She cursed herself for the thrill pulsing through her veins. For indulging in the fantasy of him. The image of Marcus—*Mr McGrath*—summoning her to his office and her kneeling on his command.

But, God, her thoughts were toeing the line of cheating. Even if everything with Marcus existed in the grey shadows of Verto's shady world. Her desire to meet him again was inappropriate.

Wasn't it?

Lana rubbed her forehead as if it could clear her muddled thoughts. She had to stay away from temptation. But the more she remembered, the more that didn't seem possible.

It was a huge mind fuck.

With Verto Veneri's next event fast approaching, Lana decided to leave work early and visit Janice at the beauty salon.

As she packed up her desk to prevent Magpie Marty from swiping her stationery, Amanda appeared from behind.

"I haven't had a chance to talk to you yet, Lana. Been stuck in meetings all morning," Amanda said, coming up beside her. "Where do you think you're going?"

She dropped her spiral notebook on the desk, clearly ready for answers.

Lana slid her things into her bag.

"Taking a half day. I've got a beautician appoint-ment." She only half lied.

Amanda arched an eyebrow.

"Who the hell was that sex on legs the other day? Where've you been hiding him? You and Rory over or something?" She fired the questions so fast, it was like a machine gun.

"Rory and I are *not* over," Lana quickly replied, her voice a little too defensive. "That was just some guy I know."

Amanda's fiery curls bounced as she shook her head.

"Some *guy?*" she repeated, sceptical. "It seemed like you wanted to rip each other's clothes off right there on the pavement. I was a gooseberry. You better be careful, girl. That kinda thing doesn't end well. Infidelity has a way of seeping out, even when you think it's buried. Cheaters never stop cheating."

Lana lowered her lashes and straightened.

Amanda was touchy because her parents had divorced when she was fifteen, and the chaos left her stuck in the middle of an ugly parental war.

The battles were more about money than custody, but the trauma still shaped her, giving her a bitter, non-committal view of relationships.

Lana rubbed her friend's forearm, trying to reassure her.

"Let's not discuss this now. Rory and I are fine. We got ourselves into something, and I'm not sure how to get out of it." Her voice dropped to a whisper. "I'm really confused."

"Tell me it's not drugs, Lan, please," Amanda said, grabbing her hand, her eyes wide with concern. "Do you owe that guy money? With that expensive suit, he looked like he was mafia or something."

Lana shook her head, holding up her hands. "No drugs...of course not. Drugs are for losers. I'm not an eejit."

But if she had to be honest, she'd admit that sexual attraction—*Marcus*—was its own kind of drug. He put her under his spell and left her craving more.

Amanda's gaze narrowed, hands resting on her hips.

"That guy reeks of heartbreak, girl. He looks familiar, though. Where'd you meet him?"

Lana turned to her desk, pushing in her chair and heading for the stairwell with Amanda trailing behind.

"He owns a few hotels. His name's Marcus McGrath."

Saying his name out loud made her heart flutter, like she was accepting the taste of the divine.

Amanda stopped dead in her tracks, slapping her hands together with a dramatic gasp.

"McGrath? Like *the* McGrath? The billionaire businessman? The biggest playboy north of the border—any border?"

"That's the one." Lana nodded, her smile threatening to break free, but she bit it back.

"Oh shit, Lana, you fancy him, don't you?"

"I'm with Rory," Lana muttered, the words sticking in her throat like a confession she didn't want to admit.

Amanda crossed her arms, lips pressed tight in that

way only a mother would understand, waiting for the real answer.

"That's not what I asked, Lana. Do you have the hots for McGrath?"

Lana exhaled a slow, steady breath, shoving the stairwell door open with her shoulder.

"I barely know him, Amanda...but I can't help it. I'm drawn to him. Like when I'm near the guy, I can't think straight."

Shoving her foot between the closing door and the frame, Amanda poked her face through the slim gap.

"First you need to be honest with yourself, Lan, then you need to be honest with Rory."

Her expression was stern, but there was a softness behind her gaze, a silent understanding that Lana wasn't sure she deserved.

"I love Rory," she rushed the words, a little too defensive.

"But are you *in love* with him?" Amanda's words hit harder than she'd expected.

Before meeting Marcus, Lana would've said yes without hesitation.

Rory was everything she'd ever needed—steady, reliable, always there when she needed him. Their lives and routines complemented each other.

But now... now there was Marcus, with his electric pull and wild energy, that made her come alive in ways Rory hadn't in a long time. Or maybe ever.

She hesitated, a lump forming in her throat. Was she

really in love with Rory or was she just holding onto the relationship because it was comfortable?

Amanda read the doubt in her eyes.

"Lan, listen to me. From where I'm standing, this hot billionaire has made you question your relationship because he's new and exciting. A crush is a powerful thing, but it's not love. Don't confuse the two."

"Well, I'm certainly not in love with Marcus," Lana corrected. "I just want him to screw my brains out."

The second Amanda's eyes widened, guilt sank heavy in her belly. "But that won't happen."

"Well, you need to figure it out. Because if you don't, you'll end up doing something you regret. And someone's going to get hurt."

Lana swallowed; her heart heavy with uncertainty. She didn't know the right answer—whether it was committing to Rory forever, giving in to a steamy night of passion with Marcus, or something else entirely.

Perhaps Marcus was just the catalyst for a change in her relationship.

"Just take a step back, okay?" Amanda said, giving her a light pat on the shoulder before moving out of the doorway. "You'll figure it out. But don't ignore what your gut is telling you."

When Amanda disappeared, Lana headed downstairs. Pushing out into the main reception area, her phone buzzed with a message from Rory.

Rather than answer, she shoved her phone back in her pocket, not having the headspace to hear him grovel all over again.

Truth was, Lana didn't know what she wanted anymore.

Deep down, her gut instinct told her she was just another one of Marcus's conquests. So she should forget all about him and Verto Veneri.

Janice threw her arms around Lana in a whirlwind of warmth and energy, air-kissing both of her cheeks before pulling her into the back office of the beauty salon.

The room was cosy, with soft lavender wallpaper and modern white furniture. Pictures of models adorned the walls, all flawless, with glossy hair and perfect skin.

Instead of the figure-hugging dress Janice had worn at the club last weekend, she wore a tailored, business-like ensemble—a fitted blazer over a silk blouse, paired with dark trousers that gave her an air of authority.

"So good to see you again, sweetheart," Janice cooed, fixing a strand of Lana's blonde hair. "Are you here for a wax? We have a brilliant—"

"Not this time, but thanks. I came to ask if you got one of these?" she whispered, glancing over her shoulder to check the office door.

Janice slid onto the plush lilac chair behind her desk and opened the top drawer, her manicured nails clicking against the metal as she rummaged through it.

"I certainly did," she replied, her voice dropping an octave. "I nearly fainted when it arrived. You know I'm not easily shaken, but this..."

She pulled out a pearly pink diary, its pages thick and pristine, and flipped through them with practiced ease.

"I've checked my records. The Verto team never plans events that closely. It's unheard of."

Lana placed the black card back into the safety of her bag.

"Who sets the dates and organises the events?" she asked, curiosity edging her voice.

Janice leaned back in her chair, tapping her chin.

"As far as I'm aware, that's Donna Marie's job. I guess Marcus has the final say, though." Her eyes twinkled as she looked Lana over. "He must have a good reason to arrange another night so quickly...in the same hotel. Perhaps he's testing the waters—seeing if the demand is there to accommodate the growing number of members."

Lana's stomach flipped at the mention of Marcus, but she shook it off.

"Anyway," Janice continued, giving a mischievous wink, her lips curving into a knowing smile, "who cares? As long as we have some extracurricular activity."

Lana sank into a velvet chaise lounge that matched the decor, its rich purple hues inviting relaxation, and held her bag on her lap.

"Did you get lucky that night?" she asked, a curious smile tugging at the corners of her lips.

Janice's eyes lit up, and she grinned.

"Sure did," she laughed. "Some young thing. Well, he was thirty-five and full of stamina. You?"

Lana sighed. "Well, one guy was a contender, but when I got to the room, my key card wouldn't work."

Janice set her elbows on the desk and frowned.

"That's unusual," she said. "What happened after that?"

Lana hesitated, the memory of the night still lingering in her mind. "It felt like a sign. Like maybe I wasn't supposed to go through with it. So I went home alone."

Janice narrowed her eyes, thoughtful.

"In a five-star hotel of that calibre, key cards don't just randomly stop working," she said.

Lana's thoughts drifted back to Marcus. How he conveniently appeared moments after her key card malfunctioned.

"Don't overthink it, Lana. Just enjoy the ride," Janice said, her smile almost secretive, as if she knew things Lana didn't. "What about your fella? How did he get on?"

"Oh, he spent the whole night with a woman. He told me her name was Jacqueline."

Janice shifted in her seat, her expression tightening as she leaned in. "Jacqueline Simpson? Black hair, in her twenties?"

Lana frowned, her brows knitting together. "Yes. Why?"

Janice's gaze became more intense. "Oh, Lana, she's an odd one, that girl. One guy told my Justin she was into weird, kinky stuff."

Lana's pulse raced, an icy shiver running down her spine. "Like what?"

Janice shrugged, a light, almost dismissive gesture. "I

don't know, sweetheart. Justin stays clear of her. Rumour has it her husband, Ciaran Simpson, is a gangster. A real bad bastard."

Lana rubbed her throat, where the memories of Rory's hands still lingered. The pieces were falling into place. How could she ever compete?

Janice stood, her movements quick and graceful as she studied Lana's face. "You've gone an unsightly shade of pale, sweetheart. Are you okay?"

Lana swallowed hard, her mouth dry, her head pounding as she tried to steady her breath. The room felt smaller, tighter.

"Could you get me a glass of water, please?" she asked, the words almost a whisper.

Janice strolled to the corner of the office, opened a mini fridge, and grabbed a bottle of water. Lana had a sinking weight in her stomach, a knot so tight it made her nauseous.

She wanted to believe Rory wasn't hiding something darker, but she wasn't sure anymore. The more she thought about the nights he'd come home late and the growing distance, the more Lana wondered if Rory was fulfilling his own kinks elsewhere.

What if he was experimenting with other women outside of the club? Was there a whole different side of him—a violent side—she hadn't met? Was joining Verto Veneri his way of introducing her to the darker parts of him?

Even though questions ran through her mind, Lana kept them to herself.

As Janice returned with a bottle of water, Lana took it without a word, her hands trembling as she sipped from it. She glanced up at Janice, meeting her gaze. The older woman's gaze was sharp, as if she could see through the mask Lana tried to hide behind.

"You're thinking too much, darling." Janice smiled. "He loves you, right?"

Lana's chest tightened. Did he?

"Yeah. Of course he does," she replied, feigning a smile and light laugh.

"Then there's no reason to worry. Just enjoy yourself."

Despite her words of comfort, Lana wondered how much longer she could keep pretending everything was fine.

20

Lana

Friday evening rolled around faster than Lana had hoped.

She sat on the edge of her bed, staring at the invitation in her hands, the black card heavy.

Her thoughts circled like a whirlwind, confusion clouding her mind. Nothing had changed. Rory was still distant and with his mates most nights.

And the pull toward the unknown, toward the world that Marcus represented, was even stronger.

But that didn't make her decision any easier. Focus on repairing their relationship or learn about the club, of everything it entailed—and take a bite of desire.

She stared at her bare complexion in the mirror, her fingers brushing over the strap of the sexy dress she had picked out. The silky fabric was featherlight against her skin, as if it didn't belong to the version of herself she recognised.

One question haunted her—why isn't she enough for him?

The thought nagged at her, unable to shake the notion that Rory needed more—more than she could give, more than she was willing to sacrifice.

Verto Veneri wasn't just about sex; it embodied power, control, desire, breaking boundaries—for men and women alike. Was that what Rory wanted all along? To mould her into someone she wasn't.

Rather than put on her makeup, she sat there, staring at her reflection.

Lost.

The prospect of meeting Marcus again left her breathless, a thrill blooming despite herself.

She wasn't naïve; she knew the difference between the dangerous allure of Marcus and the safety of what she'd built with Rory. But the vicious cycle they'd fallen into was a half-hearted attempt—a game they weren't playing on equal ground.

Was this more about Rory's adventure than theirs?

She groaned and threw herself onto the bed. Rory could fly solo if he wanted. Not that he'd miss her, anyway.

Deep down, the reality of it made her stomach twist. She didn't want him disappearing into that world without her.

Then again...what if Marcus could show her things she'd never imagined—if he could show her what she'd been missing all along?

Fear struck. What if everything she thought she knew

about love and trust was just an illusion? Would she be able to walk away from that kind of darkness unscathed?

Her breath quickened again, dread pressing in on her chest.

Rory walked into the bedroom, the soft click of the door behind him startling her. He peeled off his t-shirt, tossed it over the chair and kicked off his track shoes.

"Why aren't you ready?" he asked.

"I haven't decided if I want to go."

"Really? Why not?"

"I'm not feeling it."

"Come on, babe," he said half-heartedly, like he was going through the motions. "It'll be fun. Relax, enjoy a few drinks, maybe meet some new guys."

Lana sighed, already preparing herself for the lie she'd have to tell.

"It's my time of the month. Horrendous cramps. You know how it is."

The lie left a bitter taste, but facing Marcus while vulnerable and confused was not a smart idea.

Rory gave a casual shrug, his gaze wandering over his reflection in the mirror as he dressed in a clean shirt she'd washed and ironed for him.

"No worries, babe. Have an early night, yeah." He leaned in and kissed her lips, the gesture more out of habit than anything else. "Love you."

"Will you be home tonight?" she asked, watching him button up his shirt.

The fabric clung to his chest, accentuating his athletic build underneath. He was handsome, with his

165

new chestnut stubble giving his jawline a more rugged look.

He looked at her reflection in the mirror as he tucked his shirt into his trousers.

"I don't know, Lana. Do I have a curfew or something?" He sprayed cologne on his neck, patted his cheeks, and then turned to face her, his expression a mix of indifference and impatience. "Look, whatever happens, happens—okay, babe?"

Lana's brow scrunched, his tone condescending.

"I'm asking if I can expect you home. It's common courtesy to let me know in case something happens to you. I am your girlfriend, aren't I?"

Rory threw a hand up in the air, as if swatting away her words. His posture stiffened, and he drew his shoulders back, exasperation flashing in his eyes.

"What's that supposed to mean?" he spat, his voice rising. "Of course you're my girlfriend. You live here, don't you?"

Lana shot up from the edge of the bed, pulse thumping with anger.

"Yeah, but I might as well live here by myself for all I've seen of you lately. You could be out shagging half of Belfast, and I wouldn't have a clue. A bunch of flowers now and then doesn't build a relationship, Rory. It doesn't mean shit."

Rory's face twisted into a scowl, but he didn't seem overly fazed.

"Jesus, you're being dramatic. I'm not sleeping around, so I don't need to send you a bunch of dead flowers to make up for it. What do you want me to do, call you every five minutes?"

"No," she snapped, the frustration flooding her chest. "I want you to stop pretending like I'm not here. I want you to act like you give a shit."

He exhaled in a gust down his nose, rolling his eyes. "I give a shit, Lana. But you're acting like I've done something wrong. I'm just out having a good time, like everyone else. You could join me instead of sitting around with your woman cramps. But whatever, you do you."

Rory sighed and stepped into her, cuffing her wrists, his fingers digging in just enough to make her flinch. His eyes were intense, his jaw clenched tight, but there was something else beneath the anger. Something he was trying to keep hidden.

"We agreed to this, Lana. Me *and* you. So don't start painting me as the asshole. I've been letting off some steam, just like you need space sometimes."

Her heart lurched. He was right. She had given her approval for everything. She'd convinced herself she was okay with it, that it was just a phase couples go through.

"I just don't think I can give you what you need, Rory," she whispered. "Maybe I'm not the woman for you."

His expression darkened as he unhanded her, and for a moment, he looked almost...vulnerable. Then he sighed and stepped closer, his chest bumping into hers and that charming smile he used to flash just for her appeared.

"Look, babe, you're my girl." He thumbed her cheek. "You know that. I love you. I'm not asking for more than what we agreed on. But I need you to understand that this isn't about replacing you. You're my future."

He dipped into her face and kissed the tip of her nose, a gentle, almost affectionate gesture. Then he pulled away and stepped back, sighing, an exhale that seemed to release all the tension in his body.

"It's all gonna be fine, okay?" He grabbed his jacket off a hanger and slipped it on, already retreating into his own world.

"I'll be back later. Don't worry about it. Next time we'll go together."

He strolled out of the bedroom. Lana stood there, her heart pounding with a mix of anger and confusion. Her throat tightened, but the words wouldn't come. What could she say?

Rory wasn't hearing her, not the way she needed him to. Instead, he was just...disappearing.

The rift between them was widening with every step he took away from her.

Lana stepped out of the shower and towelled off, her mind still reeling after Rory's departure.

During her time under the hot water, she decided to level up her game. While she'd declined the opportunity to attend Verto Veneri this evening, she would make the most of her alone time with some inspiration.

She slipped into her favourite pyjama set—soft jersey

shorts and a snug tank top for comfort, then blasted the lengths of her hair with a hairdryer.

It was time to focus, unwind, and do a little research.

Moving downstairs, she poured herself a generous glass of gin over crushed ice, adding a few slices of cucumber, and settled onto the couch with her laptop open.

The first crunch of a potato crisp, followed by a sip of her drink, helped her relax. Movie night could officially begin once she'd found the perfect spicy website to browse.

One drink turned into three as she clicked on random erotic movie clips. It wasn't her first time watching porn, but tonight, with the loneliness of the house and the gin, it seemed different.

She maxed up the volume and let the sound of desperate moans and grunts fill the room, punctuated by the rough pounding of a scene she wasn't sure she could handle herself.

Although the title of the clip—'Spit Roasting Rochelle'—made her giggle, she was unprepared for the surge of heat that followed.

As her eyes remained glued to the screen and her pulse raced, a loud thump echoed from the front door.

21

Lana

Frozen, Lana's heart skipped a beat, adrenaline pumping through her hot veins. Her first thought was to ignore whoever was outside, however the knocking continued, steady and insistent.

She scrambled to click the pause button on her laptop, cursing under her breath.

Padding into the hallway, buzzing from alcohol and an arousal, she fixed the safety chain in place, unlocked the door and peeked outside.

Oh, fuck.

There, framed by the moonlight, stood Marcus McGrath. The sight of him in dark trousers, a navy shirt clinging to his muscular chest made her pulse go haywire.

His height had her neck craning to find his shadowed face, and the silver gleam of a designer watch caught the light from behind her.

She swallowed, trying to steady her panic.

"Eh...hold on...give me a minute while I unhook the

safety chain," she said, her voice sounding breathy and shocked.

Closing the door, her heart continued to hammer in her chest. She took a steadying breath, pressed her forehead against the cold wood and closed her eyes for a moment, gathering herself.

Why the hell was Marcus McGrath standing on her doorstep?

Shouldn't he be at his club, managing his empire, surrounded by members who paid him a fortune?

After a beat, she straightened and brushed crumbs off her chest. Her pulse thrummed in her throat and every breath turned shallow.

She ran a hand through her hair, trying to smooth out the mess, then took the safety chain off.

The universe was clearly playing a cruel joke.

She'd been alone, wrapped in her own thoughts and distracted by a dirty movie that was not appropriate for company.

Now, Marcus stood beyond the door, and she became hyper-aware of the paused image on her laptop and her clothes. Embarrassment flushed her cheeks. The shorts revealed her bare legs, and she was unsure how to act with him.

A quick puff of air into her cupped hand and a sniff reminded her of the salty crisps she'd eaten—thank fuck she didn't dive into the sour cream and chive dip.

Lana pulled the door wide and played it cool, pretending the sight of him didn't impress her, even though she almost went blind from the blood rush.

Marcus's broad frame filled the doorway, commanding her full attention. His gaze raked over her in one lingering sweep, bold green eyes studying every inch of her.

The corner of his mouth lifted, offering her a lazy smile. "Can I come in, please?"

Never invite the devil into your house, Lana.

The words echoed in her mind, but she didn't heed her own warning. She couldn't—he was here. And when he smiled at her like that, she couldn't do anything but step back and wave him inside.

"Okay. Sure."

Marcus McGrath—the sexiest man alive was standing in her small living room, only a few steps from her laptop. Thankfully, the screen faced the back of the couch, so she didn't have to dive on top of it.

He folded his arms, his gaze still locked onto hers. She couldn't escape him, couldn't pull her thoughts together. His intoxicating cologne surrounded her, making the room smaller, more intimate.

"Nice place," he said, even though his eyes hadn't left her for a single second.

Her stomach swooped. She reached for her midriff, to shield herself from the intensity of his stare.

"Thanks. It serves a purpose," she quipped.

A smile danced over his lips. "It's...cosy. However, you look more like a woman who'd enjoy living on a foreign property with a pool and the sun shining on your freckles."

Her fingers brushed over her lips as a helpless, shy smile appeared.

"Can I get you a drink?" she asked, her voice steady, even though her pulse had gone wild.

"Sure," he said, his baritone voice thick with something she couldn't quite place—amusement, desire, maybe a bit of both. "Water will do. I'm driving."

The words were simple, but they sent little shivers of excitement over her skin, like tiny bombs of electricity scattered over her body.

Marcus McGrath had driven all the way to her house on a club night.

"Give me a second."

She spun on her bare feet, her skin still humming with awareness of his presence, the coolness of the floor beneath her grounding her. Walking into the kitchen, she wondered if he watched her very step. Nerves burst through her.

The shorts she wore had crept up between her ass cheeks, and the last thing she wanted was to pick at them in front of him.

Out of sight, she yanked at her shorts, pulling them free from the uncomfortable wedge. Her heart was still pounding, but her hands were steady as she gripped the edge of the counter, using it for balance as she settled herself.

God, why was he doing this to her? Her body seemed to have a mind of its own, sending little pulses of heat to places that made her question her sanity.

Then, she sensed his approach when a shiver rolled down her spine. Glancing at the doorway, he leaned casually against the frame, arm resting above his head, muscles flexing in a way that made everything inside her tighten.

His green eyes were alive with amusement.

"It seems I've interrupted you," he said, his voice low and deep, like dark velvet.

A hint of a smirk made something wild stir inside her. "If you wanted action, beautiful, you should've shown up at my club. You got the invitation, right?"

Lana shrugged like it was nothing.

"Yeah, I got it," she replied. "And you haven't interrupted me at all. I was enjoying a quiet night to myself. I wasn't well earlier, that's all."

His gaze held hers, and her stomach did a full flip when he rubbed his jaw.

"I'm assuming the porn made you feel better. Because you look perfect to me."

Perfect.

The word flooded her cheeks with heat, spreading down her chest. She dabbed at the wet spot on her top with a hand towel, trying and failing to act like it wasn't a big deal.

However, her skin burned under his gaze, and she didn't know how to pull away.

Marcus took a step closer, making the kitchen walls close in. She forced a scowl, trying to cover her embarrassment, and took a sideways step. Rising to her tiptoes, she reached open a cupboard and reached for a glass.

Behind her, he cleared his throat.

"Why are you here—" she muttered under her breath, moving to the sink and flicking on the cold water. "Looking at my laptop? Don't you have better things to do on a Friday night?"

"I have business to take care of but that's not better than calling in to check on you."

Every word from his mouth, every look he sent her way, shot tiny, wicked explosions through her, jolting her from one moment to the next.

"And the porn wasn't hard to miss," he replied when she turned back to him.

His eyes drilled into her like he was undressing her with every passing second.

"I can't help but notice... Something's got you all worked up, beautiful." His voice dropped an octave.

Lana slid the glass of water across the counter, the cool condensation slick against her fingertips.

"There you go." Her voice was light, casual—too casual. "Is this a courtesy call?"

Marcus didn't answer immediately. Instead, he took a sip, and her eyes betrayed her, dropping to his throat as he swallowed. She stared, transfixed, as a bead of water escaping the corner of his mouth and rolling down through the bristled shadow of his chin.

For a fleeting, reckless moment, she envied that tiny water droplet, wanting to trace its path with her tongue, to taste him all over again.

She swallowed, the sound filling the silence.

When he finally lowered the glass and wiped his jaw

with the back of his hand, her pulse kicked against her throat.

"Why didn't you show up tonight?" he asked. "I like to meet my customers' expectations, so if there's a reason you didn't go, then I'd like to know."

His narrowed gaze locked onto hers, daring her to give him the truth.

She forced herself to hold his stare, though every nerve ending screamed at her to look away. The real reason sat between them, thick and suffocating. He knew. Of course, he knew.

Rather than give in to temptation, she played it safe, stayed in the comfort of her sitting room, surrounded by distractions and distance. And now the real reason stood inches away, messing with the heat of her body.

The flutters between her legs grew as his gaze took its time trailing down the length of her bare thighs. He wasn't subtle. He didn't have to be.

Lana straightened, gripping the counter behind her like an anchor. She couldn't trust herself around him. He made her impulsive, reckless. He made her want things she had no business wanting.

And worst of all, he wasn't Rory.

"Like I said." She shrugged. "I wasn't feeling well."

His head tilted, considering her. "And now?"

Her lips pressed together, but they twitched at the corners, betraying her.

"Much better." She swayed slightly, the warmth of the gin still humming through her bloodstream. "Just a little tipsy."

"I was looking for you in the club."

Her gaze dropped to her toes, as if breaking eye contact might ease the unbearable tension curling inside her.

But it didn't. It only made her more aware of how close he was. How easily he could reach out and touch her if he wanted to.

She wanted him to.

God help her, she craved it.

The realisation sent a fresh wave of heat through her, shattering whatever fragile principles she'd been clinging to. She'd never endured this. Not with Rory. Not with anyone.

"Oh, yeah?" she asked. "Why?"

Marcus stepped closer, the space between them vanishing in an instant.

"Were you trying to avoid me?" His voice was softer now, but no less commanding.

Lana lifted her chin, her pulse hammering against her ribs. "Would it matter if I was?"

He didn't answer right away. Instead, his eyes darkened, as if weighing something important, something *inevitable*.

Then, finally, he said, "Maybe."

His fingers brushed against the counter beside hers. Just a whisper of contact, but it sent an electric shock through her system.

She was playing with fire and deep down, she was ready to go up in flames.

22

Marcus

Earlier in the evening, when Donna Marie informed Marcus that Rory had entered the club alone, his temper spiked to nuclear.

Lana was supposed to be with him. That was the plan—the whole damn reason he'd arranged an extra night. He wanted the chance to turn a good girl bad.

He'd fought the urge to tear through the place hunting for her and considered the possibility she'd arrive later.

So, he waited.

Two hours passed.

She never came.

His patience snapped. Tension coiled through his body as he strode into the Verto Veneri lounge, every step controlled, every muscle wound tight.

It didn't take long to find Rory.

The arrogant little fucker was lounging in a corner booth, a whiskey in one hand, the other running up the bare thigh of Jacqueline Simpson—the same woman he'd fucked last week.

Rory sat there like he was fucking royalty when, in reality, he was just an asshole. The woman draped over him giggled, their laughter blending like drunk teenagers caught up in the rush of a new infatuation.

Marcus didn't give a damn that he was interrupting. He moved without hesitation, stepping into their space like a shadow swallowing the light. His presence was a silent threat—imposing, unyielding—commanding attention with the sheer force of it. The laughter died instantly.

Marcus levelled a stare at Rory. "Do you even know who I am?"

At that moment, the woman beside him leaned in, her voice hushed and reverent, "Marcus..." as if his very name were divine.

Without missing a beat, Marcus continued, "You're meant to bring your partner, Mr O'Hare," his tone low and razor-sharp, cutting through any bullshit excuse Rory might try to spin. "Where is she?"

Rory's head snapped up. His pupils expanded a fraction, betraying the flash of unease he tried to hide beneath a smirk. But Marcus saw it. He always saw it.

"My girlfriend isn't feeling well," Rory replied, lifting his drink and taking a slow sip. "She stayed home tonight. I didn't think it would be a problem if I came along given you added an extra date."

Marcus's gaze dropped to Rory's hand, tracing slow,

lazy circles along Jacqueline's inner thigh, his fingertips skimming close to the edge of her underwear.

A muscle in Marcus's jaw flexed, his teeth grinding together. A dull pang settled in his chest—something unwelcome, something foreign. He forced a quiet breath, shoving down his anger.

The woman at home was Rory's responsibility.

And he was a fucking disgrace for leaving her behind... all alone.

Marcus folded his arms across his chest, the thought settling in.

Lana is home alone.

"Is she ill?" Marcus asked, his voice calm.

Rory shrugged, careless. "Eh, yeah. Women crap. Sore tummy or something."

Marcus's fingers curled into his palm.

Lana was unwell, and this worthless bastard was here —flirting, drinking, groping another woman like he didn't have a care in the world?

Selfish. Disrespectful. Prick.

Marcus's blood ran hot beneath the surface, but his face remained impassive. Losing his temper wouldn't get him what he wanted.

To show Lana how a real man acted—how he moved, how he commanded, how he claimed, while letting her experience things she hadn't even realised she was missing.

He could have kicked Rory out. It would have been an easy snap of his fingers. In seconds, security would arrive, drag him out back, and kick him until he bled.

However, he'd crawl home to Lana like a wounded animal.

So instead, he let his authority settle over the fucker with a silent stare. He tilted his head, his sharp green gaze locking onto Rory's frown.

"We good, Marcus?" Rory asked.

"Next event you attend, bring your partner." His voice was like steel, firm and final. "This isn't a speed dating venue. This is your first and last warning."

He didn't wait for a response. Didn't give Rory the satisfaction of arguing.

He turned on his heel and strode away, leaving the little bastard in the dust.

That was an hour ago.

And now he was exactly where he wanted to be.

With Lana.

Marcus leaned against the kitchen counter, his gaze fixed on her pretty face and the way her blonde hair cascaded over her shoulders.

"Rory's occupied with a woman at my club," he said. "If he goes back there without you, I'll scrap his membership."

A flicker of hurt passed across Lana's face, replaced in a beat by a subtle sense of relief. Her fingers tightened around the edge of the counter, but she didn't ask. She didn't demand more information about the woman her fella was with.

She just nodded.

Acceptance.

When she exhaled, the tension in her shoulders

seemed to melt away, leaving something raw and exposed in its place.

Marcus took a step forward, aware of how the atmosphere grew hotter, crackling like a live wire, and when he reached for her, she didn't flinch.

"Lift your arms," he commanded, voice rough with need.

Lana obeyed without hesitation.

Her hands drifted above her head, graceful, trusting—offering herself to him in a way that sent a primal thrill down his spine. He took his time, dragging the tank top from her body, peeling it away inch by inch. The fabric hit the floor, but his gaze never left her.

Her eyes fluttered shut, lips parting to exhale a shaky breath.

Christ, she was devastating. Beautiful and untouchable, yet right here, in his hands. Fragile and fierce in equal measure, a contradiction he wanted to enjoy.

Then, as if sensing the shift inside him, her lashes lifted, and she speared him with those crystal-blue eyes—an endless ocean threatening to pull him under.

A silent plea shimmered in their depths. *Claim me.*

And fuck, he was ready.

Heat punched through his chest.

His fingertips skimmed the curve of her waist, the gentleness betraying the war he fought within himself. She melted against him, her soft belly bumping into his full, hard dick, a needy little nudge that sent fire licking up his spine.

A slow, wicked smile ghosted over her lips, and she fluttered her lashes.

"Did you come for this?" she asked.

Fuck.

His restraint stretched to its limit.

Marcus gripped her hips and backed her into the kitchen cupboards, his hands diving into her.

His mouth crashed over hers, rough and possessive, swallowing the breathy moan that slipped from her lips.

She arched, pressing her bare breasts against his chest, the friction setting fire to his already burning self-control. And when he finally tore his lips away, it wasn't to stop. It was to devour.

His hands cupped her breasts, thumbs teasing over stiff, pointed peaks before he dipped and latched onto one with his teeth.

A dirty little gasp broke from her throat as he bit down, the delicious tremble in her body sending a surge of raw satisfaction straight through him.

He sucked harder, dragging his tongue over her heated skin, getting off on her shiver beneath his touch. Goosebumps rose across her body in waves, and the reaction was so fucking intoxicating that it spread from her to him, an electric current binding them together.

His fingers dug into her flesh, anchoring her, claiming her, because in this moment, she wasn't thinking about Rory. She wasn't thinking about anyone but him.

This was how he worked—he took what he wanted, savoured it, then walked away without a second thought. He'd done it a hundred times before, never looking back.

That's why he came here tonight. To have *her*—just for one night.

At least, that's what he kept telling himself.

So why did everything about her pull him in deeper?

Marcus dragged his mouth from her breast, his breath ragged, his pulse thundering in his ears. His hands moved lower, stroking her hips, his thumbs digging into her skin.

She whimpered, and fuck, that sound was going to haunt him.

Because she surrendered.

And that did something dangerous to him.

Lana was gazing at him now, wide-eyed and breathless, pupils blown, lips swollen from his kiss. She was waiting, clinging to the moment, as if she already knew what was coming.

He could have her. Right now. Fuck her against this counter, drag her to the floor, take her in ways she'd never forget. Leave his mark so deep Rory could never touch her without sensing it.

But this was about her as much as him.

His thumb swept over the bare strip of skin just above her waistband, and she shivered. So damn responsive.

Marcus took his time, dragging his teeth along the delicate slope of her neck, savouring the way her breath hitched, the way her fingers explored, matching his hunger.

A deep, possessive growl rumbled in his chest as she pulled at his shirt and rubbed herself against his leg, chasing the friction.

"Not yet, sweetheart," he said thickly. "When you come, it'll be because I made it happen."

He wouldn't allow her to take control and rush what was his to give.

"Holy shit..." she gasped as he pinched her nipple, rolling it between his fingers before biting down just enough to make her cry out.

"God, yes..."

She liked the pain. The sharp edge of it. The way he pushed her that little bit further.

Shockwaves tore through her, her body reacting exactly as he planned—hips arching, breath hitching, fingers yanking his hair in a plea for more.

His tongue flicked out, soothing the bite, drawing another choked moan from the back of her throat. She was starving for his touch.

And that was so fucking sexy.

Skating his touch to her thighs, he yanked her shorts to her ankles in one swift motion. Her sharp gasp made his spine tingle, but before she could recover, he had her on the counter, legs spread, his body slotting between them.

Her ankles locked around his waist, pulling him in like she couldn't bear a single inch of space between them. Desperate little thing.

Their mouths hovered inches apart, their breaths mingling, heavy and uneven. His fingers tangled in her messy hair, yanking her head back just enough to expose the fluttering pulse in her throat.

"Fuck, Lana," he rasped. "You're beautiful and very fucking sexy."

She whimpered.

He smirked.

Then he lowered before her, aware of the sharp inhale from above and a slight shudder of her thighs.

His hands clamped down on the backs of her knees, pulling them to his shoulders to rest there. She was panting, her body wired so tight she might shatter if he so much as breathed on her.

"You're shaking," he said, crouched before her.

"I want you to show me what it's like on the other side of it all."

He slid a finger through her wet pussy and hummed. "You're ready to shake some more?"

"Yes... so ready."

"Good girl."

Then he spread her open and buried his face.

Her body jolted when his tongue swirled her clit, and a powerful shiver caused wrecked little moans to catch in her throat. The way her fingers clutched the counter had his dick almost weeping.

He didn't stop.

Didn't slow.

Didn't give her a second to breathe.

While she writhed for him, he thrust a finger inside her, curling, stroking, sending her spiralling to the edge.

She was close. So fucking close.

His mouth stayed on her, his tongue relentless and

his finger pumping in and out. She twisted, trembled, and gasped his name.

Then he growled against her slick heat, low and commanding, "Come for me, Lana."

His finger pushed in deeper, and his tongue pressed harder.

"Come all over my face."

She shattered beneath him.

And fuck, it tasted divine. The way her body locked up, the way her thighs clamped around his head before she let go. Her hips jerked, grinding into his mouth, chasing every wave of pleasure he wrung from her.

It had him wishing he was her man.

His growl rumbled through her, vibrating against her oversensitive flesh, dragging another wrecked whimper from her lips.

Good fucking girl.

The broken moan that followed sent heat lashing through his veins. The sound of her falling apart was a fucking symphony. His cock pulsed against his zipper, the pressure mounting, agonizing.

He let her have a moment—a second to breathe—before he rose to his full height and lightly cuffed her throat.

Her skin was hot, flushed. Her pulse thumped beneath his fingers.

"So fucking perfect," he murmured, tilting her chin up.

Her lashes fluttered as she met his gaze, pupils blown

wide, lips still parted from ragged breaths. He crushed his mouth to hers, sliding in deep, letting her taste herself on him.

The kiss was all-consuming, branding him onto her lips so she'd forget anyone else had ever touched her.

Slowly, he lifted her off the counter, letting her legs find the floor. She swayed, unsteady, her breath ragged.

Before she could fully regain her balance, he seized her waist and pulled her flush against him. A breathless sound escaped her—half gasp, half moan—just as her fingers traced the zipper of his jeans.

The first teasing brush sent a brutal shock of heat through him.

His grip tightened at her jaw, tilting her face up, forcing her gaze back to his.

"On your knees."

She obeyed.

"My belt," he ordered, voice thick with need. "Unbuckle it."

Lana hesitated for half a second—just long enough for him to catch the flicker of nerves in her eyes.

Her trembling fingers found the buckle, working it loose. She swallowed hard, her breath uneven as she reached for his zipper.

"Pull it down," he demanded.

With precise slowness, her fingers brushing over his hard dick beneath. A hiss rushed through his clenched teeth, his composure tested.

Wrapping her hand around the width of his dick, she

pulled it free. Lana peeked up at him as she parted her lips, flattened her tongue against it and dragged upward in one wet stroke.

He fisted her hair, gripping tight, controlling, guiding —reminding her who she belonged to in this moment.

"Hmmm," he said thickly, nostrils flaring as his cock twitched. "Wrap those lips around my dick."

And fuck, she did.

Heat. Pressure. Perfection.

Her wet, sucking mouth took him in, inch by inch, until the tip of dick met the tight resistance of her throat. She gagged but didn't pull away.

"Fuck..." The curse left his lips as he held her in place, watching her struggle, watching her take him.

"That's it, beautiful," he gritted out. "Suck my dick. Just like that."

Her throat vibrated as she hummed around him, the sensation sending pulses of desire straight to his spine. He couldn't stop the way his hips flexed, pushing deeper. Couldn't stop the low, guttural groan that rumbled in his chest as her nails dug into his thighs.

He pulled her off, just enough to force her to meet his gaze.

His cock, slick with her spit, gleamed in the dim light between them. Her lips were swollen, her eyes hungry.

She wanted him. Needed him.

Just like he fucking needed her.

He shoved back in, thrusting deeper, his fingers tightening in her hair as she swallowed him down.

His muscles coiled, heat licking up his spine like a violent storm ready to break.

"Fuck," he bit out, voice raw.

His balls drew tight in her palm and his whole body braced as he pulled his dick out before he exploded.

Marcus groaned at her shy smile that had no business being on a mouth that sinful.

"I nearly came too soon." His voice was rough, strained, still thick with need.

He reached for her, yanking her to her feet. A few stray strands of hair had fallen into her face, and he smoothed them back, taking a moment to look at her.

Flushed cheeks. Watery eyes. Lips swollen from sucking his cock.

His grip tightened. His next words came out low, dark. A promise. A threat.

"I'm going to fuck you now, beautiful."

Her breath hitched—sharp and unsteady. A sudden tension tightened her muscles, her pulse wild at the base of her throat.

She edged back until the counter halted her retreat.

But she wasn't trying to run.

Not exactly.

Something changed in her gaze—just for a second. A flicker of guilt, perhaps, the weight of realisation settling in.

Lines already crossed.

A choice made.

And now, the next step loomed before her—one she wasn't sure she was ready to take.

Marcus watched it happen in real time. The way her mind pulled her back, shackling her to the life she wasn't ready to admit was already dead.

Her arms folded around herself, a weak attempt at protection, but he saw the truth plain as day. She wasn't shielding herself from him—she was back tracking.

And then she shook her head.

Marcus's brow creased, irritation flaring as she attempted to sidestep him. In a beat, he had her trapped, his body crowding hers against the cabinets.

Her breath rushed out in a gust as his dick, still hard, pressed into her hip. A promise of dark satisfaction. A pleasure that would rip her apart and put her back together.

Her lashes fluttered. And then he crushed his mouth to hers, loving how she melted into him, just like before. Just like she always would.

Between teasing licks and bruising kisses, his voice dropped to a rough murmur.

"You signed a contract allowing other men to fuck you in my club." His teeth grazed her lower lip before soothing the sting with his tongue. "And technically, the owner is a member too, isn't he?"

Another kiss—deeper this time, designed to break her down.

"The highest-ranking member." His lips ghosted over hers, his words silk and sin. "And he's chosen you."

A soft, helpless sigh left her mouth, and he caught it, swallowing her doubt, feeding her surrender.

But then—hesitancy.

Her palms pressed against his chest, a weak attempt at distance, though she barely moved him an inch. Just enough to break the kiss—to steal a breath, to collect a thought that was already slipping away.

"No..." Her voice wavered, barely more than a whisper. "We can't."

23

Lana

"This is wrong." Lana's voice trembled.

The protest stuck in her throat, rough and uneven, like her body was fighting against it.

Her hands shook as she wrapped her arms around herself. "We're in my house, not the club. That makes this... something else."

But the second the excuse left her lips, doubt crept in. The words felt hollow. Weak. Even to her own ears.

Marcus exhaled, his head tipping toward her neck. He was so close, his heat enveloping her, his scent thick in the air—a heady mix of sweat, sin, and a cologne that had become an addiction.

His lips ghosted her pulse, and when he inhaled deeply, a needy whimper followed by a full body quake.

"How come he gets to play around," he whispered against her skin, his voice a molten rasp, "and you're home alone watching porn?"

Her stomach knotted. Marcus was right—but that didn't make it any less wrong.

A storm raged inside her, two forces pulling her in opposite directions. Every inch of her ached to give in, to press against him, to lose herself. But her mind warned her that this was a line she couldn't uncross.

Tonight, she'd crossed too many already. And if this was what she really wanted, then she had to talk to Rory first.

With all the strength she could gather, she set her hands against his chest and nudged.

"I'd like to be alone."

Marcus stiffened. His body remained solid, unmoving, but his eyes flickered—just for a second.

She angled away before she changed her mind, scrambling to gather her discarded clothes, her fingers shaking as she clutched her tank top against her chest.

"Lana." Her name left his lips like a warning—deep, edged with power.

Her throat tightened. She forced herself to look at him, to face the mistake she *almost* made.

"I'm sorry, Marcus," she whispered. "This—is confusing."

He just stood there, silent, unmoving. His green gaze pinned her in place.

But for a fleeting second, she caught it—that flicker beneath the surface. A brief shadow of respect tangled with frustration, maybe. Or something else entirely.

Then it vanished. Snuffed out, buried under the hard, impenetrable mask he always wore. The one that made it impossible to tell if he was about to walk away or drag her back into the fire.

A single rebellious lock of hair fell against his brow, daring her to step closer and fix it.

Her fingers twitched.

She *wanted* to.

But she didn't dare.

Marcus finally reached for his boxers and trousers, his movements measured. Even as he pulled them into place, his dick remained thick and heavy, the strain evident as he tucked himself away—but his composure never wavered.

Lana hugged her tank top tighter, hugging the fabric like it could hold her together.

"I'm not like the rest of your women, Marcus." Her voice wavered, but she pushed through, forcing steel into her spine. "I'm in a relationship with Rory, and this is our home. I can't risk ruining that for a meaningless fling. That's not who I am."

Her hands shook, but her body—traitorous and desperate—remained taut with unspent need, still aching for Marcus to take more.

"I hope he understands what he's about to lose," he muttered, running a hand through his hair, the movement deliberate as he pushed back that stubborn strand.

His breaths slowed, his chest rising and falling in a steady, controlled rhythm. A dark, raw intensity in his gaze twisted her stomach.

Maybe it was the war within him—fighting against

every instinct to take what he wanted, to finish what they'd started.

For a mindless second, she hoped he'd do it. That he'd ignore her principles and remove the choice for her.

This was her fault for letting it go too far, for sucking him off and giving him a glimpse of something neither of them could have.

Then again, he was the one who showed up on her doorstep.

And now, she had to live with it.

Marcus stepped back. Just once, then rubbed his jaw, considering her. After a slow, controlled exhale, his broad shoulders rolled back, and he gave a small nod.

"Thanks for the water," he said. "And for the record, you deserve so much more."

Lana's stomach clenched when he turned and prowled out of the kitchen, leaving her behind, not saying another word.

She pressed her hand against her belly, an ache blooming deep in her core—not just from desire, but from the gaping emptiness he left in his wake.

A few days had passed since Rory stumbled through the front door just after ten in the morning, looking pale and exhausted.

Bleary-eyed, reeking of whiskey and someone else's perfume, he'd grunted a greeting before dragging himself up the stairs and collapsing into bed.

He hadn't tried to explain, hadn't offered a half-hearted apology or even an attempt at reassurance. Just silence.

And she hadn't pushed him for details.

Instead, she'd stood in the kitchen, arms folded, waiting for some kind of reaction from herself—anger, disgust, heartbreak. But nothing had come.

Because that was their normal now.

Rory spent the night with another woman. She knew it would happen, so that wasn't counted as betrayal. And he expected the same from her. So theoretically, she should be absolved from cheating, too.

However, if that was their future, then maybe it wasn't worth holding on to.

She sank onto the couch and gathered her laptop from the coffee table, opening her web browser. Her fingers hesitated over the keyboard.

She shouldn't do this.

But she was curious.

With a deep breath, she checked the time. Rory was still upstairs, still fast asleep, as he had been every morning since that night.

Then, before she could talk herself out of it, she typed his name.

Marcus McGrath.

The search engine responded immediately, flooding her screen with results.

One headline stood out.

"McGrath dines out with Ally Doyle in Barcelona, May 2016."

Her pulse throbbed in her ears as she clicked the link, unable to stop herself.

The image loaded in an instant, and Lana's stomach plummeted.

An old photo from years ago, but fresh enough to sting.

Marcus grinned at the camera, his expression laced with that effortless charm.

The same lips that had ghosted over her skin, that had whispered filth into her ear, were stretched into an easy, teasing smirk.

The same teeth that had both bitten and soothed her to a frenzy gleamed under the restaurant's dim lighting.

He looked stunning in a jade-green polo shirt, the colour a perfect match for the wicked glint in his eyes. Relaxed. Confident.

And a stunning woman leaned against him, her smiling face angled toward his as if they'd shared a joke.

Lana studied the woman—a blonde of impossible beauty, all long limbs and high cheekbones, the kind of flawless elegance that belonged on a magazine cover.

She was laughing, her dainty hand resting possessively on his chest, her flirtatious eyes sparkling.

The sucker punch hit hard.

Lana clenched her jaw as her fingers curled around on the laptop. A burning heat sat in her stomach, equal parts jealousy and humiliation.

Who was she kidding?

Marcus McGrath avoided relationships.

He was a storm, rolling in fast and leaving wreckage

in his wake. A man who sought pleasure, took control and offered nothing else afterwards.

The hard facts were right there, and Lana was just another name on growing his list. Another woman he'd seduce, devour, and discard when the thrill wore off.

And she couldn't afford to be that woman.

Her fascination was pointless.

The cyberstalking was pointless.

This ache in her chest was pointless.

With a loud exhale, she slammed the laptop shut and scrubbed a hand over her face.

She wasn't built for fleeting affairs or hollow sexual encounters. She needed a solid foundation for the future. And that meant refocusing on the relationship she already had.

Marcus had consumed her thoughts for too long. But Rory... he was her reality.

And reality meant making a choice.

Her chest tightened as she whispered the words aloud, as if saying them would make them true.

"I have to ask him to leave *Verto Veneri*."

24

Lana

Another week went by, and remarkably, Rory had arrived home from work most afternoons and stayed at home.

He even made her dinner one evening and bought popcorn the next for a movie night in.

As if sensing the rift between them, he'd put in the effort, and in return, so did she.

It was like old times again.

And this evening he'd arranged a mid-week dinner date, claiming they needed more quality time together.

She clung to that sliver of hope, to the version of Rory she fell for in the beginning—the one who would pull her close just to breathe her in and made her a priority.

After spending extra time in the shower, she smoothed her skin with lotion and spritzed her most expensive perfume.

She applied her makeup, opting for subtle yet alluring, with a smoky flick of liner at her lashes and just enough gloss to make her lips inviting.

And the dress she chose was the one he loved—a silky, emerald-green number that hugged her figure in all the right places, the thigh-high slit revealing a teasing glimpse of her thigh when she moved.

Slipping on her heels, she cast one last glance in the mirror, willing herself to believe this night would be what they needed to get them back on track.

Rory had reserved a table at her favourite French restaurant, the one with a shabby-chic décor and a Parisian ambiance that made her heart ache for travel.

Inside, the walls were a moody, smoky grey, adorned with an eclectic mix of frames showcasing French landmarks.

The scent of food and wine drifted through the air and fairy lights twinkled overhead, casting a dreamy glow.

Their table sat nestled near the window, mismatched chairs adding to the restaurant's curated charm. A single candle flickered between them, its golden flame swaying in the quiet hum of conversation and soft music.

Lana studied the menu, trying to shake the unease in her chest. She understood they had to work through the bumpy times together because relationships needed effort. However, she questioned his commitment to her and dreaded bringing up Verto Veneri.

"Oh, the Cassoulet sounds yummy." She licked her lips, offering him a smile over the top of the menu.

Rory grinned, his blue eyes dancing with mischief.

"I'm going for the 40-Day Dry Aged Beef. Then you can have some of my beef later." He chuckled, his thumb tracing soft circles over the back of her hand. "Seriously, babe, you look good."

She rolled her eyes at his innuendo but smirked, unable to deny that he looked good too.

The low lighting shadowed his features, highlighting the defined angle of his jaw and the boyish charm in his grin.

He'd chosen a dark green shirt—whether intentional, it complemented her dress, making them appear as effortlessly in sync as they once had been.

And for the first time in weeks, Rory was being attentive. Touching her at every opportunity—his palm against her knee, the occasional brush of his fingers along her wrist, as though he needed to keep their connection alive.

And God, it was so easy to fall back into it.

She let herself enjoy it—the familiar, intoxicating pull of him when he focused on her.

She glanced down at the napkin in her lap, smoothing it between her fingers.

Rory tilted her chin up with a knuckle, forcing her to meet his gaze.

"You're quiet, babe," he murmured, concern flickering behind his eyes. "What's wrong?"

She could let this moment linger, let herself bask in the warmth of his attention, pretend that the last few weeks of distance and indifference hadn't happened.

Or she could finally speak her mind.

"We need to talk."

His smile faltered, but only for a fraction of a second.

Then it returned, soft and coaxing, as if he could charm her out of whatever she was about to say.

"Talk?" he repeated. "We're talking now."

Rory's grip on her wrist tightened ever so slightly, his thumb grazing over her skin in lazy strokes.

"Okay, hit me with it," he said, flashing that flirty, boyish grin that had once made her weak in the knees. "Because if it's about how fucking stunning you look tonight, I've got plenty to say."

His voice dipped, low and smooth, the kind that had always made her stomach flutter.

"I mean it, Lana. You look unreal." His gaze dragged over her like he wanted her to absorb every second of his attention. "That dress—fuck, you're killing me here. And your hair..."

He reached up, curling a strand around his finger before tucking it gently behind her ear.

"You always drive me crazy, but tonight? Jesus." He leaned in, lowering his voice to a husky murmur. "Every guy in this place wishes they were me right now."

Damn. Rory always knew what to say.

"I should take you out more often," he mused. "Or maybe I should just never let you leave the house dressed like this. I wouldn't want another man stealing my girl."

She forced a smile. "I can wear what I want, Rory."

"Obviously." He grinned, playful, but with a glint of something darker swimming beneath the surface. "But I'd rather you wore it just for me, babe, so I can peel it off. Nice and slow."

Lana's heart thudded against her ribs. She wanted to

believe this was real. That this wasn't just another attempt to smooth over the cracks in their relationship with sweet words and well-placed touches.

"Rory..." She hesitated, watching as he tilted his head, studying her.

His fingers laced through hers, his hold firm.

"Babe." His thumb stroked her knuckles. "I know things have been off lately. But I swear, I'm trying. I've been coming home after work and making time for us. Hell, I even made reservations at your favourite place."

His lips quirked, his blue eyes softening as he lifted their joined hands and kissed the back of hers. "Because you're it for me, Lan. You always have been."

Her breath hitched.

You always have been.

"What about the membership?" she asked, her voice quieter this time.

Rory's smile wavered for a fraction of a second. She caught the micro-change right before it reappeared.

He let out a soft chuckle, shaking his head.

"Babe, you're overthinking again." He leaned in, pressing a kiss to her knuckles. "Just enjoy the night with me, yeah? No stress, no worries. Just us."

A knot twisted in her stomach because, deep down, she knew this wasn't him fixing things. This was him stalling.

"We can't hide from it, Rory. We need to have this conversation."

Their future together depended on it. If she dropped

the subject and let Rory brush it aside, nothing would change.

Because she couldn't go back to *Verto Veneri*.

"I don't want to be a member of Verto anymore," she whispered, lifting a hand to shield her mouth from the surrounding tables.

Rory's gaze darkened. The dancing candlelight cast shadows across his face, so his expression appeared haunted.

Then, slowly, one corner of his lips curled into a half-smile.

"I know, babe," he said, his voice as smooth as silk. "I could tell it wasn't for you. How about we forget the whole thing?"

Her heart skipped.

"Really?" The word tumbled out, disbelieving. "You'd be happy to leave—for me? For us?"

"Of course." He squeezed her hand. "I don't want to lose you, babe. So, I'll do whatever it takes."

The tension in her chest loosened, and she let out a long breath.

"On one condition, though." He took his hand back. "Don't give me hassle when I go out with the guys. I deserve to let off steam, Lana. It's important to me."

Of course there would be a condition.

Rory was giving up something they'd spent months considering—something he'd been so determined to introduce into their relationship. And now, he was letting it all go for her.

A niggle of guilt crept into her chest, twisting, tightening.

He was making a sacrifice. And yet... She'd betrayed him in ways he couldn't even imagine with a guy she hadn't quite forgotten.

While Rory waved over the waiter to order, her gaze drifted outside, and her thoughts turned inward.

How long would it take until she could shake Marcus McGrath from her system?

Her body still burned with the memory of him. And no matter how much she tried to kill it; the torture was unbearable.

Whereas the guy before her was steady, dependable, if not a little wild. He knew her Starbucks coffee order, rubbed her feet during movies, and he'd asked to move in with him so they could build a life together piece by piece.

Rory was *real*.

"We'll work it out, Lan. I promise."

Marcus wasn't chasing her anymore, wasn't taking her to dinner, wasn't building a future with her—wasn't *loving* her.

Rory was her happily ever after.

Lust burned hot and fast, destined to fade. And love had no place in that equation.

"I want us to work, Rory," she said, her voice softer now. "You know I don't care if you go out with the guys. Just... promise me I'm what you really need."

His hand settled over the top of hers. "You are, babe."

It wasn't quite the declaration of love and desire she

had hoped for. But Rory had never been the best at putting emotions into words, and she knew that.

So she let it go and took a sip of her red wine.

Rory's gaze followed the movement of her hand. His silence was heavy, his expression turned thoughtful.

Then, as if in slow motion, he reached into his trouser pocket and pulled out a small black box.

The flick of the lid seemed deafening.

Lana's heart stopped.

Fairy lights illuminated the facets of a diamond ring nestled within black velvet.

Rory leaned forward. "Lana, you already share my home, so why not share the rest of my life, too? Do you want to get married?"

The room seemed to tilt.

Her pulse roared in her ears.

Every woman dreamt of this moment. For a man to surprise them with a pretty engagement ring and offer his full commitment.

So why, deep in the hollow of her chest, did something ache?

Lana's breath stuttered as she stared at the modest trio of glistening diamonds embedded in a gold band.

"Rory..." She covered her mouth, her wide eyes holding his. "Y-you want to get married?"

He smirked and waggled the box. "It would be a pretty shitty joke to ask and not mean it, babe."

Around them, the hum of the restaurant dimmed. Conversations lulled as curious diners turned their heads, waiting for her answer.

A flush of heat crawled up her neck, burning her cheeks.

If this had happened two months ago, she wouldn't have held back. She would have pried the ring from his hand, thrown her arms around his neck, and squealed.

But now?

Her heart faltered.

Doubt slithered through the cracks of her mind, clouding the clarity she so desperately needed.

The silence stretched too long. Rory's grin faltered, his excitement slipping into something more guarded.

She swallowed hard.

Marcus had never made her any promises. He hadn't offered her a future, hadn't asked her to be his, hadn't fought for her. Because he never intended to.

He was nothing more than a craving. A temptation lurking on the edges of her self-control. A test of willpower she had failed in the worst possible way.

"Well?" he asked. "You need to give me an answer, babe."

Her fingers trembled as she reached for the ring, lifting it from the velvet box. The gold band was cool against her skin as she slid it onto her finger.

"Yes," she whispered, the weight of metal anchoring her to the choice she just made.

25

Lana

The news spread like wildfire.

Amanda took it upon herself to announce Lana's engagement to anyone who would listen.

Before she knew it, a flood of congratulatory handshakes, well-wishing emails, and repetitive questions overwhelmed her.

"How did he propose?"

"When's the big day?"

"Let me see the ring!"

Over and over, she lifted her hand, letting near-strangers check out the diamonds.

Colleagues who'd rarely spoken to her before immediately acted as if they cared, when in reality, they just wanted something to gossip about over morning lattes.

It was all bullshit.

Thankfully, the buzz died down after a week and things drifted back to normal.

Lana was halfway through typing a report when Amanda peered over her monitor.

"Have you set a date yet?" she asked.

Lana glanced up, catching the curiosity in her friend's eyes, and shrugged. "Nah. Nothing set yet. We're not in a rush."

Amanda's brows pulled together. "Really? You haven't talked about what year it'll be?"

Lana's fingers hovered over the keyboard before she dropped her chin. "No, we haven't."

Since the night Rory proposed, neither of them had brought it up again. Not once.

There hadn't been a flurry of wedding plans set in motion or even a mention of special venues, favourite flowers, or a honeymoon destination.

The whole thing had been swept under the rug, as if neither of them wanted to discuss it.

And that suited her for the moment.

Amanda's chair let out an annoying squeak as she wheeled it closer, now fully invested.

"Lan." She lowered her voice. "I told you to be honest with yourself. Do you really want to marry Rory?"

Lana swallowed, staring at the ring on her finger. A symbol of permanence. Of commitment. Of a life she had agreed to without letting herself really think about it.

Amanda reached out and cuffed Lana's wrist, tugging her closer.

"You're still thinking about Marcus McGrath, aren't you? He's the itch you desperately need to scratch."

Lana's heart stumbled.

Amanda somehow unlocked the ability to crawl into her brain and sift through the mess of conflicting emotions.

Her eyes misted as she swallowed the hard knot forming in her throat.

"It's totally irrational, I know, but I can't stop thinking about him," she admitted. "Guys like him don't settle with girls like me but..."

The words trailed off as emotion bubbled under the armour she'd built to keep him out of her thoughts.

Amanda sighed, muttering something under her breath as she dug her phone out of her pocket. Her fingers danced over the screen before she thrust it into Lana's hands.

"Here. Look for yourself. He's definitely not the settling down type... With any woman."

Lana hesitated, but curiosity got the best of her.

"The guy is sexy. I'll give him that. But he's also a man slut," Amanda stated flatly, crossing her arms. "Every girl thinks she'll be the one to tame the bad guy. But, Lan... that's not how this works. Someone took that picture of him two days ago in Marbella. He's not thinking about you."

Lana's stomach twisted as she stared at the screen.

A luxury yacht. Three stunning women wearing string bikinis, sprawled across the sun deck, bronzed and carefree. And right in the middle of it all—Marcus.

He was lounging on his back, damp black hair tousled, a deepening tan across his defined torso, and nothing but ass-hugging black swim shorts covering him.

Aviator sunglasses masked his eyes, but she knew exactly where he was looking.

"Not just one girl," Amanda continued, as if reading her thoughts. "I'd bet fifty quid he's sleeping with all three of them." She raised three fingers for emphasis. "At the same time, Lana."

Lana's pulse jumped.

She couldn't tear her gaze away.

He looked handsome, at ease in his opulent world, as if everything and everyone existed purely for his pleasure.

And there she was, stuck in her dull office, tormenting herself over him while rain drummed against the city streets outside.

She clenched her jaw, willing the ache in her chest to disappear. She had no right to consider the photo a sign of betrayal when she was the one who had pushed him away.

Amanda snatched the phone back, locked the screen, and set it on the desk.

"Listen to me," she said, her voice softer now. "I get it. He's intoxicating. Guys like that always are. But you are not some lovesick teenager, and Marcus McGrath is not your future."

Lana sighed, nodding. "I know."

Amanda cocked a brow. "Do you?"

"Yes."

"Good. Because you're marrying Rory. And—" She clapped her hands together with an excited shriek. "I have a surprise for you."

Lana groaned, narrowing her eyes. "Oh God. What have you done?"

"Relax," Amanda said with a dramatic eye roll. "We're having drinks after work. A few of us thought it was very necessary to celebrate your engagement."

Lana gulped. The last thing she wanted was a big fuss.

"Who's going?" she asked.

Amanda waved a dismissive hand. "Nothing crazy. Just Richard and Fi, plus Ronny's dropping by after football around eight. Geraldine wanted to come but has to help her mum. Sophie from finance might swing by, and James from marketing said he'd pop in if he finishes his project on time. A few others mentioned it too—we'll see who actually shows."

Amanda glanced at her watch, then smirked. "And of course, me—the party planner, bridesmaid or maybe just the only best friend in attendance?"

Lana couldn't help but smile. Amanda was a damn good friend—blunt to a fault, but always there to keep her grounded.

And this time, she was right. Rory was the one who chose her, and she had to fully choose him.

"I'm not dressed for an after-work party." Lana glanced down at her plain blouse and fitted trousers.

Before she could protest further, Amanda's eyes lit up with excitement. She spun on her heel and rushed toward her desk.

"Oh, ye of little faith!" she called over her shoulder.

Lana frowned as Amanda rifled through a drawer,

muttering under her breath. Then, with a triumphant *aha*, she yanked out a plastic carrier bag, clutched it to her chest, and strutted back with the confidence of a catwalk model.

Grinning, she waved it in Lana's face. "This," she said, "is your solution."

"Oh no, what's in the bag?"

"Ta-da!" Amanda pulled out a dress, holding it up like a prize.

Lana stared at the cerise pink slip of fabric and laughed.

"Are you kidding me? That's not a dress, that's—" She pinched the material between her fingers, her eyes popping at how insubstantial it was. "—a napkin."

"Oh, relax, Lan." Amanda huffed. "You might have a ring on your finger, but he hasn't secured your shackles yet."

Lana shot her a look. "I thought it was just drinks? And this looks like we're going clubbing. I can't be arsed with shouting over music tonight."

"Oh, please. We're going to The Fitz for food and drinks. It's classy. Cosmopolitan. The kind of place where you actually want to be seen."

"You're joking, right?"

Amanda's grin widened. "Nope."

"You know who owns that place, don't you?"

Amanda's shoulders lifted in a lazy shrug.

"Yeah. And you saw that photo. He's screwing a harem of models. McGrath won't be anywhere near his hotel at five p.m. on a Friday afternoon. He's got more than business on his mind, babe."

Tonight wasn't about him, anyway. She owned the night. It was a celebration and a chance to let her new reality settle.

With a sigh, she took the dress from Amanda and held it up against her body.

Amanda clapped her hands together.

"That's my girl!"

Together, they hurried to the ladies' washroom to transform from office professionals into party girls.

Lana tugged the snug dress over her head, smoothing the fabric over her hips. The Jessica Rabbit effect was undeniable—form-fitting, yet surprisingly elegant.

Pink wasn't a shade she'd usually go for, but standing in front of the mirror, she had to admit...it worked.

The bold colour set off the warm tones in her skin, and with her nude heels, it was the kind of effortless glamour Amanda always pulled off.

Amanda, of course, looked gorgeous, as she always did. Her cobalt blue dress clung to her lithe frame, her golden tan flawless.

"You should wear bright colours more often," Amanda declared, nearly stumbling out of her narrow stall as she took Lana in. "You look seriously hot."

Lana laughed. "So do you. But then, you always do."

Amanda tossed her hair over her shoulder with a dramatic flair. "Well, obviously. But tonight is about you."

Lana rifled through her makeup bag, pulling out a mini eyeshadow palette. She dusted a dark mauve shade over her lids, blended it out, then followed with a swipe of black eyeliner and two coats of mascara.

A light sweep of bronzer sculpted her cheekbones and cleavage, and after a quick spritz of her favourite perfume, she was ready.

Before leaving, Amanda snapped a photo of them hugging.

"Right! Let's round up the others and get the hell out of here."

Lana grinned, a rush of nerves fluttering in her stomach.

Beneath the thrill of dressing up and stepping into the spotlight as the future Mrs O'Hare, she was becoming a new version of herself.

Amanda looped an arm through hers.

"Come on, let's go. You've got a party to attend, and I refuse to let you overthink it."

Lana nodded, forcing a smile as they left the office. Because deep down, a whisper of doubt still lurked, and a glimmer of hope flickered.

No matter how much she told herself that Marcus was in Marbella, somewhere in the treacherous corners of her mind, she wished she'd bump into him again.

26

Lana

"What's the craic, Lana?" Richard took a hearty sip of his Guinness, frothy foam clinging to his upper lip before he wiped it away with the back of his hand. "You guys got a date set for the big day?"

Lana traced the stem of her wineglass, a polite smile tugging her lips even though she was tired of being asked that question. She had a soft spot for Richard with his rough edges and quick wit, but at his core, he was one of the few decent ones.

Anyone with half a brain could see he was hopelessly in love with Amanda. Not that he'd ever admit it.

"We aren't in any rush. It'll all fall into place eventually," she replied.

Richard's black eyebrows shot up, forehead wrinkling in exaggerated shock.

"A girl who isn't in a rush to plan a wedding. Take a picture, everyone. This is a rare species of woman!"

Laughter erupted around the table, and Lana chuckled along with them.

"I'd rather have a long engagement, save up, and do it right." Lana shrugged, aiming for casual. "I'll grab a few bridal magazines when I'm ready and start making notes."

Fi—a curvy, bubbly girl from HR on the third floor—thudded her empty Prosecco glass onto the table and immediately poured herself another.

"I've got my whole wedding planned already, and Jo hasn't even proposed yet," she declared.

Amanda smirked. "And what if he never pops the question?"

Fi snorted. "Then he either asks me, or he dies. Simple."

Another round of laughter rang out as the group tucked into their shared tapas.

The Fitz's public bar exuded sophistication with sleek mahogany tables and intimate booths. In the corner, a pianist played a modern tune, the melody weaving through the hum of distant conversations and the occasional clink of glasses.

Amanda nudged Lana's arm and grinned as she raised her champagne flute.

"To your engagement," she said, tapping her glass against Lana's. "You deserve all the happiness in the world."

Lana lifted her glass, mirroring Amanda's toast. The diamonds on her finger caught the light, a pointed reminder of the life she was supposed to be celebrating. A knot coiled tight in her chest.

Cool bubbles danced against her lips as she took a slow sip of Prosecco, her gaze drifting absently toward the entrance—then her pulse lurched.

A tall figure stood near the doorway, broad shoulders wrapped in a dark suit, sleek black hair glinting under the dim glow.

Her lungs tightened.

But then he turned.

Her stomach plummeted.

Of course, it wasn't Marcus. He was in Marbella, stretched out on a yacht, drowning in models and expensive liquor. Meanwhile, she was here, toasting to a future her mind kept trying to rewrite.

Amanda's voice sliced through the fog in Lana's head. "Lana?"

She blinked, snapping back to the present, and forced a smile. "Sorry, what?"

Amanda narrowed her eyes but didn't press. "I was just saying—let's make a night of it."

"Yeah, okay." Lana reached for her glass and took a long sip, hoping the fizz of the Prosecco would ground her.

Her phone buzzed against the table. Rory's name flashed on the screen.

"Hold that thought." She lifted the phone in a quick wave before slipping away from the lively hum of the bar, weaving through the crowd until she reached a quieter corridor.

The air was cooler, a welcome contrast to the warmth of the main bar. Leaning against the cool, textured wall, Lana took a steadying breath, the champagne fizzing in her veins making her just a little off kilter. She pressed the phone to her ear, exhaling before answering.

"Hey, what are you up to?" Her voice came out quieter than usual.

"I'm on my way home now. Do you want me to grab a takeaway?"

Shit.

In the rush to get ready, she'd completely forgotten to tell him she was going out.

"Sorry, Rory, I'm out with some people from work— celebrating our engagement." The words felt strange, unnatural, like they belonged to someone else.

Her stomach flipped, and she let her head rest against the wall, the cool surface grounding her as the moment settled over her.

A brief sigh whispered through the line before Rory replied, his voice neutral. "Okay, cool. I'll head to the pub with Zac. I'll see ya later."

Behind her, a door swung open and shut, the hum of music and chatter spilling into the hallway before being muffled again.

"Okay, have a good night," she murmured, her thumb hesitating over the screen.

No, *I love you, babe*. Or, *I miss you*.

Neither of them had said it.

She stared at her phone for a beat too long, then let out a slow breath.

Enough.

Pushing away from the wall, she smoothed down her dress and squared her shoulders

"Lana."

A deep, husky voice rolled through the air, rich and unmistakable, shooting a shiver down her spine.

Slowly, she turned, pulse hammering, and locked eyes with the man who had haunted her thoughts since the night they met.

This time, it wasn't a trick of the light or her mind playing a cruel game.

It was really him.

Dressed in a navy three-piece suit, every fitted seam and tailored edge moulded to his powerful frame. Underneath, a pale pink shirt lay open at the collar—just enough to hint at the heat beneath all that polished control.

The contrast only sharpened the dangerous edge he carried so effortlessly.

His piercing green eyes dragged over her, setting her skin ablaze in their wake. An unspoken intensity lurked behind them, like he was already ten steps ahead.

Marcus didn't speak again as he strode toward her. Silence amplified her racing heartbeat, charged and smothering, and the overwhelming scent of his cologne curled around her senses.

Sandalwood and spice. Dark and masculine. A scent she'd never forgotten.

Lana swallowed hard, her throat tight as if her body had forgotten how to breathe.

"Damn, Lana..." His voice dropped to a rasp. "You're a fucking vision."

Her vision blurred at the edges, a haze settling over her senses as she fought to steady herself against the weight of his presence, the magnetic pull drawing her in.

"Marcus... I'm here with colleagues from work," she said, the words rushed, her heart thumping.

Marcus didn't react, didn't so much as blink, but she swore she saw his pupils expand.

As she fumbled to double-check that her phone was off, a flash of light caught her eye.

Her engagement ring.

The sparkle of it was almost taunting.

She dropped her hand to her hip, as if that simple motion could make it disappear. "I didn't think you'd be here."

"Disappointed?"

"God no," she said too quickly. "I mean... not at all. This is your hotel, after all."

"Congratulations on your engagement." His deep voice held an unmistakable chill. "I hope the two of you will be very happy together."

The words should have sounded sincere. They didn't.

Her pulse pounded in her throat. "Well...yeah, but—"

She palmed her belly and stopped speaking.

Marcus shifted, his stance widening, his hands sliding into the pockets of his tailored trousers, but the casual pose didn't mask the tension in his body.

"How did you hear about it?" she asked.

Without saying a word, his gaze jumped to her left

hand, to the three diamonds, and his expression tightened.

The green of his eyes darkened around black pupils— deep and endless, like a forest swallowed by nightfall.

"I know everything about you, Lana."

His stare stripped her bare, as though he could read every conflicting emotion she tried to shove down and knew exactly how hard she was fighting against the pull between them.

Then, as if acting on instinct, her right hand moved to cover her left, her fingers curling over the ring.

His gaze lifted to hers, and for one aching moment, neither of them spoke.

"Did you have a good time in Marbella?" she asked.

His lips quirked. "Stalking me?"

She lifted her chin, feigning cool detachment. "I saw a picture of you partying. It was hard to miss, given it was all over the internet."

"A picture can say a thousand words, Lana," he replied, his expression blank.

She folded her arms and made a silly face at him, playing cool.

"So you weren't in Marbella, on a boat, with three half-naked women?"

His lips twitched.

"Well, if you put it that way..." He paused, letting the silence stretch. Then, with a slow shrug, "...yeah. I was."

"Did you have fun?" she asked, popping her brows high.

"Not really," he shot back, rolling his shoulders.

When Marcus took a step closer, the corridor seemed to shrink, and her blood ran red-hot.

For a moment, she thought he might say something more, might ask her if she'd made the right call, might lean in and—

Instead, he rolled his wrist and checked his gold watch.

"It was... good to see you again. I have a meeting to attend." He returned his hand to his pocket. "Enjoy your evening, Lana."

The words sounded final. Like a fire door slamming shut to contain a blaze.

"I thought you liked to drive?" she asked, desperate to keep him talking.

Marcus scratched his jaw, his gaze holding, and when he exhaled, she caught it—the faint scent of whiskey on his breath.

"I gotta go," he said, then, with a firm nod, "Goodbye, beautiful."

It hit her square in the chest.

Her lips parted, but nothing came out.

She watched him walk past her, each self-assured step cutting deeper into her resolve.

For a moment, she just stood, stuck to the spot, staring after him, her mind scrambling to form words— any words—that would make him stop. But nothing came.

She wanted to scream. Shake him. Beg him to admit the chemistry between them was unreal.

That she wasn't crazy for sensing how the air grew hotter whenever they were near each other.

The urge to reach for him, to grab his powerful arms and make him look at her the way he used to, burned like a destructive flame.

A dull ache spread through her chest as she dropped her gaze to her left hand.

The engagement ring—the one she'd been so eager to wear in the past—seemed more like a lock.

Because the truth was undeniable now.

She was engaged to Rory. However, Marcus brought her to life.

27

Lana

Amanda's brow scrunched. "Jeez, Lan, you look like a ghost."

Lana flung herself into the booth, reaching for the bottle of Prosecco, her hands shaky as she yanked it from the ice. She filled her glass to the brim, desperate to numb the chaos inside her.

"And you're unusually thirsty. Everything okay with Rory?"

She didn't reply, draining the entire glass in one long gulp, breathing only when the glass was empty.

Lana forced a wide smile, the kind that never reached her eyes. "Yeah, all good. Just happy to be out, you know? This is a celebration. Let me get you a refill."

As she topped up their glasses, a bartender appeared at their table, carrying two golden magnums of champagne, his eyes searching the group.

"These are compliments of the owner, Mr McGrath.

He mentioned Ms Craig is celebrating her engagement tonight."

The table fell into stunned silence, all of them staring at her.

"Eh... Thank you," she said. "But we already have Prosecco."

"They're for you to enjoy, Miss Craig." Ice crunched as the bartender shoved them into silver buckets. "I'll bring a few more flutes."

Her gaze stuck to the bottles—the unmistakable black Ace of Spades. The same brand she'd shared with Marcus McGrath just weeks ago in his apartment. The memory of that day made her stomach flutter, her anxiety deepening.

Richard broke the silence, hauling one from the ice and shaking his head.

"Shit, Lana, you didn't tell us you knew the owner. These bottles go for four or five hundred pounds each."

Lana's chest tightened, her heart hammering in her ears. She forced another smile, but inside, everything was unravelling.

"There's more where they came from," the bartender announced, offloading more flutes from a tray. "Mr McGrath gave us strict instructions to ensure Ms Craig gets whatever she desires this evening."

Her heart, once steady, seemed to crumble, turning into a mush of blood and goo that coursed through her veins with an uncomfortable warmth.

She didn't want his generosity. Not like this. All she wanted was *him*—and the thought of accepting anything from him while she wore Rory's ring gnawed at her insides.

"That won't be necessary," she said, her voice firm but strained, as though denying his offer was an act of rebellion. "The champagne is more than generous. Thank you."

She gave a polite smile and the bartender, unfazed, nodded and retreated.

The others popped the corks and poured glasses, clinking them together with cheers. Even Richard, who was usually more reserved, sank a flute of champagne. Ronny, who had finally arrived, did the same, his face lighting up at the sight of the expensive alcohol.

Everyone seemed swept away by the decadence of it, and Lana was no exception. She raised her glass, her fingers trembling ever so slightly.

Each sip carried the ghost of Marcus. The champagne was exquisite. Sweet and fresh, but every drop was an imprint of him, a lingering presence woven into her senses.

She smiled, nodded, pretended to be present, but her mind was elsewhere—trapped in moments she should have forgotten. Memories she should have erased.

She was engaged. Her focus should be on Rory, on the life they were building together.

But Marcus—his effortless charm, his unexpected tenderness—had embedded itself deep, refusing to let go. No matter how hard she tried, he was still there, lingering in the dark corners of her mind.

The night had been a blur of laughter and flowing

drinks. Lana felt the warmth of the champagne, its gentle buzz softening the edges of her restless thoughts.

Amanda and Ronny had been in rare form, their animated storytelling sending waves of laughter through the table. Even Richard, typically the most composed among them, had loosened up, swaying slightly in his seat, grinning like a fool.

By the time they'd indulged far beyond reason, Richard took it upon himself to stumble toward the bar, ready to hear how much they owed. But when he returned, his hands were empty, and the drunken bravado had drained from his face, replaced by sheer bewilderment.

"Well," he announced, dragging a hand over his shaved head. "We've officially been taken care of."

Lana's stomach dipped. "What do you mean?"

"We don't owe a single penny," Richard clarified, glancing at the others before his gaze landed squarely on her. "McGrath covered everything. Even the food."

A fresh wave of heat crept up Lana's neck, but before she could respond, a tall, broad-shouldered doorman in a black, knee-length coat approached. He moved with the swagger of a guy who spent his breaks lifting weights.

His elbows flared outward, his shoulders pulled back like he was prepared to take on the world.

"Which one of you ladies is Ms Craig?" he asked.

Amanda, giddy from the champagne, pressed a finger to Lana's cheek with a giggle.

"Her. This little minx with the ring on her finger." She swayed into Lana and kissed her cheek.

229

Lana forced a smile. "Is everything okay?"

The doorman nodded. "A driver is waiting to take you home. I'll escort you to the car, Ms Craig."

Lana blinked. "What do you mean? I didn't order a taxi."

"Mr McGrath instructed us to make sure you got home safely," the man said, his tone calm, unwavering. "There's a private car waiting outside."

Of course he did.

Lana's fingers tightened around the stem of her glass as conflicting emotions warred inside her. She exhaled slowly, forcing her voice to stay even.

"Right. A private car." Her lips pressed into a thin line before she added, "Thanks, but I'll take the bus home."

The doorman didn't flinch. "No, Ms Craig. Mr McGrath was very clear in his instructions."

Amanda nudged her, completely oblivious to Lana's struggle. "Come on, Lana. It'll save you the fare home. I'll hitch a ride with you. The thought of sitting on a bus for half an hour, shaking up all the champagne in my belly— I'll throw up."

Lana hesitated, then sighed. "Okay. Can we drop my friend off first?"

"Of course, Ms Craig," the doorman replied. "Whatever you need."

As the car rolled through Belfast, slicing through the shimmering glow of the city lights, Lana stared out the window, her reflection blurred against the night.

The streets were alive, pulsing with late-night energy, but all she could think about was *him.*

Where was he right now? Was he out there somewhere, drinking and laughing with someone else? Was he alone?

The warmth of the champagne still tingled in Lana's veins, though it did little to steady the restless energy buzzing inside her.

Amanda stretched her legs out, kicking off her heels with a groan.

"God, I love rich people's fancy cars," she mumbled, rolling her head back against the seat. "Everything's so bloody sexy. No rattling, no smell of stale chips or sweaty lads."

Lana huffed a quiet laugh.

Amanda turned her head, eyes gleaming with drunken curiosity. "Alright, spill. What's happening inside that head of yours, girl? You've been in another world all night."

Lana continued to stare out the tinted window at the blur of streetlights. "I had a great night. Thanks for organising it. I have a feeling Fi will die a death tomorrow. She finished the champagne straight from the bottle."

Amanda snorted. "She'll suffer a hangover from hell. And I'm not drunk enough to forget my question. Are you going to tell me why you're not yourself?"

"It's nothing, honestly."

"Nothing? Please. You've been twitchy ever since those champagne bottles landed on the table. And don't think I didn't notice you checking over your shoulder all night like you expected *him* to show up."

"Him who?" Lana rolled her eyes. "I don't know who you're talking about."

Amanda shot her a look. "Don't insult me, girl. *Marcus McGrath.* It's my fault for picking The Fitz for our night out. But he's got you rattled. Hell, he practically owned your night, and he wasn't even there."

Lana opened her mouth to protest, but Amanda shook her head.

"Don't bother denying it. He paid for our dinner, sent over ridiculously expensive champagne, and now we're riding in one of *his* cars because *he* decided that's what you needed." She folded her arms. "That whole show of wealth? It was just a game, Lana. A way to get inside your head."

Lana swallowed, her mouth dry and her mind spinning. "It wasn't—"

"Oh, it was. Men like him. They don't just give. They carefully plan everything they do. He wanted you to spend the night thinking about him instead of your fiancé. And guess what?" She lifted a brow. "It worked."

Lana blew out a long sigh and pressed her back into the seat. "Or maybe that was his way of congratulating me."

Amanda hummed. "You really think that?"

Lana hesitated. "It's just... chemistry. That's all. Some weird pull that I don't even understand. But it's not *real.* Not like what I have with Rory."

Amanda tilted her head. "So, you're saying you have

this crazy, electric thing with Marcus, but it's meaningless?"

"Yeah," Lana said firmly. "That's exactly what I'm saying."

Amanda smirked. "And you're also saying that what you have with Rory is forever love?"

"Yes," Lana repeated. But this time, the word didn't come as easily.

"So why is Marcus the one in your head right now?"

Amanda sighed, rolling her head back against the seat again. "Because you took me to his hotel and now I'm indebted to him."

"Look, I'm not saying you should run off and shag him in the nearest hotel room—though, honestly, if you did, I wouldn't blame you." She smirked, but then her expression softened. "I'm saying...don't confuse lust with love.

"Okay... Let's say, hypothetically, I think I'm doing the wrong thing by marrying Rory. Because Marcus makes me—" She swallowed. "—think there's more out there."

Amanda's eyes widened, but she said nothing, letting Lana keep going.

Lana bit her lip, choosing her words carefully. "Do you think it's possible to love a guy and be obsessed with another?"

Amanda sighed. "Love is the endgame. It's picking up your boyfriend's gross socks even though you *hate* feet. It's pretending to care when their football team scores a goal or cooking him another fucking meal even when you're exhausted."

She wrinkled her nose. "An obsession, though? That's all heat and urgency. It's skin on skin. A burning ache that grows stronger if you don't get your hands on them. And over time it fades...well, it did for my parents and then they realised they actually hated each other. Do you have any of that with Rory?"

Lana's lips parted, but nothing came out.

Amanda sighed, tilting her head.

"Look, if this billionaire guy stirs something in you that Rory doesn't..." She let the words hang, her meaning unmistakable. "Maybe he's just the wake-up call you've been avoiding. Maybe your relationship is already over."

Lana turned toward the window, watching the city lights smear into streaks of gold and red.

Somewhere out there, Marcus was sipping whiskey, a beautiful woman draped over his lap—utterly unaware of the storm he'd unleashed inside her.

28

Lana

Lana groaned as sunlight pierced through the gap in the curtains, stabbing at her eyes. A cruel punishment for drinking too much.

Her head throbbed in sync with her pulse, each beat a dull, relentless hammer against her skull.

Nausea rolled in her stomach. She squeezed her eyes shut, gripping the sheets as if that alone could steady the slow, merciless spin of the room.

She'd made it home before Rory, collapsing into bed in a haze of drunken exhaustion. Even in her half-conscious state, she'd heard him stumble in around one a.m., hitting the mattress with all the grace of a felled tree.

The sharp tang of whiskey and stale smoke clung to him, thick enough to make her turn away, burying her face in the pillow.

Now, the sound of running water from the shower room next door filled the room, punctuated by his off-key whistling. He seemed far too chipper for someone who'd had less sleep than her.

Lana groaned again, dragging herself onto her side. She needed something to ease the spreading ache behind her eyes.

Reaching for the bedside drawer, she fumbled through the mess inside—loose bobby pins, an old lip balm, a tangle of phone chargers—before finally grasping an empty blister packet.

"Wonderful," she muttered, flopping onto her back.

Rory always kept paracetamol in his drawer. With a sigh, she rolled over and tugged it open, expecting to find his usual stash. Instead, her fingers brushed against something crisp and folded.

A jeweller's receipt.

It wasn't fair to put a price on an engagement ring, and she knew better than to look. But curiosity clawed at her, overriding the small voice of reason.

She smoothed the paper open.

Two items.

A three-stone, gold ring and a diamond pendant.

Her pulse stuttered.

The necklace was cheaper than her engagement ring, but still significant. Rory wasn't the type to pre-plan gifts. Her birthday was months away, and he had never been one for grand romantic gestures either.

A cold prickle crept down her spine.

Maybe he got a deal on both and was holding onto the necklace for later. Maybe. But something about that didn't sit right.

The shower was still running, water drumming against the tiles.

Lana sucked her lips between her teeth and shoved the receipt back where she found it. Then, on impulse, she searched deeper, pushing aside balled-up socks and stray coins, fingers skimming the corners of the drawer in search of a small velvet box.

Nothing.

Either he'd hidden it well. Or he'd already given it away.

A ripple of unease settled over her, thick and insistent.

In the background, the shower stopped and just as the bathroom door creaked open; she shut the drawer and rolled over, schooling her features into careful indifference.

Rory strolled in, his lean torso still damp, a towel ruffling through his hair. Droplets clung to his skin, catching the morning light. His gaze cut to her, sprawled and unmoving.

"Why are you still in bed, Lana?"

She propped herself up on her elbows, every movement sending a fresh wave of pain through her skull.

"I have a headache," she murmured. "Feels like a migraine."

Rory walked to the edge of the bed, leaning down to press a quick kiss to her temple. His lips were warm, but his touch felt empty, absent-minded.

"I'll grab you a couple of tablets from the kitchen. Hold tight."

With that, he turned and strode out, leaving his damp towel in a heap on the floor.

As soon as he disappeared down the stairs, a low vibrating buzz stirred the silence.

Lana frowned, scanning the room. The noise came from his bomber jacket hanging on the back of the door.

She debated her next move.

The logical part of her—the one that still wanted to trust him—told her to leave it alone. But instinct clawed at her, warning her that something wasn't right.

The receipt. The missing necklace. The distance that had crept back into their relationship.

Too many red flags that were easy enough to ignore on their own. But together, they formed a noose, tightening around her, forcing her to confront the lies she'd been avoiding.

Her pulse quickened as she slid out of bed and tiptoed across the room. Slipping a hand into his jacket pocket, she wrapped her fingers around the phone, carefully pulling it free before swiping at the screen.

One unread text from J.

> Will b late. Same place @ one instead.
> J. xx

A weight settled in her stomach.

Who the fuck was J?

Her fingers moved on their own, tapping into the message thread. More texts appeared, a string of casual, flirty exchanges.

> Got something new. U will luv it! J. xx

And then Rory's response.

> I have something 4 u 2 R. xx

A stinging moment of clarity hit, cutting through the fog of her hangover.

Did her fiancé buy jewellery for another woman? Was this the proof she needed to stop lying to herself? A missing necklace and secret messages with kisses at the end.

Her heart pounded as heavy footsteps made their way up the stairs.

Shit.

The bedroom door swung open, and Rory strolled in —completely naked, his skin still wet from the shower. His gaze cut to the phone in her hand, his relaxed expression turning tight.

"What are you doing with my phone, babe?"

Lana forced herself to stay still, keeping her expression indifferent despite the storm raging inside her. "It buzzed."

A beat of silence.

Then, without missing a step, Rory reached forward and plucked the device from her fingers. "Right. Thanks."

He tossed a box of pills onto the bed, then, without hesitation, pressed the power button, shutting his phone off.

No explanation. No excuse. Just a simple, silent shut down.

The final red flag went up.

Lana stared at him, her fingers trembling as she padded to the bed and reached for the pills.

She popped two out of the packet and climbed across the bed on all fours to reach the bottle of water on the nightstand. Swallowing them whole, she wiped her mouth and angled around to face him.

She couldn't ignore this anymore.

"Who was messaging you?"

He didn't look at her as he pulled open his bedside drawer, rummaging for something—probably a fucking weak excuse.

"Zac's mate," he said. His shoulders were stiff, his body tense like a wire about to snap.

"And he ends his texts with a kiss?"

That got his attention.

Rory's head snapped up, eyes narrowing into slits.

"Is this an integration, Lana?" he bit out. "What the fuck are you trying to say?"

"I'm only asking," she said.

Anger swirled inside her, white-hot, and mixed with the ache of betrayal. She pushed up onto her knees, her fists digging into the mattress.

He snatched his phone off the bed and shoved it into his jacket pocket before grabbing a clean pair of boxers.

"No, you're not asking. You're prying like a fucking police officer."

Lana let out a bitter laugh, shaking her head. "Are

you serious? I'm allowed to ask, Rory. We're engaged, aren't we?"

For a second, he went still.

"And what a fucking mistake that's turned out to be." He stuffed his legs into a pair of jeans. "I can't even have friends without you snooping around like Miss fuckin' Marple."

His words hit like a slap, but the sting barely registered. Instead, she observed the tightness in his jaw and the way he yanked his t-shirt over his head, edged with frustration.

This wasn't the man she had loved.

The real Rory—the one she thought she knew—would never cut so deep, never look right through her as if she were nothing.

But this version was a stranger. A liar.

He shoved his arms into his jacket, already moving for the door, but Lana was faster. She threw off the covers, her pulse roaring in her ears as she planted herself in front of the exit, refusing to let him slip away so easily.

"A mistake?" she hissed. "Really?"

Lana pulled the ring from her finger, her chest heaving, and thrust it into the cold, empty space between them.

"Here," she spat. "Just take the stupid thing. Clearly, the sentiment means fuck all to you. And if we're being honest, I don't want to spend the rest of my life with a guy who lies."

Rory's gaze settled on her outstretched hand, to the small golden band glistening in the morning light. For a split second, something flashed across his face—regret, maybe even guilt.

But it vanished as quickly as it came.

"Fuck you, Lana," he bit out, his voice dripping with venom. "You're such a child. Try living in the real world and grow the fuck up."

Her jaw clenched, nails digging into her palms.

"We both know you want to get married," he continued, slipping effortlessly into condescension, his lips curling in disgust. "That's all you wanted, wasn't it? A ring on your finger and a chain around my fucking neck."

Bastard.

Was that really what he thought? That she was some desperate little fool, clinging to him for a wedding?

If anything, she'd overlooked red flag after red flag. Ignored the gnawing pit in her stomach, convinced herself that love meant compromises and sacrifices—like waiting for him to become the man he used to be.

Despite her patience, he wasn't that man. And maybe he never had been.

Lana's fingers curled around the ring one last time before she hurled it at his chest. It bounced off his collarbone and dropped onto the floor, rolling toward his feet.

"I don't want your ring," she said, voice cold, steady. "And if I'm being really honest? I should have turned you down."

Rory didn't even spare it a glance. He just pushed past her, his shoulder clipping hers as he stormed out of the bedroom. Heavy footsteps thundered down the stairs, followed by the violent bang of the front door slamming shut.

Good. Let him run.

She sucked in a shaky breath, pressing her palms to her cheeks as the reality of it all settled in.

Their relationship was pathetic.

Over and over, she'd tried to trick her body into reacting to him. But the only way she could get turned on was by delving into her Marcus fantasies.

The thought sent a pulse of heat through her veins, a stark contrast to the ice settling in her chest.

None of that mattered now, because Marcus didn't want love and commitment.

And this thing with Rory was over.

Lana dragged a hand down her face, her eyes dry—no tears, no lingering heartbreak. Just a steady certainty settling in her chest.

There was nothing left to fight for. Nothing worth salvaging.

It was time to stop pretending, stand tall, and walk away.

29

Lana

"Thanks for letting me crash on your sofa," Lana slurred, tilting her head back to drain the last drop of Prosecco from her flute.

Amanda curled up in the armchair across from her, tucking her knees to her chest. Her oversized chequered onesie all but swallowed her petite frame as she cradled a full glass of wine.

"Anytime, Lan. You know that," she said, smiling. She took a slow sip before adding, "I'm sorry it ended this way. But honestly? You did the right thing leaving Rory. A relationship without trust is already over. It just takes longer to admit it."

Her apartment was small but inviting. A warm, cosy haven illuminated by a mushroom shaped table lamp and the glow of scattered vanilla candles.

The compact kitchen blended into the living space, while two doors branched off—one leading to the bedroom, the other to a tiny shower room that doubled as a closet.

Lana shook her head. "God, how blind was I?"

Amanda clucked her tongue. "You weren't blind. You just wanted to believe in him. But come on, Lan, you've known something was off for ages."

Lana tugged the fleece blanket tighter around her shoulders, hugging her knees to her chest, too.

She wiggled her empty flute in the air. "Top me up. I need to drown my sorrows."

Amanda snorted but obliged, filling her glass full. "If we're ranking sorrows from mild inconvenience to full-blown existential crisis, you're barely at mildly inconvenienced."

Lana shrugged.

"I just got fed up with the constant nights out and the way he rarely made plans with me. And the sex—" Lana groaned, palming her face. "There *was* no sex. Not since the night he proposed. And even that was half-assed because he got wasted at the restaurant."

Amanda grimaced. "Yeah...that's not normal for a guy in love."

"And then the messages on his phone. How long had that been going on behind my back? Weeks? Months? He even had a receipt for a necklace, Amanda. A fucking necklace that I sure as hell didn't get."

"So that fucker was fooling around all this time and buying his mistress jewellery while you were planning a future with him? God, I could slap his smug face."

Lana sighed. "And I let him gaslight me. My gut told

me something was wrong, but every time I asked, he flipped it on me. Like I was crazy for questioning it."

She swallowed, her voice cracking. "I let that happen because I was fighting my own guilty conscience."

Amanda shook her head. "No, girl. That's what guys like him do. They twist shit so you doubt yourself while they're off screwing around. You were only trying to fill the void he'd left behind."

Lana rubbed circles at her temple, mentally back-tracking through the weeks.

"It wasn't just the texts, was it? It was all of it. The way he was constantly on his phone, grinning at messages but never sharing the joke. Disappearing after work and staying out. To be honest, he always seemed checked out when he was with me." She let out a humourless laugh. "Fuck, even when he kissed me, it felt...empty."

Amanda reached for her hand, almost toppling off the armchair. "Listen, you got out before the wedding planning started. And honestly? I think you just needed the final push out the door."

She took another sip, thinking as the bubbles settle on her tongue.

"It's weird, though. I'm angry—but more than anything—I can finally breathe." Her shoulders eased as she exhaled.

Amanda lifted her glass. "To breathing again. And to never letting a lying asshole gaslight you into believing his bullshit. I'm here for you, girl."

Lana reached across the divide and clinked her glass

against Amanda's, a slow smirk curling at her lips. "Amen to that."

"Amen."

"Don't worry," Lana began. "I'll move into my own place soon. Gotta hit the reset button and start over. I'll be out of your hair once I find a place. I might even take up knitting or some other random hobby. You know, live my best life."

Amanda raised an eyebrow. "Knitting isn't exactly living your best life, Lana. Now, telling Marcus you're single? That might just lead to the best night of your life. Unless..." She smirked. "You already slept with him?"

Lana snorted, downing the rest of her drink in one go. "Please. Of course not. That would make me a hypocrite."

She set the glass down with a thud. "Besides, I need a break from men, including Marcus. That guy throws me so off balance it's like being on a rollercoaster—except I'm the one puking at the end. So, let's just drop it, okay?"

Amanda smirked. "What are you scared of?"

Lana hiccupped, sloshing her drink onto the blanket as she topped up her glass.

"Scared? Me? Nah, I'm not scared of him...or his monster cock."

Amanda leaned in, eyes glinting with mischief.

"Oh, girl, that's a big thing these days. It's called monster smut. There's a whole genre for it. Like, people love it." She winked.

Lana stared at her for a second, then burst out laughing, her hiccups making her laugh even more.

"Wait, seriously? People are out there reading about...that? Damn. I'm behind the times."

Amanda leaned back, laughing too. "You've been missing out, girl. It's like...huge. Like, literally. And by that, I mean their monstrous cocks. You wouldn't even believe some of the...plots."

Lana wiped tears from her eyes.

"Monster cocks and plotlines? God, who knew my life was already trending?" She hiccupped again, her laughter filling the air.

Amanda burst out laughing, covering her face with her hands.

"God, you're a mess. But a cute mess. Seriously, though, he's hot and well-hung. What are you waiting for? Having a one-night stand could help you move on from Rory and get Marcus off your mind. Rebound sex, no strings. Zero hassle, zero commitment. You've just broken up with your fiancé, and Marcus is basically allergic to commitment. It's a win-win."

Having a mind-blowing night of sex could be a good idea. Maybe the carefree, non-committal Lana vibe wasn't such a terrible idea.

"Maybe I should—"

Amanda didn't let her finish, launching forward with a dramatic shriek that sent her curls flying off her shoulders as she grabbed Lana's phone.

"Call him. Plant the seed that you're in Single Town! Let him know you're on the market and let it play out. Make him do the legwork."

Lana let out a long, exasperated breath. "I don't even have his number."

"Lan, a guy like Marcus must have a secretary or something to handle everything. He's too important to not have a go-between."

Lana's eyes widened, realisation flickering in her tipsy mind.

"Wait... There is someone who could pass him a message." She leaned back, a drunken grin creeping onto her face. "Alright, fine. Maybe I will plant a little seed."

Amanda high-fived her in a burst of enthusiasm. "You've got this."

Lana scrolled through her contact list, her finger dragging across the screen as she squinted at the blurry names.

"There she is," she drawled, each word coming out with a slow slur, her focus wavering.

The phone rang, and a female voice with an edge answered, "Donna Marie speaking."

Lana blinked, trying to focus. "Oh... Hi. I need to speak to Mr Marcus—I mean, McGrath. Marcus McGrath. Please."

There was a noticeable pause on the other end, then Donna Marie's voice cut through, colder than ice. "Who am I speaking with?"

"Lana Craig, here. Is he there?" she asked, her voice a little unsteady.

Donna Marie's response was sharp, seemingly unimpressed by the drunken nonsense. "Lana, Mr McGrath handed the running of the club to me, so if you have any queries, direct them my way."

Lana's eyes narrowed, her patience running out.

"It's not about the club. It's a personal matter. I'd like to speak to him. Tonight," she pleaded, the desperation seeping through her words.

"I'm sorry, Ms Craig," Donna Marie's tone remained cool. "Mr McGrath isn't available."

Silence hung between them for a beat.

"Oh right, have you got his number then? I'll just call him directly," she pressed, determined.

"No, Ms Craig, I can't give out Mr McGrath's personal information to every woman who calls him. Good night."

Lana stared at the phone, her mouth agape in disbelief, then dropped it like it was on fire. "That witch hung up on me. How rude."

Amanda, who had been chewing on her knuckles, burst into laughter so hard her face turned a shade of red that almost matched her hair.

"Oh my God, Lana, you sounded like a Muppet."

The two of them erupted into giggles, and Lana, in her tipsy state, managed to spill more drink, squealing as it trickled down to her fluffy slipper socks.

While she peeled off a wet sock, a shrill ring from her mobile made her jump. She patted down the blanket, searching for her phone, finally slapping her hand on it.

A withheld number flashed on the screen.

Lana scowled. "Who the hell is this?"

Amanda threw her arms up, stretching and yawning.

"Might be lover boy returning your call," she teased. "Or Rory. Maybe you should let him know you're safe?"

"Well, it can't be Marcus. He doesn't have my number." Lana tapped the answer button with an exaggerated sigh, fully expecting Rory. "Hello?"

"Lana, are you okay?"

The voice on the other end was deep, gravelly—velvet wrapped in thunder. It rumbled through the phone, sending a shiver straight down her spine.

Marcus sounded tired, yet commanding. Still impossibly sexy. Every nerve in her body tightened, every hair stood on end.

"Donna Marie said you were looking for me."

Lana's pulse raced.

Fuck... Shit... Fuck.

"Marcus... Hi... Ah, yes, I—I um, just called to say hi." She almost jumped off the chair in shock. "How did you get this number?"

A low, almost predatory growl rumbled through the line. "Are you drunk?"

"I'd say tipsy more than drunk." Her stomach flipped.

Oh God, this was a mistake. Perhaps guzzling three-quarters of a bottle was excessive.

"Where are you?" His tone was laced with a frustration he didn't bother to hide.

Heat crept up Lana's neck. She'd called him—tipsy, sprawled on the couch in an old cami set and only one sock as if a powerful businessman like Marcus had nothing better to do than drop everything and come running.

"I'm staying with my girlfriend, Amanda. Well, she's not my girlfriend, she's my best friend. I don't have a girlfriend or a boyfriend, not even a fiancé, for that matter." The words spilled out in a blur, her nerves betraying her.

For a split second, it seemed like he was about to comment on her relationship status, but an awkward silence stretched instead. When he finally spoke, his voice was lower, rougher.

"Get some sleep, Lana. Tonight isn't the time for this."

The line clicked dead.

Lana stared at the phone, swallowing hard. She tugged the blanket over her legs, burying her face in her hands.

"Holy shit. He hung up, too. I'm mortified," she muttered, reeling from the ridiculous, humiliating conversation.

Amanda struggled to hold back her giggles, but couldn't. She wheezed, snorted through her nose, and collapsed into uncontrollable laughter.

"Lan, you're *so* funny. That was one hundred percent painful to watch," she cackled, reaching over to hit reshuffle on her iPod like nothing happened.

Hours later, Lana drifted into sleep, her mind fixated on Marcus—as it had been far too often these days.

She dreamt about his rugged, stubbly jaw, those piercing eyes, and his sinfully soft lips trailing hot, teasing kisses along the inside of her thigh.

But then, a loud knock yanked her out of the best sex

dream she'd ever had. She jolted upright and, in the process, rolled off the sofa with a graceless thud.

Groaning as she scrambled to her feet, Lana glanced at the kitchen clock. Just after seven-thirty in the morning.

"Amanda? Some crazy person is at your door!" she yelled, wincing at the headache pulsing behind her temples from the volume of her own voice.

But Amanda didn't stir. The knocking persisted, relentless.

Lana frowned and rubbed her temples, wondering who the hell was at the door so early. Tough luck if it was a window cleaner or another debt collector, she didn't have any cash.

Lana caught a glimpse of herself in the mirror: pale face, dark circles under her eyes, and bright red, dehydrated lips.

Her appearance was disastrous and impossible to fix before meeting whoever was still fisting the goddamn door.

When she opened the door, Marcus nodded and strode in with the confidence of someone who owned the place. He carried a brown paper bag and wore a black sports cap that shadowed his eyes.

The sight of him made her heart race, a surge of excitement mixing with utter embarrassment.

As if the failed late-night booty call wasn't dreadful enough, there he was—looking so damn sexy in loose-fitting grey track pants and a white tee, his muscles shifting with each step, and his jaw clenched in that signature way of his.

And there she stood, looking like she'd been hit with two bottles of Prosecco rather than drinking them.

"How did you find me?" she asked, palming her belly to settle the flutters.

Marcus moved through the small sitting room, reaching to pull the curtains open a little wider, letting in more light to chase away the dark shadows.

He didn't say a word, but the way his eyes lingered on her, checking her out, making sure she was okay, despite her dishevelled state—made her skin tingle as if the only thing in his world that mattered at that moment was her.

"Sit down," he commanded.

He guided her toward the couch with a hand on her back, steadying her when she wobbled.

The touch, though light, sent a bolt of warmth through her, and tingles burst over her scalp.

"Here." He handed her a bottle of clear liquid and a small sachet. "Mix the powder and drink it. You'll feel better."

As he straightened and stood over her, there was something possessive in the way he hovered, as if he was keeping a close eye on her.

Once she'd swallowed a few gulps, he folded his arms over his chest and widened his stance.

"You should get dressed," he said, leaving no room for debate.

"Why?"

"You're coming home with me," he said, his eyes locking onto her legs with unmistakable intent.

Lana's breath hitched. There was no mistaking the smoulder in his gaze, the way he stared like he was already imagining what came next.

He leant into the side of her face, the peak of his cap touching her temple.

"Just so you know," he continued, his deep voice dropping lower, "the way those shorts are sitting... They're giving me ideas I don't think your friend in the next room would appreciate hearing. So grab your stuff and let's go."

30

Marcus

"Just throw on sweats and track shoes, and let's go," he said, his voice husky from lack of sleep.

Marcus finally arrived at the small city apartment following a long night of waiting. Finding Lana hadn't been easy. It had taken a series of well-placed calls and leveraging favours from people who owed him.

He wouldn't let anything stand in his way—no distance too far, or price too high for the information he needed.

Lana sat on the couch, sipping the pain relief and vitamin combo that he swore by for hangovers. He had sent it ahead, knowing it would be the first thing she needed.

As she swallowed the bitter concoction, her face twisted in distaste, and she shuddered from the aftertaste. Her eyes watered, making the vibrant blue even more striking.

He could never get enough of those dazzling baby blues.

Her bed-tousled hair and skimpy sleepwear made every part of him tighten. He couldn't help but appreciate how beautiful she was—vulnerable yet still alluring.

His dick stirred, an involuntary reaction he couldn't suppress. The second he'd heard her voice on the phone last night, everything had shifted.

There were no rules to break when she was single—no commitments to honour, no boyfriend to manage.

Now, he had to focus on keeping his hands to himself when they itched to touch her, to fist the lengths of her hair, press her cheek against the sofa, and hammer into her from behind.

He cleared his throat, reminding himself the moment would come.

But not yet.

Lana stood, a playful glint in her eyes despite the haze of a hangover still lingering.

So damn beautiful, he thought, taking in the way her body swayed a little, the way her flimsy shorts clung to her ass at the back and her pussy at the front.

Fuck, his veins ran hotter.

"We're going to your place?" she asked.

"We are." Marcus deadpanned. "That's why you rang me, right?"

She nodded.

"How long will I be there?"

God, she was testing him.

"I'd like to know what you have planned for me?"

She folded her arms, trying to act nonchalant, but the act just shifted her braless tits and captured his full attention.

"Let's wait and see," he replied, his voice low and teasing. "You called. And I came."

His eyes locked onto hers, daring her to defy him.

She raised an eyebrow, lips curling with curiosity. "What sort of things? What if I'm not into whatever you have in mind?"

A confident smile tugged at his lips. "You'll be into it. Trust me."

His words hung in the air, thick with promise, as he saw the faint tremor in her eyes—just a crack.

"Okay, I need to get a few things," she replied, unbothered, ducking beside the couch.

She rummaged through a kit bag, unaware of the little things she did that drove him wild.

As she bent over, the hem of her shorts rose higher. His body temperature spiked, heat pooling in his chest and spreading fire through his veins.

Every inch of her was calling to him, but he knew he had to wait—had to be patient.

At least, for now.

Marcus studied her as she tossed a pair of jeans aside and reached for a loose pair of sweatpants that sat low on her hips. She wasn't trying to impress anyone, but to him, she was magnetic and irresistible in a way he couldn't explain.

Her skin was bare of makeup, and freckles scattered across her nose, a natural beauty that drew him in even more. The soft curve of her jaw, the mess of her hair falling around her pretty face—everything about her drew him in.

She pulled a cropped hoodie over her head; the hem sitting just at her midriff, leaving a sliver of skin exposed when she moved. His body tensed.

The urge to reach out and pull that hoodie off her tested him in ways he hadn't expected.

But he forced himself to stay rooted in place, arms folded, trying to ignore the hook of his desire as it pulled tighter with each passing second.

She caught him staring.

"What?" she asked, her voice teasing, but there was a slight flutter of uncertainty in her eyes.

"Nothing." Marcus shrugged. "You'd look good in anything."

She smiled, that bright, wide smile that lit up his chest, then rolled her eyes before finishing adjusting her hoodie, pulling the strings tight around her neck.

Once she was done, she turned toward him, her eyes lifting to meet his with that same unguarded warmth.

Truth was, he still wasn't looking for anything long-term, and he sure as hell wouldn't give her that impression. But the temptation to have more—to claim her, taste her, keep her for longer than just one night—haunted him.

One night had always been enough before. He wasn't sure it would be this time.

"Ready?" His voice came out sharper than he intended.

Lana nodded, slipping her feet into a pair of old sneakers. She was so damn sleepy. Hair a little wild, eyes still heavy with the remnants of a hangover, yet she carried herself with confidence.

"Yeah." She slung the bag strap over her shoulder.

Before her next step, he gently but firmly took the bag from her.

His gaze locked with hers, as though everything she owned was his to take.

"I'll carry that. Let's go," Marcus said, taking the lead.

As they walked to the car, Marcus kept his hand on the small of her back, fingers just brushing the soft skin beneath the fabric of her hoodie. The whisper of contact was enough to send a shockwave through him.

He fought the urge to kiss her as they reached the parked car at the side of the road. The urge pulsed through him with every step, and he wasn't convinced he could stop once he started.

Marcus pulled open the door for her, stepping aside as she slid into the passenger seat. He couldn't help but watch the way she settled in, the curve of her hips shifting just enough to drag his gaze downward.

Then came the seatbelt—her fingers fastening it with an effortless click, exposing that same teasing sliver of skin above the waistband of her sweatpants.

She glanced up, catching him staring, and smiled. A mix of anticipation and nerves. He fucking loved it.

Without a word, he tossed her bag into the backseat before rounding the hood and sliding into the driver's seat.

As the engine rumbled to life, her gaze settled on his side profile.

"Thanks for covering my bill at The Fitz the other night, Marcus," she said. "You didn't have to do that."

He leaned back, one hand resting casually on the wheel, the other draped along the console. His gaze flicked to hers.

"No need to thank me," he said.

She tilted her head, a teasing glint in her eyes. "Guess I'll have to return the favour. A few drinks on me next time?"

Marcus let out a low chuckle, shaking his head. "You don't owe me anything."

She held his stare for a beat, then smirked. "Good. I'd rather buy you a drink because I want to, not because I have to."

Marcus shifted gears. "Fair enough, beautiful. Just don't expect me to let you pay."

Something settled within him. She wasn't trying to play him, wasn't looking for a payout. No calculated sweetness, no batting her lashes in expectation. Just a woman who meant what she said.

And damn if that didn't make her even harder to resist.

She laughed and stared out the side window. "You're impossible."

He gave a slight shrug, his voice a low rumble. "I guess so. And you're impossible to forget."

His eyes flicked to her for a brief second before

focusing on the road again, as if the words tumbled out without him thinking them through.

Beneath his calm exterior, though, a strange sensation churned in his gut. He wasn't used to caring, not past surface level, but there was something about her that brought out a protective streak even when he'd never admit it aloud.

As if he could hear himself saying her name in his future.

It made little sense, but then, neither did she.

All he needed was one night. That was it. Then she'd be out of his system once and for all.

Except, as he drove towards his city apartment, he took another exit and veered away from the city instead.

31

Lana

Lana made herself comfortable in the sleek leather seat, stretching as the hum of the engine filled the car.

Beyond the windscreen, the first hints of dawn painted the sky in soft shades of blue and gold, making the car ride almost dream-like.

Blinking away the haze of tiredness, she caught sight of a green road sign up ahead.

She frowned. "Why are we going away from the city?"

Marcus, calm and focused, kept his hands steady on the wheel. "My home is in Fermanagh. I'm taking you there for the weekend."

"The weekend?"

The plan had been a single night. No expectations, no strings. Just enough time to scratch the itch and slip away before things got complicated.

"Did you have other plans?" he asked.

"No..."

It wasn't a lie. The only person who'd be waiting for her was Amanda. Despite her nerves, a dirty weekend sounded better than mindless internet shopping and another night on a tiny couch.

A weekend, though, that idea had its merits... and its dangers.

However, Monday would come soon enough. But for now? Carpe fucking diem.

Her body relaxed as the car glided along the open roads. The rhythmic motion, combined with the warmth of the heated seat, made her eyelids heavy again.

Marcus glanced at her, a small smirk tugging at his lips. "Go back to sleep, Lana. We've got a long drive ahead of us."

She turned her head and stared at his perfect side profile. "What if I snore? Or worse—what if I drool?"

His smirk deepened. "Then I'll consider it a souvenir."

Lana laughed. "That's gross."

He flicked her a sideways glance, eyes full of amusement. "You think a little drool would turn me off?"

Her stomach flipped.

Marcus chuckled, low and rough, his grip tightening on the wheel. "If anything, it's the opposite."

Heat curled in her belly, a delicious mix of anticipation and butterflies.

Could she really handle a man like Marcus?

The thought sent a wicked shiver down her spine, but before she could dwell on it, her lashes grew heavy, and she fell asleep.

A warm weight settled on her thigh, rousing her. Lana's eyes sprung open to find Marcus watching her, his handsome face close, a hint of a smile teasing his lips.

"We're here, beautiful."

Blinking, she took in the sight before her. Marcus's home sat among sprawling green fields, with dense spruce trees framing the long, winding driveway.

An elegant row of silver birch lined the path, their pale trunks standing in perfect symmetry as they led up to a modest yet striking Georgian cottage.

The classically proportioned house had soft grey stone construction, with its white front door framed by glass panels, offering a glimpse of the warmth within.

Wispy clouds drifted across the clear blue sky; their images captured in the many windowpanes.

It wasn't over the top or flashy—just peaceful. Idyllic. And not what she imagined for a billionaire jetsetter.

The car crunched to a stop on the gravel drive. Sunlight dappled across the vast countryside beyond. A strange sense of freedom swelled in her chest.

As Marcus stepped out of the car, she followed, her sneakers sinking into the tiny cream pebbles underfoot. He led her to the front door, pushing it open to reveal a wide hallway bathed in natural light.

Large flagstones lay underfoot, their earthy tones grounding the space, while sage walls and ashen cornicing added an understated elegance.

"This used to be the coach house," Marcus said, letting her inside first. "Dates back to the 1800s. The stables and courtyard really sold it for me. I've extended it quite a bit out the back."

Lana glanced up at him. She wasn't sure what surprised her more—the house, or the man who owned it.

Marcus sauntered ahead, pushing open another door and gesturing for her to enter. "This used to be the kitchen. I added on the rest."

The space was breathtaking—an expansive, airy room with exposed stone walls and towering windows that framed the shimmering waters of Lough Erne.

Sunlight streamed through a glass lantern ceiling, warming the air and coaxing the sweet scent of jasmine from the potted vines climbing toward the light.

Looking left and right, she took it all in. From a rope-suspended sofa buried in silk cushions and angled toward the lake view, to the handcrafted kitchen units wrapped around the space, anchored by a massive wooden-topped island.

Overhead, bronze pendants reflected the sunlight, adding an opulence to the otherwise understated design. Every detail was intentional—elegant and expensive.

Lana let her gaze sweep the space, taking it all in. "I love this room."

He strode to the corner, crouching to toss a log into the wood-burning stove. She followed, the crackle of kindling and the smoky scent sparking memories of winter nights by her grandfather's fire.

"Can I help?" she offered.

Marcus straightened and placed his hands on her shoulders, his emerald eyes gleaming.

"Relax for a few hours. I need to handle some work calls. The rescue powder can leave you a little groggy, but trust me—it works wonders."

His fingers drifted down her arm until they cuffed her wrist. The simple touch sent a shiver through her as he guided her toward a low armchair beside the log pile.

"Sleeping on the way here helped," she admitted, sinking into the chair when his hand slipped away. "I'm ten times better. Thanks."

"Freshen up if you like." Marcus crossed his arms over his chest, that unreadable look firmly in place. "Then I'll show you around later."

"Sounds good," she replied, then frowned, realising all her toiletries were still at Amanda's.

Sinking back into the chair, she let her gaze drift. "This isn't where I imagined you living. But it's miles better than your city crash pad."

Marcus tossed another log into the burner. The fire-light casting shadows across his face.

"I have plenty of places to stay, but this is home. My father and brother live nearby. When I need to think—to recharge—I come here."

Her gaze settled on the distant lake. "I can see why. It's... very peaceful. A little slice of heaven."

"Exactly." He nodded. "I'll show you to your room now."

He offered his hand, and she took it, the heat of his palm grounding her as he pulled her to her feet.

Her brow scrunched. "I'll have my own room?"

Marcus led her from the kitchen, his grip firm yet distant, keeping her close but not too close.

"Yeah, you'll have your own bathroom, too. My housekeeper stocked the cabinets for you. But if there's anything else you need, I'll arrange for it to be delivered."

"I'm not staying with you?"

He didn't answer. Instead, he slid his hand to her shoulder and gave a small tug, leading her along a wide corridor. They stopped at a door, its polished brass handle shining in the daylight.

"This is your room," he said, reaching for the handle.

Without another word, he stepped aside, gesturing for her to enter.

"Make yourself at home."

The door swung open, revealing a space as tranquil and sophisticated as the rest of the house—an enormous bed sat in the middle, framed with simple but elegant furniture.

As he turned to leave, her mind whirled. A part of her had expected... more. She'd imagined them tangled in sheets, not staying in separate rooms.

She wasn't here for a love story, and yet, the idea of him pulling back when everything between them had been so electric... it stirred something she wasn't ready to acknowledge.

"Marcus... Wait."

When he glanced back over his shoulder, the reality hit her all at once. This was his way of keeping things casual. Separate rooms ensured she understood that, without saying the words aloud.

"Why did you bring me here?" she asked. "Rather than your city apartment? It would have been easier for me to leave in the morning."

Marcus paused, his back to her. His hand rested on the doorframe, the silence stretching long enough for her to second-guess herself.

Slowly, he turned to face her, his expression shadowed, but his eyes—those damn eyes—seemed to strip her bare.

"I told you—this is where I come to think and to recharge. I'm giving you space, Lana. A place to gather your thoughts. And... We want to keep this simple, remember?"

Her stomach fluttered, but she couldn't let it show. "I don't need space."

32

Marcus

"Take a shower while I deal with business."

She opened her mouth to respond, but the words caught in her throat. As he moved into the corridor, doubt settled in his mind.

This was supposed to be simple. But nothing about Lana was simple.

"Don't overthink it. Find me when you're finished," he added.

Without looking back, he walked away, each step heavier than the last.

Marcus returned to the kitchen, trying to refocus on the stack of work waiting for him. He was a self-confessed workaholic and that wouldn't change for a woman.

Calls, emails, deadlines—they all needed attention.

That's how people make billions. Dedication.

However, his mind kept drifting to the woman he'd

brought home. His phone rang, but the conversation didn't hold his interest for long.

The image of her naked drowned every click of the keys on his laptop and every sound from the outside world.

Fuck, he was too distracted to concentrate.

Marcus paced back-and-forth in front of the roaring wood burner, his next phone call slipping past him in a blur.

Pressure from work and ambition usually preoccupied him, yet today, things were different.

Lana had just broken things off with her fiancé, and that wound was still raw. She needed space, time to regroup—but waiting had never been his way.

In his world, he made deals, solved problems, and saw hesitation as a sign of weakness.

Still, he told himself he'd be the gentleman, even as restraint burned through his veins like a volatile fuse.

However, he respected her just as much as he wanted to fuck the sadness right out of her.

His gaze followed the length of the hallway, lingering on the closed door. And a new thought bubbled up—*Fuck it, she was his to play with now.*

The realisation struck him harder than he expected. She was here, in his house, because she had chosen to be —but no matter how much he told himself to be patient, every instinct in his body was pulling him toward her.

With a determined stride, Marcus headed for the guestroom. Keeping her on the other side of the house was the smarter choice. There would be plenty of time to take her apart when the moment was right, but that didn't mean she needed to be in his bed.

Truth was, bringing her here had been a last-minute decision, completely unplanned. And for a man who thrived on control, that was damn near unheard of.

Marcus couldn't help himself. Whatever self-control he'd been clinging to had just snapped.

His feet carried him to her bedroom door, his blood pumping hotter.

He didn't knock—he didn't need to.

Moving inside, he pushed open the adjoining bathroom door and stepped into the steam-filled room.

His pulse kicked up, but outwardly, he remained composed, every movement measured, controlled.

Leaning against the doorframe, he let his gaze drift over the blurred outline of her body behind the glass. The curves of her hips, the slope of her back—she was putting on a show without even knowing it.

He smirked, his voice low and controlled.

"Hope I'm not interrupting, beautiful."

Marcus yanked his tee over his head, the fabric snagging briefly against his jaw before sliding free, revealing the bold black numerals inked across his left pec.

He kicked off his sneakers, sending them tumbling aside. In one fluid motion, his track pants followed, discarded without a second thought.

With only one thing on his mind, he strode toward the glass cubicle and stepped inside. His gaze locked onto hers, drinking in the way her pupils darkened, her wet, glistening breasts rising and falling with each quickened breath.

Her bottom lip caught between her teeth when the glass door shut behind him, trapping them in.

In a single step, he was inches from her, his breath heavy with desire. But she didn't let him get any closer. Her palm pressed to his chest, a silent warning to keep the distance.

She reached for the body wash, squeezing it between her hands before lathering it against her curves. The creamy soap slid over her full breasts, traced the soft dip of her belly, and drifted lower.

It took everything in him not to reach out. To take a fucking bite.

Lana kept up her slow, torturous tease, turning every movement into a sensual performance. Heat licked through his veins, his entire body tightening with need.

The aching throb in his dick intensified, almost unbearable, as she made him wait—made him suffer.

A low growl rumbled deep in his chest as their eyes met—hers heavy-lidded, full of unspoken promises. For a fleeting second, her gaze dipped to his cock, her lips parting just enough to feed his hunger.

She was toying with him. Testing his restraint.

Enough.

In one swift move, he surged forward, caging her against the cool tile. Water cascaded over his shoulders as he pressed his body into hers, the heat between them scorching.

The teasing was over. He was in control now.

She gasped when her soapy breasts pressed against him and his fingers dug into the soft flesh of her waist, anchoring her to him.

"You want me now, beautiful?"

"Yes," she breathed, her fingers diving into his hair.

"No backing out?"

Lana shook her head. "No backing out."

"Then beg me to fuck you, Lana." His teeth scraped along her jaw, his breath hot against her damp skin. "Beg me."

She swallowed hard, her pulse hammering in her throat as her lips parted on a shaky breath.

"I need you, Marcus," she whispered, voice thick with longing. "I've needed you for so long."

She let her hands skate over his chest, tracing the ridges of muscle slick with steam. Her mouth followed, pressing hot, open-mouthed kisses to his throat, his collarbone, tasting him like she was starved.

Her nails scraped over his stomach, stopping just shy of where he ached for her most.

"Please," she whispered again, voice breaking with need. "Fuck me. Make me yours for the weekend. Finish what you started in your office that night."

Fuck, she had never looked more beautiful—desperate, needy, completely at his mercy.

"You want me that bad, beautiful?" His voice was dark, teasing, edged with the hunger clawing at his insides.

"Yes," she said, all breathy and raspy.

He caught her wrists and pinned them to the cool tile

behind her head. His dick, hard and heavy, nudged her stomach, making her whimper.

Christ, he loved the sound of those needy little gasps.

"Then tell me," he murmured against her jaw, his lips grazing the delicate skin just below her ear. "Tell me how much you need me."

"I need you so bad it hurts," she whispered, rolling her hips, desperate for friction.

He dipped into the side of her face, his breath fanning over her wet skin. "And you think I'll just give you what you want?"

She let out a frustrated groan, her fingers flexing against his hold.

"Yes," she challenged, voice breathless, eyes full of heat. "Because you want this just as much as I do. Stop holding back."

His control snapped.

With a growl, he crashed his mouth against hers, swallowing her moan as he finally gave in to the hunger that had been burning between them for too damn long.

Their kiss was fire. Untamed, desperate, a clash of hunger and control. His tongue swept into her mouth, claiming her, his grip tightening as he pulled her flush against him.

Her hardened nipples dragged against his chest, every brush sending electric shivers down his spine.

A strangled moan slipped from her lips as his hand moved, fingers teasing the heat between her thighs. She arched into him, needing more, but he took his time, drawing out her torment.

His touch was restrained—just enough to make her squirm, just enough to remind her who was really in control.

He swallowed her whimpers, deepening the kiss as his fingers slid inside her heat. His other hand gripped her hip as he pressed his palm against her most sensitive spot, forcing her to take exactly what he gave.

He hummed against her lips. "So fucking wet for me."

Lana gasped, her nails digging into his back, her body tightening around his hand as he worked her closer to the edge. But he didn't give in—not yet.

He wanted her desperate, wrecked, begging for him to finally give her what they both craved.

She was on the verge of shattering, her breath quickening in a staccato rhythm, her body tensing for release.

Her dirty little whimpers and breathless moans sent a raw pulse of hunger through him, his blood running molten, thick with need.

His dick throbbed, aching to claim her, to bury himself so deep she'd forget the man before him.

Breaking the kiss, he leaned back just enough to take her in. His gaze roamed over the soft curves of her wet, swollen breasts that moved to the same rhythm as her ragged breaths.

Each subtle movement betrayed the frantic beat of her pulse.

She was wrecked for him already, and fuck, she had never looked hotter.

Gritting his teeth, he wrenched his fingers from her

soaked heat, every muscle in his body tightening with the effort to hold back.

The sudden absence made her groan, a desperate, needy sound that made him smile.

Her lips parted in stunned disbelief, her body trembling, hips shifting instinctively, as if searching for his touch.

Fuck. Keeping control was torture. But watching her fall apart for him? That would be worth every second of restraint.

"Marcus..." she whimpered, a plea wrapped in a single breath.

He tilted her chin up with the rough drag of his knuckles, his voice a dark command.

"Be a good girl and wait a bit longer."

33

Lana

Lana blinked through the steam, her body was thrumming and her veins burning.

Her brows pulled together as Marcus stepped away.

"What's happening?" Her voice was breathless, laced with confusion. "Where are you going?"

He glanced over his shoulder, those wicked green eyes gleaming with power.

"Patience, beautiful." His voice was a slow drag of heat down her spine. "I'm not going anywhere."

Her thighs clenched as she swallowed hard, the pulse between her legs throbbing.

Marcus stepped out of the shower, water dripping, every muscle flexing, as he reached for a towel and dabbed his face.

The black ink sprawled across his chest shifted with the movement, the Roman numerals carved into his golden skin only making him look more untouchable, more lethal.

The ridges of his abdomen glistened beneath the bathroom lights. Drips rolled a slow path down his taut stomach before disappearing into the dark trail of hair leading lower.

She exhaled when he prowled toward the vanity, his movements smooth, unhurried, every step oozing masculine control.

The crinkle of foil had her heart racing as he tore a condom wrapper open with his teeth and rolled the latex down his thick length with expert precision.

When he finally lifted his gaze to hers through the mirror, the hunger in his emerald stare sent a violent shiver down her spine.

"You sure you still want this, beautiful?" His voice was deep, gravelly, full of dark promise.

Lana's lips parted, her throat dry, her body screaming for more. "Yes."

His mouth curled into a slow, devastating smirk. "Then come here."

Lana's body moved before her mind could catch up. The desperation clawing at her insides drowned out everything else—the past, the broken engagement, the doubts.

None of it mattered. Not when Marcus stood there, waiting.

Adrenaline pumped through her every step, the cool air prickling against her flushed skin as she exited the shower.

Marcus caught her wrist before she could close the distance, halting her advance. His finger traced slow, lazy circles around her nipples, teasing her as his smirk deepened.

"Not so fast, beautiful. I want to savour this."

She let out a soft, frustrated whimper, her body wound too tight, strung out on the unbearable need coiling in her core. "Marcus—"

He pressed a finger to her mouth, dragging her bottom lip lower, then slid it past her teeth. "I like you like this... desperate, aching, ready to beg."

Lana sucked his finger, holding eye contact. He was playing with her, tormenting her, but she didn't care. She wanted him to.

"Forget every moment before this one. Right now, the only thing that exists is you and me," he said.

"I already have," she whispered.

"Good."

He smiled, just a little, then tugged her flush against his chest and growled low in his throat, his control fracturing.

His hand jumped to her ass, squeezing hard. She gasped, her head falling back, and he was on her—mouth at her throat, tongue dragging fire over her sensitive skin.

She clawed at his shoulders, loving how his lips trailed lower, across her collarbone, and down to her breasts.

He flicked his tongue over her hardened peak, then bit down just enough to make her cry out.

The sound sent a wicked gleam through his eyes.

"Hmmm... You like that?" His fingers slipped between her thighs.

His thumb swirled over her swollen clit, making her whimper. "Fuck, Lana. You're so ready for my dick."

She moaned, gripping his forearms to steady herself as he worked her into a frenzy, her body shaking with every pump of his finger.

He was relentless, pushing her closer, unravelling her piece by piece.

Her past was gone. And her ex? He was a faded memory. The pain, the betrayal—none of it existed. Marcus had erased it all, replacing every scar with fire.

Her hips bucked into his hand, desperate for friction, but he pulled back, a devilish grin curving his lips.

"Not yet," he murmured. "I want to watch you come apart when I'm inside you."

Lana whimpered, nails digging into his shoulders. "God, yes—"

Marcus lifted her in one swift motion, carrying her to the vanity as if she weighed nothing.

He placed her on the cool marble countertop, parting her legs and lining himself up between them.

Teasing her with the glossy head of his dick, his gaze locked onto hers. "Keep your eyes on mine, beautiful."

She did, her breath catching as he pushed into her inch by inch, stretching her, claiming her.

A strangled moan tore from her throat, and Marcus groaned, his hands tightening around her hips.

"Fuck, Lana."

"So... Deep," she whimpered.

And then his hips moved—slow and powerful. Each thrust sent white-hot sparks shooting through her.

He quickened his pace, driving into her harder, faster. The soap bottle clattered into the basin, the water pounding relentlessly in the cubicle behind them.

But none of that mattered. All she could focus on was the way he filled her, the reality of it far surpassing anything she'd imagined in the weeks of longing.

A raw, breathless cry escaped her as the intensity of her climax consumed her, every wave of pleasure crashing over her, leaving her lost in the moment.

Her inner muscles clenched around him, her thighs trembled, and the rush spiralled while Marcus held her firm, his name tumbling from her lips in a breathless moan.

Every nerve in her body ignited, every sense overloaded as the intensity hit, unlike anything she had ever experienced.

A guttural groan rumbled from his throat as he followed her over the edge. His muscles tensed and he came hard and fast.

Lana peered up, her breath still erratic, and let out a soft, dazed laugh before tipping her forehead against his chest.

His skin was warm and slick, the steady thud of his heart drumming against her ear.

Her heart thundered, too, but something else stirred beneath the bliss—a dangerous, unsettling emotion.

She had never been so sated and utterly consumed in this way.

How could she leave him after experiencing a connection so fierce it left her craving more?

She cursed herself for mixing lust with emotions.

A soft exhale escaped her, and she tightened her arms around him, clinging to something she knew wasn't hers to hold on to.

Marcus said nothing, but he didn't let her go either.

His arms curled around her waist, strong and possessive, and he rested his cheek against the top of her head. For a moment, they just stood there, their thoughts unspoken.

Once her breathing had regulated, his arms fell away. He backed up, grabbed a towel and handed it to her, then peeled off the condom and disposed of it.

Lana dragged her fingers through the ends of her matted hair, squeezing the excess water into the towel.

Something about the way he stood back, silently observing, sent a slow heat curling in her stomach. He seemed... Relaxed.

It was strange how he eyed her—almost unsettling, yet there was no judgment in his eyes.

Marcus wasn't the type to linger. She knew that. He didn't strike her as a man who hung around after sex, waiting for a woman to fix her hair or towel off her skin.

And yet, he was still there, his eyes following her every move like he wasn't quite ready to leave.

"So, what's the craic between you and the fiancé?" His tone, although casual, concealed a sharp edge.

"You mean my ex-fiancé," she corrected.

Her gaze dropped to the Roman numerals inked over his heart.

"I regret agreeing to marry him." She shrugged.

"We'd been growing apart for a while. Long before we joined your club. I just didn't want to admit it."

Lana dropped the towel and stepped into him, her bare skin moulding against the hard planes of his body.

"Or maybe," she whispered, tilting her head up to meet his gaze, "I only realised there was more out there when a certain sexy-as-fuck man forced me to climax in his office."

Before he could respond, she leaned in and grazed his nipple with her teeth, tugging just enough to earn a reaction.

A low, masculine chuckle rumbled through him, dark and knowing, as his hands came up to cup her cheeks, thumbs stroking the damp skin beneath her jaw.

"You loved every second."

"Yeah, I did. And you knew it."

Pushing up on her toes, she ran her tongue along the dip in his throat, before pressing open-mouthed kisses along the strong column of his neck.

His breathing deepened, the tension in his muscles coiling tighter.

Trailing tiny kisses down his chest, she stopped when she reached the dark ink stamped over his heart. Her fingertips skimmed the numerals.

"What does this stand for?" she asked.

His back stiffened. "It's the date of my mother's death. November 10, 1987. The day my life changed forever."

Lana stilled. A chill ghosted down her spine, raising goosebumps across her damp skin.

Her hands flattened against his chest, needing to steady herself, as if his words had altered the ground beneath her feet.

"Marcus..."

"What?" His brows pulled together. "What's wrong?"

Her fingers traced the inked numerals again, reverent now, almost hesitant.

"I was born on November 11, 1987." A pause. A heartbeat of silence thick enough to drown in fell between them. "The day after."

Marcus cleared his throat, his expression shifting—guarded now, distant.

"I'll leave you to get sorted. Once you're ready, come find me in the stables." His voice was steady, but there was something off about it.

Raking a hand through his damp hair, he took a step back.

She reached for him, her fingers curling around his wrist before trailing up his forearm. Pressing her lips to the ink over his heart, she tilted her chin and peered up at him.

His jaw tensed before he offered her a tight smile.

Undeterred, she slid her hands around his neck, rising onto the balls of her feet. Soft, damp kisses grazed his stubbled cheek, inching toward his mouth. The moment their lips met, his muscles relaxed a fraction.

"See you at the stables," she whispered, letting her hands fall away, nibbling the inside of her lip as uncertainty crept in.

Marcus nodded, silent, before turning and striding out the door, a towel slung low around his hips.

Lana watched him go, her heart pounding against her ribs, an uneasy weight settling in her stomach.

He was pulling away and there was nothing she could do about it.

34

Lana

When Lana walked out of the bathroom, she froze.

Spread across the bed was a selection of clothes—delicate satin lingerie, smart trousers, designer jeans, and an array of tops in soft fabrics and elegant cuts.

A strange mix of emotions twisted inside her. The gesture was both considerate and over-the-top—entirely Marcus.

The man dealt in offerings, not commitment.

Despite his billionaire status, he had anticipated her needs before she even voiced them. However, his thoughtfulness made it impossible to forget she was in his world now and far removed from reality.

She traced a fingertip over the lingerie, her pulse quickening at the skimpy panties and intricate filigree bra —nothing like her usual practical, semi-padded variety.

The thought of him picking it out for her sent a little shiver down her spine.

Steeling herself, she slid into the set, the lace moulding against her skin, then picked a pair of designer pale blue jeans.

They hugged her hips as if he'd known her measurements down to the last inch.

For the top, she picked the bubblegum pink cashmere pullover. The second she pulled it over her head, she sighed at the luxurious texture against her skin.

Five boxed pairs of shoes sat at the foot of the bed, waiting for her to choose. Instead of unboxing them, she reached for her own well-worn white sneakers.

He'd told her to meet him at the stables, and she didn't mind getting them mucky. Besides, she needed to hold on to a piece of herself in all this.

To remember, this was nothing more than a fling.

Following the stone-floored corridor, she wandered into the kitchen, halted by the breathtaking view outside. The lough stretched endlessly before her, glass-like, reflecting the light.

To the right of the house, a black horse weathervane commanded a small clock tower. She figured the stables were there and went outside.

A winding pebbled path twisted through clusters of shrubs, the air carrying the scent of fresh-cut grass and blooming flowers.

Everything about this place had a hideaway, private vibe. Similar to Marcus, it was a world of its own. Controlled, immaculate, yet wild beneath the surface.

And she was walking straight into it.

Marcus' tattoo played on her mind, the odd coincidence of the date being a day before she was born.

She tried to shrug it off as nothing more than a strange fluke, but deep down, a weird emotion settled in her chest.

Fairy tales weren't true, though. She knew that. The notion of Marcus waiting for happiness—for her—since then was ridiculous. She wasn't naïve, or stupid.

By Monday, it would all be over, anyway.

Lana stepped into the stone-built stable yard, passing through a large archway paved with cobbles.

Curved passageways mirrored one another, each fitted with wide stable doors that looked straight out of an equestrian dream.

In the centre of the courtyard stood a grand fountain, crowned by a rearing bronze horse, its powerful stance frozen mid-motion as a jet of water poured from its mouth into the pool below.

Then she heard him.

"Lana."

Marcus' husky voice rolled across the yard, seeping into her skin like a lingering caress.

Her breath hitched as she turned toward the sound, catching sight of him at the farthest stable.

Golden light from the late afternoon sun framed his silhouette, making him appear almost unreal, like some god carved from stone and shadow.

Smiling, she drifted toward him. Her pulse thrummed when he vanished inside the stable. Following him, her eyes adjusted to the low light, and what she saw stole her breath.

Marcus sat on the rubber floor, his long, powerful legs stretched out in front of him.

But it wasn't just the sight of him that tugged at her heartstrings—it was the small, tubby tan dog curled up beside him on a cushion.

His large hand moved with surprising gentleness over the sleeping animal, his fingers smoothing over the round swell of her belly, rubbing her ears with a quiet affection that made something warm stir inside Lana.

Damm him.

"This is Varia," he announced, his voice lower now, like he didn't want to disturb the little dog. "The love of my life."

Lana's stomach flipped.

She had seen him powerful. Ruthless. All orders and dominance. But this?

This was something else altogether.

The sight of such a commanding man, sitting on the cold floor, caring for a pregnant dog—it struck her in a way she hadn't anticipated. It was utterly disarming.

Lana stood there, frozen, her head and heart at war. She could *fancy* him, yes. But this left her exposed and caught in a storm of emotions she hadn't prepared for.

His eyes gleamed as he continued stroking the dog's ears. "She's going to have a litter soon. The vet says she needs to rest as much as possible, not that she can waddle too far."

Lana stepped closer, crouching before them. "What breed is she?"

"Border Terrier," he said, rubbing a slow circle over Varia's belly. "I had her mother before her and kept Varia from her only litter."

Varia snorted out a soft, contented breath, her little tail wagging lazily. The sight made Lana smile, spreading warmth to her chest.

Marcus gave the dog one last affectionate scratch before rising to his feet and extending his hand toward her. "I thought you'd like to meet her."

Taking his hand, she stood, only to curse herself the second he let go. With a last glance at the dog, he stepped into the golden sunlight streaming through the open stable door.

She crossed her arms over her chest as soon as he moved, her thoughts retreating inward.

He'd changed into khaki cargo trousers and a crisp white shirt that clung to the sculpted lines of his chest.

God, he was something else.

She followed him out into the yard, stepping aside while he secured the stable door behind them.

"My yard staff are watching her day and night."

She stepped closer, a smitten smile tugging at her lips. "She's well taken care of. And a very lucky girl to have the undivided attention of Marcus McGrath."

She tilted into him, just a fraction, testing the waters.

He let her.

Then, with a featherlight touch, he ran a finger along

the curve of her jaw. The gentle stroke sent a bolt of electricity straight through her.

"There's another girl who has my attention, too."

"Oh, yeah?" she breathed, barely able to find her voice.

He smirked, stepping even closer, the heat between them thick and heady.

"Yeah," he said in a teasing rumble. "And she's playing a very dangerous game."

Catching her face in his large hands, Marcus lowered his head and captured her mouth in a slow, deep kiss that sent a rush of fire through her veins.

The idea of a one-night stand evaporated like smoke in the air. Right or wrong, she couldn't bring herself to care.

His fingers tangled in her hair, the grip firm enough to anchor her in place as he pulled her closer, deepening the kiss. Her body pressed into his, and for a moment, everything else disappeared.

The heat of his mouth on hers consumed her, stealing every breath, every thought. His lips moved with hunger, demanding, as if he couldn't get enough.

She melted into him, her heart racing and her stomach flipping with every soft bite and teasing lick of his lips.

In his arms, there was only this. Only him.

When he finally broke away, his gaze held hers, the depths dark and unreadable.

"You have my attention, beautiful."

Her heart betrayed her, whispering dangerous thoughts, but she pushed them aside.

His arms came around her, strong and sure, wrapping her in warmth. It was a lethal mix—safety and desire tangled together, making her crave something she knew she shouldn't.

He pressed a lingering kiss to the crown of her head. "Do you like horses?"

She smiled against his chest. "I love them."

"Good. Let's take a walk through the fields before the sun sets. They're out in the pasture now. The ones in this yard belong to my brother, Jamie. Mostly retired racehorses."

She tilted her chin up at him. "Do you ride?"

"I used to. Haven't been in the saddle for a long time now. Maybe tomorrow we could go for a ride."

"I've never ridden before." She grinned. "I'd love to try—if you promise I won't fall off."

She nudged his shoulder, enjoying the heat of his body against hers.

His arm slid lower, tightening around her waist as his smirk deepened. "I'll protect you, beautiful. You have my word."

The way he said it—low, smooth, laced with a promise that held more weight than it should—made her stomach flip.

Marcus McGrath wasn't the kind of man who made empty promises.

As the sun dipped below the horizon, they made their way back to the house.

It was the first time she had seen Marcus this relaxed, the hardened businessman momentarily replaced by the man beneath—the guy who didn't need to command a room or strike a deal to be powerful.

"So, tell me," he said, his voice casual but with a glint of curiosity, "why did you break it off with him?"

"He was cheating," she began, her tone heavier than expected. "But it wasn't as simple as that."

Marcus guided her along the path, his arm slung over her shoulder, holding her close. "I'm listening."

She sighed, kicking at a stray pebble along the path, trying to settle the storm brewing inside her.

"I wanted to make it work," she admitted. "I thought if I gave enough and tried hard enough...then maybe I could fix things. But then—"

She trailed off, not quite knowing how to put the rest of it into words.

Marcus stopped walking, his body blocking her path. His arm slid to her hip and turned her to face him.

"He's an idiot, Lana. Any man would be lucky to have you. Hell, maybe you're a little too much for someone like him."

Lana blinked at him, unsure of what he meant. "Too much?"

"You're just too damn impressive for a guy like him to handle," he said, his voice rougher, but there was a spark in his eyes that made her pulse speed up.

"You know what I think?" he asked, not waiting for

her to respond. "I don't think he ever really saw you. Not the way I do."

Lana tilted her head, curious but guarded. "How do you see me?"

"You're a woman who knows exactly what you want. You don't follow anyone's lead, and you don't need anyone's approval to go after it. I think you like to take risks, push boundaries, and handle the fallout like it's nothing." His gaze never wavered as he watched her. "But at the end of it all, what matters most is that you're loyal. That's something few men appreciate... but I respect it."

She met his gaze, a shiver running through her at the intensity she saw there. "I didn't realise I was that transparent."

Marcus gave a half-smile, his eyes never leaving hers.

"You're exactly as you should be," he said, his tone low, a hint of admiration in his voice. "And that's what makes you so damn sexy."

Lana offered him a shy smile, her heart fluttering at his words.

"Shame you don't commit, Mr McGrath," she said, her tone light but carrying a hint of challenge. "Guess I'll have to find myself another man who agrees with you."

She shrugged casually, her eyes never leaving his. "I'm sure he'll turn up one day and sweep me off my feet."

Marcus' muscles visibly tensed, a flicker of annoyance flashing across his face. But just as quickly, he masked it with a smirk, shrugging it off.

"Good luck finding a man as rich as me," he said, his voice thick with arrogance. "Not sure anyone else could offer you the same perks."

Lana raised an eyebrow, unfazed. "Money isn't everything, Marcus. Not for me, anyway."

He stared at her for a beat longer, his eyes narrowing, and for a moment, the playful banter seemed to evaporate, replaced by something unspoken.

Finally, Marcus broke the silence, his voice softer but still carrying an edge.

"I'm getting hungry." He leaned in, his lips brushing against hers in a slow, dirty kiss.

Lana swallowed, her body responding to the heat. She wasn't sure if he was talking about food anymore.

"Me too," she whispered.

She could see the shift in his eyes, the subtle darkening of his pupils, and it took everything in her not to let her thoughts run wild.

With a breath that sounded like a low growl, Marcus kissed her. It was slow—intentional, like he was savouring every second.

His lips lingered at first, and then the pressure deepened, causing flutters to explode in her chest.

When he finally pulled away, the world around her spun, her thoughts tangled and hazy. Her breath was shallow, her heart pounding against her ribs.

Marcus grinned, watching the struggle play out on her face.

"Come on, beautiful," he said. "You need to eat to build up your stamina for later."

A soft laugh slipped from her, the tension easing just a little. As they walked hand in hand toward the house, one thought pushed its way into her mind.

She was falling for him.

Hard and fast.

Deep and unprotected.

35

Lana

In the kitchen, Marcus moved with an intense focus, expertly preparing dinner with the same commanding precision he'd shown earlier in the shower.

She perched on a tall stool by the island, a large glass of red wine in her hand as she watched him toss pasta into boiling water.

"I've been thinking," she said. "Do you believe things happen for a reason? Maybe I was born after your mother's death so the universe could bring us together."

Marcus's eyes flicked up, locking onto hers with a look that made her stomach swoop. He stopped tossing the salad leaves, his expression thoughtful, as though he was considering every word.

"And what do you think the universe wants me to do with you, Lana?"

The question washed over her, his sultry tone igniting a warmth that spread through her body.

"Oh, I don't know," she said, attempting to play it

cool, holding her glass to her lips. "It was just a silly thought."

Marcus moved around the island, his steps slow and confident. His palm settled against the small of her back, the firm pressure sparking a wave of heat that pulsed deep within her.

"Or maybe," he murmured, his voice low, gravelly, "you're right, Lana. The universe wants us to fuck. All day. Every day."

He leaned in close, his lips brushing against her ear, and her body responded before she could stop it. His words were a command, not a question. "I want to fuck you. Right here. Right now."

Marcus spun her around, his body moving between her thighs. He tilted his head and brushed his thumb over her lips, the pad of it gentle yet possessive.

His emerald eyes sparkled, reflecting the soft twinkling lights above them like glistening beads of dew.

He dipped his face closer to hers, their breath mingling. Slowly, he slid his tongue into her mouth, teasing her lips before taking full control. She moaned into his mouth, her body on fire as his kiss deepened.

His hands slid under her pullover, the heat of his palms sending tingles over her skin as they drifted upward and squeezed her lace covered breasts. The growl that rumbled from his chest was low, dark, a sound of approval.

In an instant, he yanked the garment over her head, their gazes locking again as her hair cascaded in soft waves around her shoulders, framing her heaving chest.

He leaned back slightly, his gaze roaming all over her.

"You're so fucking beautiful," he said, the words scraping over her skin like velvet.

Lana pressed into him, her body aching for more, before quickly sliding off the tall stool. Her fingers fumbled with the button on her jeans, popping it open as desire surged through her.

She needed him now, the heat between them building faster than she could control.

"I should thank you for these, too," she said, her hips angling toward him as she slid her jeans past her hips to reveal skimpy panties.

Marcus's gaze darkened, his breath shallow as he stared. "You don't need to thank me, not when I'm going to rip the fucking things to shreds."

As she bent forward, slipping her feet free from her jeans, Marcus grabbed a blade from the island, prowled closer, and hacked at the lace. The thrill ignited her, making her blood burn red-hot.

His fingertips dug into her ass cheeks, rough with violence and need, before he moved behind her and swatted her bare skin.

She stayed bent forward, hands braced on the countertop to steady herself when a second swat landed, sending a jolt of heat through her.

"Spread your legs, Lana," he commanded.

Her heart pounded in her chest. She craved him, but it was clear his intention was to tease, making her ache for what he was yet to give.

Marcus was savouring the moment, playing with her,

enjoying every inch of her skin before finally giving her the release she desperately needed.

Dropping to his knees, he buried his face between her ass cheeks, his tongue sweeping up and down with hungry, frantic movements. It was thrilling, scorching, and better than anything she'd ever experienced.

He palmed her ass cheeks roughly, spreading them wide and exposing her tight back passage further.

"Fuck," she gasped, struggling to swallow the pounding pulse in her throat. "Uh... I've never had anything in there before."

The pressure of his palms disappeared, and his mouth pulled back. He stood, his hands trailing over her prickled skin.

"Stand," he ordered.

Shaking and panting, she obeyed, pushing herself upright.

"Climb onto the kitchen island." He pointed to an empty space on the surface. "I want to see that ass as you climb, then stay on all fours."

The tingling between her thighs intensified as she followed his orders, exposing her most intimate flesh to him. She purposely taunted, moving with exaggerated slowness, showing him everything as she climbed.

Once on her knees, she waited, almost panting. From behind, his hands squeezed her ass, sending a shiver through her, and then, without warning, he smacked the same spot, no doubt leaving her skin pink.

Lana shuddered, a startled yelp escaping her, only for the wet warmth of his mouth to soothe the sting. A tremor raced down her spine, and she instinctively pressed her ass harder into his face.

He continued to seduce her with swats and licks, each one driving her closer to the edge until her legs wobbled beneath her.

She whimpered, desperate for release.

"God, Marcus... please," she begged, and his hand met her ass once more with a sharp, resounding smack.

Whipping her head around, Lana locked eyes with his, stormy and intense.

"Please... fuck me," she pleaded. "I want more."

After another swat hit her ass, the raw need in his eyes almost palpable. His voice was a dark growl, thick with desire.

"Such a beautiful sight," he murmured. "Don't you dare move. I want to watch you tremble."

His face lowered and his lips fluttered over the burn, kissing, grazing and worshiping her with his mouth. When she groaned, he nudged her knees further apart and slipped a finger inside her pussy, driving it in deep.

"Rub yourself, Lana," he commanded, his voice a low growl that vibrated through her chest.

As her fingers moved between her thighs, circling and rubbing her clit in perfect sync with the rhythm of his pumping finger, he leaned in close, his breath hot against her spine.

"Come for me, Lana," he said, his voice low and possessive. "I want to hear you lose control and know how badly you need my dick in your hot little pussy."

The raw intensity behind his words was the spark

that set her on fire. The ache in her core twisted and snapped, releasing in a rush that shattered her composure.

As her body shook with the intensity of her release, Marcus let out a deep, satisfied groan. His hands gripped her hips, steadying her as she rode the wave of pleasure.

"Hmm... That's it," he breathed, his voice rough with approval. "Such a dirty girl. I knew you'd be this perfect."

He pressed a kiss to the base of her spine, his lips lingering with reverence.

"So fucking responsive," he murmured, swatting her ass gentler this time. "Fuck, I can't get enough of this ass."

Marcus stepped back as she panted, still basking in the aftershocks of a release.

"Off the island, beautiful."

When she turned to face him, he reached for her hand. Gently, he swept her naked body into his arms, holding her close for a moment. He then lowered her to her feet, positioning her before him.

She stood there, her breath shallow, fully aware of how completely in control he was, yet attuned to every inch of her. And then he smiled—a single smile that melted her insides, leaving her breathless.

"Kneel for me," he commanded, his tone both a challenge and a demand.

She lowered and gazed up at him, her lips parted, heart pounding in anticipation, waiting for the next command. It wasn't just submission—it was how it was meant to be.

The fierce chemistry, the raw power of his dominance, a real man taking control in a way that made her ache with need and hunger.

Marcus took a slow step toward her, his fingers brushing the waistband of his pants.

"Unbuckle my belt," he said, his voice thick.

Her hands trembled as she reached for him, her fingers working the buckle. She unzipped him slowly, knowing what he expected next.

"Now," he murmured, his tone hungry. "I want your mouth on me before I fuck you."

Lana's breath hitched, her pulse going wild as she obeyed. She pulled his boxers lower and freed his full, hard dick. Wrapping her hand around the base, she locked eyes with him and licked the tip before she took him into her mouth.

The taste of him, the weight, the way he filled her senses—everything was delicious.

His hand threaded into her hair, guiding her as he groaned, the tension building again.

"Fuck, yeah. That's it." His grip tightened. "Take it all, just...like...that."

The room hummed with the sound of deep grunts, his pleasure building as she surrendered to the rhythm, her hands steadying herself on his thighs. As he neared the edge, ready to explode, he suddenly pulled away, slid his hands beneath her armpits, and hauled her to her feet.

"I'm going to fuck you now, Lana." Marcus kicked off his shoes. "Walk to the sofa. Slowly."

With every command, she responded. There was

something about his deep voice, the power in it, that aroused her deepest, most secret desires.

The thought of what he wanted to do next sent a thrill through her, awakening a curiosity he'd set a match to when they first met.

Lana knew, deep down, she would do anything he asked.

She placed one foot in front of the other, taking her time, swaying her hips with deliberate, seductive grace. A little nervous, she glanced over her shoulder.

Marcus stood there, stripped of his clothes, his broad chest rising and falling with each measured breath. His muscles were taut, defined—every inch of him radiating strength and mastery.

His dark, intense eyes never left her, tracking every movement with unwavering focus, hunger simmering beneath the surface. He held his jaw tight, but his presence pulsed with raw energy.

He was ready. Everything about him screamed he wanted her, but he wasn't rushing, appreciating every moment until she reached the leather couch.

"Bend over and offer your pretty pussy to me, Lana."

There was no hesitation. She lowered her head, bent over the arm of the couch and widened her stance. She was exposed—vulnerable—and yet, in that moment, there was a power in her submission.

"Such a needy little pussy." Marcus' voice grew louder and then he was behind her, his fingers moving through her wet heat. "What do you want me to do with this, Lana?"

"I-I want you to fuck it."

"Hmm, good. I want to fuck it so badly, beautiful," he said, his voice thick with desire.

"Please, Marcus," she whimpered, the ache inside her growing with every passing second.

"The universe wants us to fuck all night." His finger-tips dug into her skin, marking her. "Do you think you can handle my dick again?"

He paused, waiting for her answer.

"God... yes," she pleaded, her voice desperate as she rocked back, offering herself to him.

His hands fell away, and when she glanced over her shoulder, he was rolling on a condom. A lock of dark hair draped his brow and shadows kissed his features, giving him a dangerous edge.

"Eyes forward and wait for it," he said, placing a hand on her waist.

With his other hand, he guided his dick to her entrance, and with a low, gravelly grunt, he pushed deep. Hard and unforgiving.

He fisted her hair and tugged her head back to expose her throat as a subtle reminder of the control he held over her. However, she didn't fight it. Fully embracing the rush, surrendering to him with no regrets and craving everything he offered.

As the pressure built, he pulled out, spun her around, and pushed her backward onto the sofa. Without a pause, he spread her legs and drove his dick in deeper this time, claiming her again with an urgency that left them both breathless.

His fingertips found her jaw, securing her face as their gazes locked. He crushed his mouth to hers in a violent, hungry kiss that bit, tugged, and tasted.

Each kiss devoured as he pounded into her harder, his movements relentless.

"Fuck... I'm gonna come," he bit out, his voice hoarse.

"Yes... Do it... come for me."

Lana ran her nails over his skin, sensing his muscles tense. He pulled back for a beat, staring at her with dark, heated eyes, his breathing ragged, and then he slapped her breasts before thrusting in deeper.

His jaw tightened, a low, guttural snarl broke from the back of his throat and his body went rigid, every muscle straining with the force of his release. He remained still for a moment as he hovered over her.

"Jesus fuck..." he panted. "The second time was even better."

Marcus leaned in, his lips finding hers. He drew in her lower lip with a gentle suck and hummed into her mouth. Her arms folded around him, bringing their chests together.

This time, the kiss was different.

Sensual and slow with teasing, slippery licks.

This kiss was sexy. A silent invitation, and a dark desire that could fool her into believing it meant something more.

The way he held her, the way his mouth moved with hers, whispered little lies she wanted to cling to.

Maybe, just maybe, they had forged a genuine

connection, and lying beneath him, she wondered if he was considering more than just a dirty weekend.

36

Marcus

Marcus pulled the duvet over her, his fingers brushing a lock of hair away from her face. He'd carried her to his bed, fed her pasta, and then taken her in ways he hadn't planned.

Afterward, they both fell asleep.

But truth be told, he'd developed a taste for her—a hunger that only grew. He'd gone back for seconds, thirds... hell, he'd kept taking until they were both too exhausted to move.

It should have been simple. No complications. She would stay in a room on the opposite side of the house with a measure of distance between them to make the inevitable cut-off easier.

But he wasn't ready for that. Not when she was in his bed, so warm and close, stirring something he hadn't expected.

She let out a soft, dreamy moan, stirring something

primal inside him. His thumb traced the curve of her cheek, his heart thumping in a way he wasn't used to.

Those sweet, innocent sounds had him captivated.

Everything about this woman was addictive.

The thought of her walking away, leaving his home, made knots form in his stomach.

He wasn't sure what to make of the unusual sensation. This was unfamiliar territory. Lana wasn't just a beautiful body, a stunning face with the most seductive voice that could make his blood run hot.

She could become *his* woman...if he was ready to stake a claim.

But things could spiral out of control, and Marcus knew he'd end up hurting her once the initial rush faded. Commitment had never been something he needed, and deep down, he wasn't sure he had the ability, or the desire, to live up to the expectations that came with it.

His phone buzzed on the nightstand, dragging him out of his thoughts. He reached for it, expecting it to be Roger, the stable manager, with news about Varia's puppies.

However, the name on the screen made his gut twist: Donna Marie.

"This better be good," he muttered, throwing off the duvet and jogging to the adjoining bathroom so he wouldn't wake Lana.

"Marcus, we have a situation. One of the club members was murdered."

His heart stuttered and his muscles tensed. "What... Who?"

"Jacqueline Simpson. Someone strangled her."

"Verto wasn't on this weekend, so why is this my problem?" he snapped, trying to mask the growing unease in his chest.

It was tragic, sure, but a death wasn't supposed to land on his doorstep.

"She was with Rory O'Hare, in The Fitz, Marcus."

The words hit him like a punch to the chest. His blood ran cold, and for a second, he couldn't speak. The name 'Rory O'Hare' echoed in his mind like a distant drumbeat.

"Did he do it?" Marcus muttered, pressing a hand to his forehead. "Are you sure it was him?"

"Donovan caught them on the hotel security footage that evening. Hours later, Rory left the suite after emergency services were called by an anonymous male."

"Where is he now?"

"We don't know. But I doubt he'll get far with her husband hot on his tail."

Marcus froze. The air seemed to leave the room. *Her husband.*

He exhaled slowly, the weight of the situation crashing down on him. Jacqueline's husband was Ciaran Simpson—the notorious Belfast cartel boss, a man who didn't just punish betrayal, he annihilated it.

Marcus had crossed paths with Ciaran in the past, a complex relationship built on mutual benefit. The two men had their own dealings, a web of unspoken understanding that ran deep in the criminal underworld.

They shared connections, assets, and at times, even loyalties—until those loyalties had faltered.

And now, Ciaran would come for Rory and anyone associated with him. If he discovered Lana had been engaged to Rory, she'd be marked as a target for revenge.

His mind raced back to the past, recalling the cold, methodical way Ciaran dealt with enemies—gunshots to the knees, threats hissed through balaclavas, lessons of respect taught with blood and pain.

Unless Marcus moved mountains to protect her, she'd get caught in the crossfire.

The thought of her in danger made his blood boil. Fuck Rory for putting her at risk.

"Where is Ciaran now?" Marcus demanded, his mind falling into darkness.

"We're trying to track him. But, Marcus, this could escalate fast. You need to prepare for the fallout."

Marcus ran a hand through his hair, every muscle in his body tight. Prowling back to the bed, he stood over the object of his desire, knowing exactly what he had to do next.

Backing away, he grabbed clothes from his closet and left the room in the dark of night.

He scribbled a note, left it on the kitchen counter, and texted his chef to prepare her meals while he was gone. But even as he went through the motions, something gnawed at him.

His body ached. The urge to return to bed, slide under the sheets beside her and lose himself in the comfort of her warmth, pulled at him.

But he couldn't. Not until he knew she was safe. He wasn't the type to show it, but anyone who threatened the people close to him would pay the price. And beneath it all, as much as he resisted, he'd cared about Lana.

This mess went beyond a murder in his hotel. It was a test of loyalty and alliances, one that would force him to make deals with dangerous consequences.

And the woman he'd left sleeping in his bed? She wasn't just an innocent bystander.

She was a part of this world now—*his* world.

And no one could steal her from him.

37

Lana

A muffled clatter echoed from below, stirring her. In her haste to see Marcus, she padded down the stairs, still in a blissful naked daze.

Strolling into the kitchen, she came face-to-face with a young guy wearing a hessian apron.

His hazel eyes widened in shock as they locked onto her bare chest.

"Holy shit!" Her arm snapped to her chest, and the other hand flew lower to cover between her thighs. "You're not Marcus..."

Heat flooded her face.

"Sorry to disappoint you, honey. I'm his chef. Freddy," he said, pointing to the counter. "Marcus left a note for you."

"I'm so sorry." She hunched forward as if it that would hide her. "I didn't realise anyone else was here."

Freddy's smirk widened, and he pressed his fingers to his mouth as though trying to stifle a laugh.

"Maybe you can read his note later when your hands are free," he teased, turning away. "I'm making waffles for your breakfast. They'll be ready in a few minutes if you want to come back when you're... sorted."

Lana backed out of the kitchen with a mortified curse under her breath.

Of course, Marcus had left. It must have seemed like the easiest way for him to move on—use her, then quietly slip away even though he'd promised her the weekend. The *weekend*, for God's sake.

And now, here she was—in his house—and he was gone. The note was just the final insult.

She returned to the room where her clothes were, showered and tried to shake off the hurt settling deep in her chest. As the warm spray hit her, she realised she'd walked straight into this with her eyes wide open. Still, she couldn't shake the emptiness.

Dressing in the same sweatpants and hoody she'd arrived in, she checked her mobile phone, hoping for some kind of distraction.

Rory had left loads of voicemails and sent numerous messages. Lana rolled her eyes and tossed her phone onto the bed, a mixture of frustration and resolve bubbling inside her.

She wasn't about to fall for his mind games again.

Just as she headed to the bedroom door, her phone buzzed. She pulled it from her back pocket, and Marcus' name lit up the screen.

"Marcus," she answered, her tone unbothered.

"Mornin', beautiful. Did you get my note? Apologies

for leaving so early." His voice sounded different, more strained than usual, with a tension beneath the surface that didn't go unnoticed.

"No, I haven't read it yet. However, your chef got an eyeful when I wandered into the kitchen naked, thinking I'd find you."

She gave a small chuckle, masking the hurt behind a shield of sarcasm.

"Lucky he's into guys, or I'd fire him for staring at you. But he's worth his weight in gold and he'll make sure you're fed and watered." His tone was flat, detached. "Listen, Lana, I've got urgent business in the city today."

"It's fine. I get it. I'll be out of your house before you get back," she said matter-of-factly, not letting her disappointment show.

"Lana." His tone shifted, more insistent now with a thread of frustration. "Don't leave. I'm not sure what time I'll be back, but I need you there when I return."

For a second, her chest tightened, but she kept her resolve intact. She wouldn't let him pull her in that easily. He wasn't the only one who could control the situation.

"Marcus, I have to work tomorrow," she replied. "I'm not going to hang around here waiting for you."

"Come on, beautiful, it's not like that," he said. "I'm asking you to wait for me and I'll make it up to you."

The way he said it made her pause, but she pushed the hesitation aside. She had her pride, and Marcus wouldn't see her give in so easily.

"I'll think about it," she said coolly.

"Lana." His tone shifted to something resolute, but there was a slight edge of distraction.

Muffled voices muttered in the background, a conversation happening on the other end. Then his voice cut through the noise, more focused now. "Please don't leave, beautiful."

He sighed, and then his tone turned sharper. "Fuck off until I'm done. This call's important."

Lana's heart skipped a beat.

"I need you to stay," he added, his attention firmly back on her again.

"Fine, I'll stay, but I'm not waiting around indefinitely." She kept her tone steady, even though she had a stupid grin on her face. "I have a life, too, Marcus."

"I'll make it up to you," he replied, his voice more controlled now. "There's a car at the house if you want to get out and explore, but please don't go too far. Varia might need you. So do we have a deal? You promise to wait for me?"

She pressed the phone to her ear, the sound of his voice still lingering in her mind.

"I promise, Marcus," she said, splaying a hand over her chest. "But don't think I'm going to sit here like a good girl, waiting for you to show up and fuck me."

Marcus' voice dropped to a dark, commanding whisper, sending a shiver down her spine. "When I return, I'll fuck you however I want. Be ready for me."

"Okay then." She grinned. "I'll wait for you."

The line went silent for a beat. "I really enjoyed fucking you, Lana."

Her breath hitched, a flush creeping up her neck. "I really enjoyed being fucked by you."

"Then I'll look forward to spanking your pretty little ass when I get there. See you later, beautiful."

The line went dead, and Lana sat on the bed. In a moment of weakness—or perhaps madness—she climbed over the sheets, inexplicably drawn to his pillow. The faint, intoxicating scent of Marcus McGrath still clung to the fabric, as if his presence had left a mark on it.

She took a deep breath, pulling the pillow close. A smile tugged at her lips, but with a frustrated shake of her head, she threw it aside, trying to ignore the excitement building inside her.

This was getting out of hand.

The sweet aroma of waffles drifted through the house, pulling Lana back toward the kitchen. She slid her phone into her pocket and joined the chef, offering him a small, embarrassed smile.

"Hey, Freddy," she said, glancing at the food he'd set out on the island. "Don't worry, no surprise naked entrances this time."

He chuckled, a mischievous glint in his eye. "I wasn't sure if I should offer you a tea towel or a handshake."

A black tee hugged his narrow waist and broad shoulders beneath his apron. Russet hair was tied back in a small knot at the nape of his neck, adding to his effortless charm.

"Your breakfast will be ready in a sec, Ms Craig."

"Please, call me Lana." The idea of having a personal

chef still felt foreign to her. "Do you prepare all of Marcus' meals?"

"Mostly, yeah," Freddy replied, expertly layering sliced kiwi onto an oval platter. "But he's a great cook himself. I take care of things when he's at his other properties—when he's working or partying. He likes to be alone when he's here, though. The cleaners show up the second he leaves. They're never here when he is."

The thought of Marcus' partying tightened a knot in her stomach. The image of him with three women, like that photo of him in Marbella, hit her with a sharp reminder of the man he was.

When Marcus carried her to bed last night, something had shifted—though she couldn't tell if it was real or just his charm working its magic.

She still remembered the intensity in his eyes, the way their bodies moved together—slow, sensual, completely in tune. For a moment, everything between them had felt hotter, closer.

Doubt crept in. He'd likely fooled the others too—seduced them with his charm, made them wish they were the one, then left them behind.

Her fingers brushed absently over the note with her name.

"Does he party much?" she asked.

Freddy stopped his task and turned to face her, a teasing pout playing on his lips.

"He's the best boss I've ever had," he said with a wink, "so it's probably best if I don't get into too much detail. But yeah, the guy likes to party...hard."

Climbing onto the tall stool, Lana tapped the unopened note in her hands.

"I wasn't prying. It's just..." Her voice wavered slightly, unsure of how to explain her curiosity.

Freddy's palms shot up dramatically.

"Oh, stop the bus! You're head over heels in love with him?" He gasped, his eyes widening as if he'd uncovered a scandal. "I *knew* it. Marcus never brings women back here—like, *never*! This place is his private getaway from everything and everyone."

Lana's eyes brows snapped together. "Really? He's never brought a woman here?"

Freddy stroked his cleft chin, his expression exaggeratedly serious. "Nope! Not during my five years of employment. It's only ever been me, his dad, or the gorgeous Jamie. And believe me, if he brought someone here, I would have heard about it."

She blinked at him, absorbing the information. Her stomach did a little flip. "Wow. I don't know what to think now. I mean, he's made it very clear that this isn't anything."

Freddy gave her a funny look, then with a theatrical flourish, waved his arm across the spread of food before her.

"This is for you." He wore a proud smile as he continued. "Marcus wasn't sure what you'd like, so he told me to make a selection. I've got tropical fruits, homemade granola, dairy-free yoghurt, and of course, waffles—because why not? Drizzled in maple syrup, naturally."

He gestured to the stacked waffles as if they were a

work of art. "And there's a carafe of freshly squeezed orange juice and a pot of coffee."

"Wow, Freddy, all of this for me. You'll have to join me. This all looks amazing, thank you. You really didn't have to go through all that trouble, though."

She smiled at him, still clutching the note in her hand, then sighed. "It's Sunday. I'm sure you have better things to do than hang around here making food for me. I can take care of myself if you have plans today."

Freddy's grin spread wide, his teeth gleaming as he casually shrugged one shoulder. "Thanks, Lana, but this is my job. Marcus calls and I come running. He pays me well, so I can't complain. Anyway, I could think of worse ways to spend the day."

The note in her hand pulled at her attention again. She flipped it open, her fingers trembling slightly as she read Marcus's handwriting:

Sorry to leave without waking you first. You're beautiful when you're sleeping. Freddy will get you whatever you need. I'll be back later. When you hear the chopper land, get naked.

Freddy cleared his throat. "How about a mimosa?"

Lana furrowed her brow. "Uh—"

"You know, the drink. Champagne, orange juice—*classy* breakfast stuff." He leaned in closer, his eyes twinkling with mischief. "Or do you need something a little stronger after reading that?"

"Sure, sounds good, thanks."

Clinking glasses in a low-level cupboard, Freddy peered over the counter. "As long as you're not planning to drive anywhere? Marcus would kill me if I let you drink and drive."

"I wouldn't dream of it."

Her phone buzzed in her pocket, and when she slid it free, Rory's face flashed across the screen.

She grimaced, her thumb hovering over the screen before she declined the call.

"Something up?" Freddy asked, raising an eyebrow as he poured champagne into a coupe.

"Just my ex." Lana rolled her eyes, annoyed. "He's been phoning all morning. I should probably take his call, have a calm, rational conversation with him, but I can't be bothered. He'll just kill my vibe. All I want to do is enjoy the breakfast you made for me before I get dragged back into that mess."

Freddy's eyes narrowed. "Get back with him?"

"God no!" she nearly choked on her own saliva. "I'm falling for..."

Her voice trailed off, the words hanging in the air.

Freddy's eyes sparkled, and he hummed his approval. "Just as I thought. You really do love him."

He clapped his hands together. "I'm happy for you. It's about time that man found his match."

Lana froze, her heart pounding as a cold flush crept

up her neck. She lowered her eyes. She hadn't meant to let it slip, not even to herself.

"Please, Freddy..." she pleaded, her hands coming together in a mock prayer. "Say nothing to Marcus. He won't want to hear the *L* word. This is just a weekend thing."

"Oh, honey, I'm staying out of it," Freddy said with a wink as he poured the orange juice. "Although, I'm guessing he really likes you, too. Otherwise, we wouldn't be standing here together."

"There's a big difference between liking me and loving me."

"Did I mention you're the first woman he's brought home?"

Lana's mind wandered. The idea of a man like Marcus being in love with her was absurd.

Her phone buzzed again, tugging her back to reality.

Another text from Rory appeared on the screen.

Lana, please. I need you. It's urgent. I'm in so much trouble. Pick up.

38

Lana

Her heart dropped.

Rory had never been one to show his emotions, but his message was raw and desperate. It twisted something inside her.

Freddy flicked his wrist, dismissing the phone with a wave. "Just call him. Put the poor guy out of his misery."

Freddy was right. The longer she delayed the inevitable, the harder it would be. She owed it to herself to move and put the past behind her.

The phone buzzed again. Rory was certainly persistent in his pursuit. Taking a slow, deep breath, she answered.

"Rory, can I call you back? I'm—"

"Fuck, Lana, I'm in so much shit right now," he said urgently. "I really need your help. This is crazy, Lana. I swear it wasn't me."

The panicked tone in his voice made her uneasy. "What wasn't you, Rory?"

"I didn't kill her, Lana. I didn't kill Jax... Well, I didn't mean to if I did. Oh, I don't fucking remember," he croaked, the words coming out in ragged gasps.

Killed? Someone was dead?

She palmed her belly and slipped off the stool, moving out of earshot. "I don't understand. Is Jax the woman you were cheating on me with?"

"Her name is Jacqueline."

"Right, and she's dead? How?"

"Look, Lana, let's meet face-to-face. I still love you, and you're the only person I can turn to. I need to sort this out before the police find me...or worse." He went quiet for a beat. "I just need a fucking chance to prove it was an accident or get the fuck out of Northern Ireland— I just can't remember."

"Why can't you go to the police now and tell them what happened?" she demanded, confusion and frustration bubbling in her chest.

She couldn't understand how she, of all people, could help him now.

"Lana..." Rory's voice cracked, sounding more fragile than she'd ever heard it. "Please, just help me. I didn't murder her. I woke up, and she was..."

The tremor in his voice made her heartbeat thump. "She was so fucking cold. Her eyes were open, just staring at me, but she wouldn't answer. It was just me and her, alone in the room... Oh fuck, Lana. Please, babe. I'm begging you."

His desperation slammed into her like a physical blow. Her fingers tightened around the phone.

325

"Rory, I—I don't know what you want from me. What could I possibly do? This is too big to run from. Go to the police. You can't handle this on your own."

"Please, I'm begging you. I didn't murder her."

"Were you taking drugs?"

"No, I swear. Can you to go to the house and grab my passport...clothes... Fuck, money, too."

Her thoughts spun as she tried to piece it together. This wasn't the Rory she knew. This man—this version of him—was terrified. But it still made little sense.

"Rory..." she started, her voice barely above a whisper, "I can't help you."

"Oh, really?" His voice dropped, turning dark and venomous. "You'll help me when you find out that Marcus McGrath set me up."

Lana's stomach churned. "What do you mean?"

"Marcus threatened me, Lana. Said I'd pay for what I did to you." His words spilled out in a rush, desperate, like a man clinging to his last hope. "And then I wake up next to a dead woman? You really think that's a coincidence?"

Lana recoiled, her hand tightening around the phone as disbelief surged through her. Marcus wouldn't do that. He was powerful, controlling, even ruthless. But framing her ex for murder? No. It didn't add up.

"You're lying," she snapped. "You're trying to pin the blame on anyone but yourself."

But Rory wasn't done. His voice grew softer, more menacing. "That's for the police to decide, isn't it? And if

I go down for this, guess who they'll come after next? You and that fucker, McGrath."

An icy shiver spread through her body as the threat sank in. Marcus's name would also be dragged into this if the police arrested Rory.

They would investigate his past, his businesses, and his underworld ties. It wouldn't matter if Marcus was innocent. And if they couldn't get evidence to prove Rory killed her, even as an accident, they'd go after Marcus next.

She swallowed hard as the walls seemed to close in on her.

"I won't let that happen," she said, almost to herself, before speaking louder, more forcefully. "Marcus has nothing to do with this. I know him, Rory. He didn't—"

"Yeah, Lana, I know you *know* him," Rory said, his tone darker. "Jax's husband told her Marcus had a new woman on the go—*you*, Lana."

Guilt knotted in her stomach. "This whole time you were blaming me for fucking up our relationship when you were fucking him."

"How dare you—"

"Listen, Lana," Rory's voice cracked with desperation. "Do you really think I could murder someone? I messed things up between us and I hurt you. But I wouldn't strangle a woman to death. Please, help me."

Lana's breath hitched. She didn't want to help him. She couldn't. But the threat against Marcus forced her to take a deep breath and think about the bigger picture.

"Fine, I'll grab your stuff. On one condition," she said firmly. "You keep your bullshit lies about Marcus to yourself. He had no reason to kill an innocent woman and blame you for it. You either did it yourself, or someone else did."

She wasn't sure if Rory heard the finality in her tone or if he just knew how screwed he was. Either way, the urgency in his voice turned to a more resigned, pleading note.

"Please, babe. Help me find out what the fuck happened."

Lana closed her eyes for a moment, her heart in turmoil. She still hated Rory for everything he'd put her through, and the idea of being caught up in his mess was suffocating. But she had no choice now.

The pull to protect Marcus, to keep him safe from the lies, was stronger than anything else.

"You're on your own after this, Rory. If Marcus gets hurt because of you..."

Her voice trailed off, but her meaning was clear as she hung up on him.

Her mind raced as Freddy packed the hamper into the Lexus.

Despite her telling him she wasn't hungry, he still put together a picnic lunch of cold meats, crusty bread, basil pesto, and spicy chutney. He even filled a flask with hot coffee.

"Thanks, Freddy. It was really nice to meet you," she

said, her voice casual, though her thoughts were elsewhere.

"No worries, honey. Hopefully, we'll see a lot more of each other." Freddy winked as he finished loading the car. "Make sure you tell Marcus you're heading back to the city. And drive safely."

Lana thought about calling Marcus to tell him she was leaving Fermanagh, but she knew how that would play out. He'd try to stop her—and, knowing Marcus, he'd likely succeed.

But she couldn't let him take the fall for Rory's mistakes. She had to make sure his lies didn't stick, no matter what it cost her.

During the endless drive along the motorway, Lana mulled everything over. Marcus had no reason to frame her ex. He didn't need to bring anyone down to stay on top.

Rory was just trying to save himself. He would throw anyone under the bus to get out of trouble, and he didn't care who he dragged down with him. Especially not Marcus.

Rory had to be lying.

Lana's stomach churned as she neared the house she used to share with Rory—the place she once called home, now only holding memories.

The closer she got, the angrier she became.

She wouldn't let Rory manipulate her with his bullshit.

Parking the car, she took a deep breath and made her way to the front door, her hand hovering over the knob.

Memories of time spent here with him flooded her thoughts.

Before everything had gone to hell.

Before Verto Veneri.

Before the chaos had seeped into their lives and made everything about survival.

Her life had turned upside down. And Rory? His life was unravelling, and she wouldn't let him drag her down with him—or Marcus.

To her surprise, she found the door unlocked. The hairs on the back of her neck pricked, and an uneasiness settled in her stomach.

She hesitated, her mind racing, but then, knowing she had no choice, she moved inside. The house had a stale smell, and the silence was off-putting.

Her gaze darted to the living room door, left wide open. Beyond it lay a scene of devastation—furniture overturned, the television smashed on the floor, and possessions scattered in a frantic search.

She glanced at the door, listening. Silence. Whoever had been here was long gone, but someone had come for Rory. It couldn't have been the police—they would've sealed the house off.

Eager to leave, she raced up the stairs, the old wooden steps creaking in the silence. Reaching the top, she darted into the bedroom, her brows furrowed in confusion.

On her bedside cabinet sat a bouquet of vibrant yellow roses in a crystal-cut vase. The same style of flowers that were sent to her office weeks ago.

She froze, a creepy chill running through her. The

sight of the roses made her stomach drop. It couldn't be a coincidence.

And that wasn't all.

Someone had strewn their clothes across the room, pulled the drawers out of the chest, and tossed aside the bedsheets, as if rifling through everything.

Then her eyes fell on the black dress—the one she'd worn on her first night at Verto Veneri. It was the only item carefully laid out on the mattress, with her stilettos aligned on the floor beneath it.

Her chest tightened. The sight, the memory of that night, made her stomach turn. She swallowed hard, trying to steady her breath, but panic surged.

A floorboard creaked. Her head snapped to the landing.

Lana pressed a hand over her mouth. Her knees buckled, but adrenaline forced her to stay upright.

Another muffled thud from the stairs. Someone was moving through the house.

It couldn't be Rory. He'd told her to grab his things— he was in hiding.

Her pulse hammered in her throat as she scanned the room for an escape route. There was nowhere to go. She had no place to hide.

Footsteps came closer, climbing the stairs.

She darted behind the door, pressing her back flat against the wall. Her muscles braced with fear, and she held her breath.

The soft thud of footsteps followed the unmistakable sound of a body moving into the room.

A deep, almost amused voice called to her.

"Lana," he said, in a deep, singsong voice. "I know you're in here."

That familiar voice...

Her mind scrambled to make sense of the situation, but before she could react, a hand shot out, gripping the door and pulling it away to reveal her hiding place.

Her heart stuttered in her chest as her eyes met his.

"What are you doing here?" she asked.

Before she could gather her thoughts, the man stepped closer. "Shh, Lana. It's okay. You're safe now."

"I don't understand—"

Her eyes locked onto his, but there wasn't the reassurance she hoped for. Instead, a broad, sanctimonious smile stretched wide across his face, almost mocking her.

"You will soon." His expression twisted like a mask.

Before she could react, the man's hand shot out like lightning, gripping her by the arm. He spun her around to face the wall, his body a wall of muscle pinning her in place.

The shock of contact made her gasp, and when she tried to fight back, his grip only squeezed harder.

His other hand came around her wrist, twisting it painfully, forcing her arm up behind her. A searing pain shot through her as she struggled, her breath coming in ragged bursts.

"You really think you can get away, Lana?" His voice was low, mocking, almost bored as he easily subdued her resistance.

The sting of a needle scratched her skin. Before she

could even process what was happening, it pierced her bicep, searing through her like fire.

Her body went rigid, and the pain exploded, blurring her senses for a split second.

"Get the fuck off me!" she yelled.

As if obeying, he let go and stepped back as her legs trembled, unsteady as the drug coursed through her veins.

The world around her tilted. Her knees turned to jelly, and she swayed. Every muscle turned weak, giving way under the influence of the chemicals in her bloodstream.

"Why?" she whispered.

The room appeared blurry, and the floor seemed unstable.

Darkness crept around the edges of her vision, slowly swallowing everything in its path.

Her head spun, and despite her best efforts, her eyelids grew heavier. Her mind screamed at her to stay awake, to fight, but the pull of unconsciousness was too strong.

The last thing she heard was the rapid thump of her heartbeat fading into nothing.

To be continued...

Find out what happens next in book 2, His to Keep

ALSO BY AUTUMN ARCHER

The Unforgettable Series
His to Steal
His to Keep
His Addiction

Vow Duet
Vow of Revenge
Vow to Protect

Hostile Kingdom: Jungle Oasis
Vengeful Captor
Vengeful Obsession
Vengeful Lover

Hostile Kingdom: Souza Cartel
Hostile Heir
Hostile King
Hostile Vows
Hostile Bond
Hostile Secret
Hostile Devil
Hostile Rival
Hostile Love

Sign up to Autumn Archer's Newsletter for more details
on upcoming releases.

About the Author

USA Today bestselling author Autumn Archer writes dark and gritty romance with guaranteed happily ever afters.

A lifelong daydreamer, late diagnosed autistic ADHDer, romance reader and music obsessive, she dedicates her waking hours to romancing the darkness, using fictional words to weave raw emotion into morally gray men and the feisty women who capture their hearts.

Whether it's a mafia boss, a cartel criminal or complex anti-hero, she delivers page-turning stories that will leave you hungry for more.

Connect with Autumn directly when you follow her on Instagram @autumnarcher.author

For more information on her work visit:
www.autumnarcher.com

Made in United States
Cleveland, OH
21 July 2025

18700088R00198